GRAB

BAG

8

A Gay Erotica Anthology

BarbarianSpy

FOR LITERARY HEAT

This book is copyright © habu 2015
habu asserts his right to be known as the author of this work.
Published by BarbarianSpy in 2015
Cover design © BarbarianSpy 2015
Cover image: Manipulated, © Wrangel | Dreamstime.com
ISBN: 978-1-925190-56-4
All rights reserved

BarbarainSpy
Toronto, Australia

Grab Bag 8

by

habu

Table of Contents

Introduction

Habu's *Grab Bag 8*, a collection of fifteen standalone short stories habu wrote in the spring and early summer of 2015, is the latest in a series of short story anthologies with eclectic gay male settings and plotlines presented in the order in which they were delivered to habu by his muse. The inspirations for habu stories are as random as are his story themes and settings, but those in the *Grab Bag* collections usually reflect where habu has traveled and what he observed or read or music he listened to during the writing period.

Thus there are stories here inspired by a trip to Charleston for the Spoleto music and dance festival; to Savannah, always a favorite inspirational trip for habu; and to Richmond. Also a couple inspired by books habu was reading, a historical one dredging up the provenance of a painting in habu's den, a few connected with the news headlines, and even one inspired by listening to the soundtrack of an old, favorite movie, *Who's Afraid of Virginia Woolf?* As always, there's one from habu's intelligence work past and a hardboiled promiscuous NYPD detective mystery. One, "Galician Guitar," is the opening chapter of a nostalgic book on the Galician region of Spain in writing process with habu's coauthor, Sabb.

Variety and setting are always important in habu's stories, and, as usual, the settings of these stories span the globe from the United States—mostly the East Coast in this collection—to Italy, Germany, Argentina, an isolated, foreboding desert in Southwest Asia, and Japan. Time periods also vary. Although most of these stories are in current time, one moves to Germany at the end of WWII and one is set in Germany and one in Richmond in the 1920s. And, as always, there are unusual stories that take fresh approaches to men unabashedly taking their pleasure with other men. Habu's men rarely agonize over their gay lifestyle; they embrace it.

The overarching motivation for a habu story is that it try to be different in some way from ones he has written before, a tall order for a writer who has some 800 short stories published, but a goal we think has been achieved here. As with the previous *Grab Bag* series, we hope that readers will find stories to entertain, arouse, amuse, and evoke thought in this collection.

This collection opens up with a hardboiled NYPD murder mystery, "What the Singer Saw," and then immediately spins out to Tokyo, in "Shunga World," where a young transvestite in a show review is caught up in the ancient pillow talk art of Shunga and the world of gay pornographic films. In two prison-related stories, first, in "On the Lam," a man is emotionally enthralled to a young lover who has repeatedly fleeced him in the past and thus is running from the law, and, second, in "Two-Year Stretch," a young reporter volunteers to be jail bait to help uncover a prison drug ring and quickly gets in over his head—although not beyond his own desires.

"Galician Guitar," chapter one of the forthcoming *A Season in Galicia*, coauthored by habu and Sabb under the pen name Shabbu, introduces a Washington, D.C., lawyer, retiring young and at loose ends, coming under the spell of a Spanish guitarists and choosing to set off on the adventure of his life.

"The Madison," set in Richmond of the 1920s tells the story of a returning WWI soldier working on the staff of a posh Richmond hotel and being pulled into the clutches of male prostitution. "Covered" is the story of a young male model also being suborned to sexual submission, this time on the shores of Lake Como, in Italy, as a cover model for racy gay novels. "Mountain Memory" takes us back to Bavaria at the end of WWII, where a chance encounter with a starving artist leads to an American soldier's lasting memory in the form of an oil painting.

In "H003," the collection's spy story, a Las Vegas male brothel ranch prostitute, who is recruited to service the guards at a remote interrogation center in one of the "Stans" of Southwest Asia, is also serving as an agent—and double agent—in pinpointing the location and activities of the torture prison.

"Who's Afraid of Stan Snodgrass?" is a bow to the scathing Edward Albee college world play, *Who's Afraid of Virginia Woolf?* As with the original, this story is a free-style, cut-throat, sharp-tongued sexual running of the faculty college promotion gauntlet.

"Come the White Stallion," an "art piece" early twentieth-century story set in a Black Forest hunting lodge, deals with overwhelming guilt at sacrificing a flamboyant lover for a comfortable, but sterile life.

"Men of Thunder" is out of the headlines on domestic terrorism and minuteman militias. A young man, escaping from a dominant and cruel predator, winds up captive in a secret, fanatical militia camp in the mountains of Tennessee.

"Retreat to Savannah," takes the reader back to one of habu's favorite haunts and memories of sexual fulfillment. Escaping the shadow of a famous dead artist wife of convenience, a young artist returns to his arts school in Savannah and, he hopes, to his mentor professor. Once in Savannah, though, his life and will are

9

overtaken by a sexy black bull sculptor and gay bar owner. Maintaining a college setting and the theme of lost partners, in "Lek's Diary," a reclusive academic, still grieving for the loss of his dominant professor partner, requires the shock of the suicide of his neighbors and the tugging of a construction foreman to acknowledge what he wants and needs. And concluding the collection and staying in the college town mode, in "All That Argentine Jazz," a young music student at Charleston College picks up a new life-long mentor and two lovers at the Spoleto music and dance festival.

Being jacked off inside his shorts by a stranger in a crowded auditorium during a jazz concert? Oh my.

What the Singer Saw

"OK, you can take him down now."

The police techs went to work in releasing the body of the young man from the restraints on his wrists that had held him suspended from the ceiling. The ball gag in his mouth and the lash marks on his back, chest, and thighs—and the fact that he was naked and a well-formed pretty boy—made clear to Cassidy what he was being subjected to when he died. He'd been entertaining one or more people who were into BDSM.

What he'd died from wasn't clear yet. From Cassidy's experienced eye, the marks on his body indicated there had been a certain amount of pain involved, but he was young and his body was in good shape. What Cassidy could see wasn't enough to show cause of death.

Such a pity. He'd been quite a good-looking young man. Hispanic, dark, sultry looks. Maybe no more than twenty years old.

Cassidy's partner, Jack, was busy at the door into the room interviewing the custodian who had called in the death. He could see that Jack wasn't getting very far with the man, but that probably was because there wasn't much the janitor could help with. He wouldn't know much about who hired him to clean this place up, if Cassidy knew anything about operations like this—a couple of dungeon rooms tucked away in otherwise abandoned buildings in warehouse districts by the river, like this one was. Playrooms for guys who got off on bondage and S&M on other guys. The janitor would be paid through a series of cutouts and wasn't the chatty type, or he wouldn't be willing to clean up the messes he found after these rooms were used—not that the mess had included a dead body before. That was pretty sure, at least where the custodian was concerned.

The custodian had called the death in, so there was a certain level of honesty about him. The river was nearby. His nightly cleanup could just as easily have entailed a short body carry across a deserted parking lot to the river. He'd probably even have found his paycheck a little heftier the next Friday, if, indeed, the owners of the building had any idea what had happened here. They probably didn't.

Cassidy made a mental note, though, to do the detailed tracing of who owned what around here.

While Jack talked with the custodian, Cassidy moved around the room, taking it all in and salting what he saw away in his brain. You never knew when some little observation at a crime scene would match something else that started the why and who unraveling.

The room—two rooms really—was about thirty feet square—the other one the same. The rooms were pretty much identical. The doors to both were out to a corridor rather than between the rooms. A large window visually connected them. Drapes could be pulled across the window on this side. Cassidy presumed such a curtain existed on the other side, too. The window was fully exposed now, though. The walls were cinderblock, painted a light gray-green color. The floor was concrete, slopping slightly from all directions to a central drain. There were hooks everywhere—in the walls, ceiling, and floor—and piles of restraint cording in the corners. The rooms probably had once been used to hang animal carcasses for curing. Mostly recently they were being used to hang an entirely different kind of meat. The cords were all a sickly green color. Cassidy had never seen them in that color before. He made a mental note to check where that could be bought.

Various S&M apparatuses were scattered about equally in the two rooms. Cube platforms, stocks, mats, X-bars, slings. Everything, in Cassidy's view, to entertain for hours. Or to make movies. There was every indication these rooms functioned as movie studios. There were no cameras or light poles—the users obviously would need to bring their own along with the smaller, more intimate toys—but there were frames around on the walls for mounting video cameras.

"OK, I've seen enough for now," he said as he breezed by Jack and the custodian and headed for the stairs. The street level was one flight down. These two studio playrooms were the only rooms in the building that appeared to be in use—in use up to now. These rooms would be stripped now when the investigation was complete.

The first order of business was to identify the victim. Cassidy had been around enough, though, to have some ideas about that. If the victim hadn't been a club pole dancer, Cassidy would be very much surprised. The gay red-light district was nearby.

"I'll wait for you in the car, Jack," he said as he moved down the stairs. Jack wouldn't be pissed or even feel pressured to curtail his interview. This was Cassidy's style—observing the scene and then isolating himself to get it all cataloged in his mind.

"If you'll work on tracing who's managing that operation, checking back through who owns the building to who they rented that space to," Cassidy told Jack as they entered the bull pen at police headquarters, "I'll work on who the victim is."

"Deal," Jack said as he moved to the homicide section. There weren't separate squad rooms in this station. It was just one big area they called the bull pen, where the detectives had to work their various specialties.

Cassidy's movement was arrested in the major crimes section as Jack continued on toward the back of the bull pen where their desks were wedged together.

"What are you watching there, Leo?" he asked, leaning down behind a seated detective and staring into a computer screen.

"Proof of snatch film from a kidnapping," Leo answered. "Pretty gruesome stuff. The family paid right up after receiving this. Kid sent back home. Now all we have to do is find out who's spending the money."

"Hey, could you run it again, please?"

Leo did so.

It was a BDSM hook-hanging scene, much like what Cassidy had just seen, which is probably what had caught his attention. It was an active session scene, though. A young guy was suspended from the ceiling, restraints binding his wrists together and dropped from a ceiling hook. His legs didn't reach all the way to the floor, though. They were pulled straight out at the hips from his sides, with ankle restraints on leads that ran to the walls on either side. The victim was facing the camera. A ball gag was in place, but otherwise the expression on the young man's face could be seen and was followed closely for short periods by the camera honing in on his face while he was being tortured.

He was a good-looking kid. Blond, on the smallish side but with a great build. He looked a little spoiled—groomed—which was in keeping with being a worthy subject of a ransom demand.

Cassidy looked away from the camera briefly to ask Leo, "How old is the kid?"

"Nineteen. He's OK, but is in the hospital for observation. His father is that automotive sales king,

14

Franklin Dorsey. Several franchises. A regular King Midas, which is probably why they snatched his kid."

Cassidy looked back at the video, which ran for some fifteen minutes in all. Pretty grim stuff for anyone not used to seeing S&M. The dominator was a naked black guy. Powerful body, big dick, in erection throughout. He obviously was enjoying himself. He was wearing a black balaclava hood, and he must have had distinguishing tattoos, because various parts of his body were taped over to hide whatever was underneath. He held a flogging whip in one hand and an electric wand in the other.

The video started off slow and pretty tame, with the black guy dancing around the bound one and taunting him in a voice that was altered and slowed down to sound like he was talking underwater. But the action picked up, with the black guy flogging the victim and zapping him on the legs and chest, back and balls, with the zapper. The victim's nipples were clamped, with a chain running between them, which the black buy pulled on occasionally, producing whatever writhing the young victim could do within the limits of his restraints. Weights hung down from the young man's balls. The tormentor sent these swinging from time to time, which had the victim writhing again.

As the video was coming to a conclusion, the black guy was behind the victim, gripping the victim's waist, and pulling the victim's ass on and off his cock. The expression on the victim's face was in keeping with an experienced, but taxed, bottom being fucked in the ass by a big black cock—right up to near the end, when the expression changed to an intense look into the camera that Cassidy could only describe as a look of horror. Then the video abruptly cut out. It was probably this last expression on the young man's face, Cassidy thought, that had immediately opened his family's bank account.

"Can you send a copy of this to my computer?" Cassidy asked when the coverage had stopped.

"You've seen it twice," Leo said. "You starting some sort of personal faggot porn collection?"

If that stung, Cassidy didn't show it. "Just send me the fuckin' film, Leo. I have some ideas about it. Might close your case for you."

Leo clammed up and just worked the keypad for a few seconds. Cassidy had a reputation for closing cases, so he wasn't about to turn away the help. "There you go. Sent."

"Thanks. I'll let you know if anything pans out. OK if I visit the victim? Don't need to talk to his family, I don't think."

"Sure, you can talk to him if you like. He's in the hospital for at least tonight. Wasn't returned until this morning. He's at Saint Thomas'. Here's his address. He's in college and has his own apartment. The family's rich, and my impression is that he's been indulged. Has a band that plays the Blue Parrot Club."

"Where's mine?" Jack said when Cassidy finally made it back to the Homicide section.

"Your what?"

"My coffee. I thought you'd been getting that. So, where you going now?"

"Not for coffee," Cassidy said. He hadn't sat down, he'd just transferred the video Leo sent to his desk computer to his laptop and was ready to roll again. "I'm going back out. Got to see a guy about an erection."

"Whatever," Jack said, with a laugh.

* * * *

Dean Dorsey woke with a start, taking a moment to realize he was in a hospital bed, not that there was any reason other than routine caution for him to be here. He turned over to see that there was a thuggish-looking

16

man—a very nicely thuggish-looking man—sitting in a chair at the wall, looking at him. He looked back, seeing a strong, chisel-featured face under a buzz cut, piercing steel-blue eyes, thick neck, bulging chest and arm muscles fighting to split a white dress shirt under a black suit coat. He looked both comfortable and out of place in a suit. Better in gym gear. Better yet naked.

"So, did I die and go to heaven?" Dean said, showing a smile.

"I'm a cop," came back the answer, conveying so much to Dean, enough for him to go hard under the hospital sheeting. Not only did it mean to be wary, but it meant power and control. Threat. Violence. Strength and dominance. Dean laid his hips flat on the bed, using his elbows to pull the sheet tight across his pelvis, wanting the cop to see that he was hard. "Name's Cassidy. Just Cassidy. I've come to ask you a question."

"Yeah? OK. Shoot. Ask me the right question and the answer's yes."

"What was it you were looking at in that torture chamber. . . what did you see at the moment the camera cut out?"

"See? Camera?"

"I saw the video they sent your folks. Of you trussed up. Being beaten. Getting' the shit fucked out of you. I want to know what you were lookin' at when the video was cut off."

No "How are you doing?" or "What a traumatic experience." No "Your parents and we were so worried for you and horrified by what we saw the kidnappers do to you." Just a question of what he'd seen, not what he'd experienced. Dean's eyes narrowed, and he muttered, "I'm not feeling well. Maybe you can call in the nurse for me. Just thinking about it . . . it was—"

"You liked it just fine. You're feeling good. You're coming on to me now, so it's a little late to pretend you weren't into this shit. I asked you a question. What did you see?"

"I didn't see nothin'," Dean said. He turned toward the wall.

Cassidy stood. "OK, play it that way. But I'll be back to ask the question again. In the meantime you might be getting a visit by guys who will really do for you—not just do what I saw on the video. Think on that."

When Dean turned back, the thuggish cop was gone. The sensations of desire mixed with fear flowed back into his bones. He shivered with the delicious thoughts he was having.

Stopping outside the hospital room, Cassidy flipped open his cell phone and made a call.

"Jack, It's Cassidy. Any news on our hanger's cause of death."

"Yep, Natural causes. His ticker exploded."

"Not that surprising under the circumstances," Cassidy said. "It's still a murder. He wasn't walking in the park when it happened. It's still our case."

"Yeah, guess it's still murder. But I'm glad it may not have been an intentional snuff. Any leads on who the victim is?" Jack asked.

"Not specifically. But I've got ideas."

Jack laughed. "Then it's as good as got."

"I might have something before the night's out, yes."

"Till tonight, then. Ciao."

Later that night, Cassidy showed up at the Blue Parrot Club, a seedy boy band joint on Vine, not far from the warehouse where the body had been found. He sat close up front, where Dean Dorsey, who had been released from the hospital and who was on stage singing as front man for the band, could clearly see him. Dean had no trouble picking Cassidy out, now dressed in black leather pants and a dark-blue mesh muscle shirt, and he sang directly to the cop, showing that he thought Cassidy was there for him and not in an official capacity. Dean was shirtless, proudly displaying welt marks on his chest and back.

Cassidy paid special attention to the other members of the band. A couple of them were black. Cassidy particularly liked scanning the tats on the muscular drummer.

Dean particularly liked making love to his mic as he sang directly to Cassidy.

Cassidy left though, before the set was over, and started to cruise the gay bars and clubs in the warehouse district down near the river, even closer to where his homicide scene was located. He hit pay dirt at the Brass Knuckles Club.

He was sitting at the bar, observing not just the entertainment, where, on stage, a small, cute Filipino guy was bound to a X-frame and being flogged by one black bull while he was being fucked from behind by another black bull, but also scanning the crowd.

He was able to identify about half the clientele, but most of his attention was going to Ross Strang, one of the local gang bosses, who was sitting at a table close to the stage, his eyes glued to the entertainment, and licking his lips. His usual array of thugs surrounded him.

"Haven't seen you for a week or two, Cassidy," a voice cut in from the side. Cassidy turned his head to see the club manager, Phil Davis, looking spiffy in his gray-striped suit with a red scarf hanging out of his breast pocked, standing beside him. "The bartender said you wanted to see me?"

"Yeah, Phil, I wanted to talk to you. I wondered if any of your dancers had walked off the job in the last week."

"Yeah, a couple of them. You know the dancers here. Some of them can't take more than a couple of nights—which is fine. The customers like to see fresh tail. Sometimes hard to find, though, and very expensive."

19

"Right, Phil. We all got problems. I've got one myself. Do you have photos of these guys who have taken a powder?"

"Sure. Back in the office. You're not here to make trouble, are you, Cassidy?"

"If I was, you'd already notice the trouble. There will be no trouble if you show me your photo book."

The two sat, slugging back bourbon neat, while Phil pulled out a photo album and Cassidy went through the mug shots—all promotional photos highlighting the young men's claims to fame.

"This one, the dark-haired Hispanic, looking like he was lookin' for fun, what's his name?"

"Oh, that's Sonny Rodriguez. Great dancer. A fine lay too, so I heard."

"So you heard?"

"OK, so I know. Sorry to lose him, but haven't seen him since last Tuesday night."

"Did you just lay him, or did you do more to him?"

"You know what kinda club this is, Cassidy. He liked what he got. He came to this club because he liked what he got."

"Did you see him leaving with anyone that night—Tuesday night?"

"No, I don't think so. Someone was askin' about him, though—what he'd do and for how much."

"Ross Strang, maybe?"

"Not direct. One of his boys, though." There was a pause and then Phil said, "You're tellin' me that Sonny's not coming back to work—ever—aren't you?"

"Yep, that's what I'm tellin' you Phil. Sorry."

"Too bad. He took it like a champ—both on stage and off. So, did you like the Filipino trick being put through his paces tonight? Want to take him for a couple of rounds? Maybe even on stage? You're a favorite around here, you know."

"Sure, don't want him tonight, though. I have another visit to make."

* * * *

Dean Dorsey answered the door to his apartment, clad only in bikini briefs, stifling a yawn, and looking drowsy eyed. The fist to the chin caught him completely by surprise and he hit the rug on his knees. Cassidy leaned down, picked the much smaller young man up, slung him over his shoulder, and propelled himself into the room, kicking the door shut behind him.

Slinging Dean down on the living room sofa the length of the cushions, Cassidy had handcuffs out, cuffing Dean's wrists behind his back and a ball gag in the young man's mouth before Dean could recovered from the surprise blow to the chin. He writhed under Cassidy, as the cop pulled the young man's briefs down and off his legs. He was thrashing his legs out at Cassidy until the detective got his ankles into handcuffs as well.

He seemed to give up and lay there panting until, stripping off his own trousers and briefs, Cassidy pulled his belt out of the pants loops, snapped it enough times to get Dean's attention, and then gave Dean a few good, but not too hard, whacks with it on the back and buttocks.

"Stop fighting it or I'll stop whipping you," Cassidy growled. "Yes, I'll stop if you resist. I know you want it. And I won't fuck you if you don't calm down and just take it. I know you want that too." Young Dorsey settled right down. He moaned and whimpered, but he held steady as Cassidy gave him a few more controlled floggings with the belt. He turned his face to Cassidy and flashed him a "yes, do me like this" smile, went up on his knees on the sofa, and widened his stance, presenting his buttocks for mounting.

If there ever had been a question that he wanted it, all that evaporated when he smiled and presented his hole for the cock.

Cassidy laughed and whacked him a few more times before sitting behind him on the sofa, grabbing and spreading the young man's butt cheeks, and burying his face in Dean's crack. Dean groaned deeply, and then even more deeply, as Cassidy reached around and grabbed Dean's hard cock. After a few seconds Cassidy's hand went to Dean's balls, which he distended down from Dean's body and crushed in his fist until Dean was writhing and sobbing. After twenty seconds of this Cassidy went back to milking the young man's cock and eating his ass out.

When Cassidy came up on his knees behind Dean's buttocks, Dean held steady, buttocks raised, as Cassidy, still reaching under Dean's waist and pulling at the young man's cock, entered Dean's ass hard and fucked him in long, cruel strokes. Cassidy made a loop in the belt with the belt buckle, pulled the loop over Dean's head, tightening the loop around the young man's throat, and then using the belt tail as reins to pull Dean's head arched back toward Cassidy's chest as he rode the young man's ass and listened to Dean gagging. He first brought Dean to an ejaculation with his hand and then withdrew, ripped his condom off, and shot his load up Dean's back.

Cassidy reached down for Dean's calves, pulled them so that the young man collapsed along the sofa cushion. Cassidy came down on top of him, and the two lay there. They would have been cooling down, but Cassidy was biting Dean on the back of his neck and had worked hands under the young man's chest and was pinching and twisting Dean's nipples, to feel him writhing ineffectually, grunting, and sobbing quietly.

The torturing wound down. When they were both breathing regularly, Cassidy pulled the ball gag out of Dean's mouth. The first words Dean uttered were, "God, that did me great. You've got one fuckin' big cock. But how did you know . . . ?"

"How did I know you took it hard and with pain?"

"Yes."

"I told you I watched the video. You had one hard erection throughout, and I could see it in your eyes. You were having a great time. It's how you wanted it. And how did I know you wanted it from me?"

"Yes."

"The same look in your eyes when you looked at me in the hospital—and then in the music hall. The erection you wanted me to see. It was as good as flat out telling me you wanted me to punish you."

"Are you going to fuck me again?" And then when Cassidy didn't answer fast enough, "I want you to fuck me again. Punish me."

"You've done something you should be punished for, Dean?"

No answer, so Cassidy continued. "I don't care about any of that. Not my business. I want to know what you saw, what made your expression change to one of surprise and horror right before the video cut off."

"Who's to say I saw anything?"

"You're to say, but I can tell you what you saw."

"You can?"

"Yes. You saw another young man hanging from the ceiling, just as you were and being flogged and tortured. Beaten and fucked to death."

"Fucked to death? What do you mean. The Mexican was killed?"

"He was Puerto Rican. Had a name. Sonny Rodriguez. So they pulled the curtain between the rooms before you could see that he was dead?"

"Yes. But, how did you know?"

"I was there this morning. I recognized the room from your video. Gray-green cinderblock walls and those bright green restraints on you. The same were on the stiff in the other room. You've seen a murder. There's just one thing I need you to do. I want to show you a photo and have you tell me that's the man who was flogging and fucking Sonny Rodriguez in the room beyond the window."

"Just that one thing?"

Cassidy laughed. "I'll fuck you again if you'll look at the photo and tell me the truth. I'm thinking your bed has restraints on the four corners doesn't it?"

"Yes, it does. OK, show me the photo."

Cassidy hadn't freed Dean from the handcuffs or taken the belt collar off his throat. He reached down and pulled a photo out of the back pocket of his trousers. Cassidy traveled with an album in the trunk of his car with photos of "all the likely suspects" in his area of the city. It saved a lot of time.

"Yes, that's him. Who is he?"

"That's Ross Strang, a local gang kingpin. You don't want to mess with him, and you don't want him deciding to come looking for you because of what you saw him doing through that window the other day. You want us to put him away for some time."

"OK, I've done what you asked. Now, will you—?"

Cassidy laughed. "You got a one-track mind, don't you?"

"And you got a dick and body to die for," Dean countered.

Better than restraints at the four corners of Dean's bed, Cassidy found hooks in the ceiling over the foot of the bed, as well. He trussed Dean up spread-eagled on the bed, with his arms spread and raised toward the top two corners of the bed, his buttocks on the end of the bed, and his legs raised and spread, tied off from the ceiling hooks.

Cassidy, hunched over Dean's body at the foot of the bed, pushed his left knee under Dean's right butt cheek, arched his torso down toward Dean's, with their foreheads touching. Cassidy wanted to hold the expression in Dean's eyes, watching for every indication the young man was about to come. He gripped the back of Dean's neck with his left hand, holding the young man's head in place, and, with a super-lubricated middle finger of his right hand inserted in Dean's ass, worked the young man's prostate from the inside.

"Let me come, please let me come. Stroke it with your hand," Dean cried out whenever he was coming close to ejaculation. Cassidy would, time and again, hold off in his expert manipulation of Dean's prostate, making the young man's cock burble with teased-out come, but neither bringing him to conclusion by stroking his cock or leaving him with hands free to finish himself.

Cassidy brought Dean to the brink again and again with the prostate work and then backed off, leaving Dean to whine and whimper and beg for relief. The glorious torture went on for some thirty minutes until Cassidy felt that all of the come that was going to ooze out of Dean's cock had done so. Cassidy turned, moved his cock head to Dean's hole, and pressed in.

Dean writhed within the confines of his bindings, arched his back and cried out, "Yes, yes. Nail me. Screw me. Fuck me!"

Cassidy gave him three long, deep strokes, and then pulled out of Dean's ass.

Dean whimpered. "Give it to me. Give it to me hard."

But then Cassidy left the bed and dressed, while Dean whined for the fuck to be completed.

"Oh, you're gonna be royally fucked sometime soon," Cassidy said as, dressed, he released Dean's hands and headed for the door, knowing that he'd be long gone before Dean could free his legs.

Cassidy drove to the Brass Knuckles Club. For that particular entertainment, the night was young.

25

"Ah, you're back," Phil Davis said when Cassidy walked up to the club's bar. "If you're here to pick up Ross Strang, he's already gone. Don't really want this brought down in the club anyway."

"I didn't come for Strang. I'm strung out. Is the Filipino still available?"

"For you, of course."

"Got a chamber free with stocks in it?"

"For you, yes. But I can fit you in for a slot on stage, if you like."

"Even better."

* * * *

When Cassidy entered the bull pen the next morning, Jack saw him from the other end of the big room and stood up from his desk. Cassidy gave him a smile and a thumbs up, but he stopped at the Major Crimes section and leaned down over Leo's shoulder.

"A little birdie in your ear, Leo," Cassidy said in a low voice.

"Yes? Chirp for me."

"Look for the money in your Dorsey kidnapping case. Look for the Dorsey kid with the money."

Leo gave a low whistle. "You think the kid set his parents up himself? You have reasons for—?"

"Giving you what's on the silver platter, not the platter itself here, Leo. You've got to connect the dots yourself. But I know they're there. Go visit him at the Blue Parrot Club when his band is playing. Look hard at the drummer. He's the guy doing the torture in the video. And take another look at the kid in the video. He's got a 'I'm lovin' this' hard on in the video almost to the end. He didn't just set it up; this is what he likes."

"OK, you're never wrong about these things, but—"

"No buts, Leo. The kicker is that I want him too—as a witness to the murder I'm working. He was there. Look at the video again, where it is. Then go look at the murder scene in my case. You'll see it. Same scene. We can put Ross Strang away for this—for a very, very long time. A double win."

"Sounds great to me. Anything I can do for you, I'll—"

"There is, as a matter of fact. You can investigate for a couple of days before picking the Dorsey kid up. I'm not finished interrogating him for my case yet."

Cassidy was whistling as he strode back toward the Homicide section to give Jack the good news. The test run with the Filipino and the stocks last night went real well. Dean Dorsey was sure to go wild for that treatment too.

Shunga World

A swirl of beauties moved around the stage at Joou in the red-light Shinjuku Ni-Chome district of Tokyo. The entertainment had moved into the evening gown portion of the night, where the lovelies paraded around, lip synching to a Peggy Lee song. Each of them had a moment in the spotlight at center stage, where the audience's favorites received the most applause—and where bids could be made in an auction "for later," if any of the patrons were so inclined.

This was Dayea's first performance at the club, the name of which translated from the Japanese into English as "Queen." She was dressed in a stunning electric-blue sheath that barely covered her melon breasts and went nearly to the floor. Movement was enabled by a slit in the side that rose all the way to her hip. Underneath were a gold lamé thong and gold spike heels. Even with the heels she stood slightly less than five-and-a-half feet. She had only recently arrived from the Philippines and had taken as her stage name Dayea, as it meant "goddess of secrets" in Tagalog. She picked the name because she had a secret, although it wasn't much of a secret in this club.

A strikingly beautiful Filipina with long, straight black hair flowing down her back, she had more than one secret. A prominent one, though, was that her melon breasts were only recently acquired, paid for her by a procurer in Manila.

The set done, she was finished for the night—at least on the stage. She had to await the possibility there would be a winning bid on her further attentions in her dressing room, a private room that was furnished with a divan and its own small bathroom with shower as well as a clothes rack and her makeup table. Having just arrived, this was Dayea's home until she was able to find a small apartment rented by other performers like her who needed another roommate.

But Dayea's working day wasn't over. She heard the gentle knock on the door, which opened before she could do more than rise from her dressing table and turn when the club manager, Natsume Yawata, leaned into the room and said, "You have a visitor."

He didn't name the visitor. There would be no names, although the tall, slightly heavy-set, middle-aged man in evening dress who came into the room would soon enough be known to her as Tajema Eicu.

Alone with him in the room, Dayea didn't quite know what to do, so she offered him a glass of scotch from the watered-down Johnny Walker Black bottles the management provided to help entertain the clientele. Not having learned much Japanese yet and too nervous to try what little she had learned, she spoke in English.

"No, I don't want liquor," he answered in English, although he was Japanese. "I want what I paid for."

She was leaning over the divan, supported by her fists pushed into the divan's surface, as the man, fully clothed, knelt behind her, parted the skirting of her gown at the slit, pushed the butt string of the gold lamé thong aside, and buried his face in her buttocks crack.

She moaned for him as she knew he wanted. She was not a virgin to this. She had been well broken in to it in Manila clubs before she'd been sent to Tokyo. Lubricant and packets of condoms were close at hand,

and it didn't take long before he was hunched over her back and fucking her from the rear.

As he fucked her, he slowly peeled what clothes she was wearing off her. He unzipped the bodice of the gown at the side and slid it down to her waist. His hands went up under the cups of her skimpy gold bra and squeezed her new breasts. The fastening on the bra straps gave way, and it slipped off to the side. While still stroking inside her and squeezing her breasts alternately with one hand, he cupped her chin with the other and pulled her head back into the hollow of his neck.

The man reached through the slit in the gown with the hand he'd been working Dayea's breasts with, grasped Dayea's cock, and continued stroking in her ass while he jacked the transvestite to completion. Dayea had been born a Filipino male, Jabol, and had only made a partial transition so far. The Joou club he was working in was a drag queen show theater. This was the big time for him in comparison to the clubs in Manila. He'd come to Tokyo for the much higher pay.

All it took to strip Dayea naked as the man continued pumping her ass was to undo a couple of buttons at the waist of the gown and it fell away to the floor and to unsnap the sides of the thong waistband.

Dayea gave the man the sighs and groans she knew he want, as, still fully clothed himself and still bending Dayea over the divan, he approached and then realized his own climax. Before he released Dayea, though, he reached into his pocket and pulled out a packet that he slit open with his fingernails, pulling out a pad giving off a pungent odor, which he brought up and held over the young Filipino's nose and mouth. Dayea's eyes rolled up into her head and she collapsed, unconscious, in his arms.

"Jomo, assistance now," he called out. The door to the corridor opened, and the hulking and thuggish bodyguard who had been standing outside the door stood on the threshold, taking a look in both directions down the corridor.

"All clear. Do you need help?"

"Yes, you bring her."

The bodyguard entered the room, took Dayea's limp and naked body from Eicu, and held her while Eicu pulled a silk robe off the rack and wrapped it around her. Then Jomo threw the limp body over his shoulder, and when Eicu saw that the coast was clear, they carried her out of the room and out of the theater, threw her in the backseat of a black Mercedes parked in the alley behind the theater, and drove away.

* * * *

"Look at the art on the easels. What do you see?"

"A couple embracing, wearing old Japanese robes and in some sort of old Japanese tea room." Dayea was trembling less than when she'd been brought into this room. The man from the previous evening—introduced now at Tajema Eicu—was sitting, embracing her close to him, at a low tea table. He had a hand inserted into the folds of her robe and was gently stroking her breasts.

"In a setting just as we are in? Dressed as we are?" Tajema asked.

"Yes," Dayea responded.

They were dressed in the style of ancient Japan, Dayea in elaborate robes as a Geisha. Her hair was taken up and arranged in Geisha style, her face was powdered white as snow, her features had been drawn into a Japanese caricature, and she was dressed in two layers of brocade robes, a scarlet-red under robe and a burgundy-colored outer robe with white and gold Chrysanthemums embroidered on it. Under the robes she was naked except for the white Japanese tabi socks, which separated the big toe from the rest. Tajema, without the wig he'd worn the previous night gone, was bald on top with hair around the

31

sides and back that was long and pulled back in a pigtail. He was wearing a simple brown-and-white striped cotton robe—and nothing but an erection underneath.

When Dayea had awakened that morning, she found that she was lying on a tatami mat in an old-style Japanese room walled with shoji screens and opening out to a small walled garden with the finger-leaved miniature maple trees in shades of burgundy, green, and yellow, weeping over a small carp pond. A stone bench was at one side of the pond, and sitting on the bench was Tajema Eicu, naked other than that brown-striped robe, parted and flowing behind him, and slow-stroking his erection.

"Come here," he commanded when he saw that Dayea, herself lying naked on a lush blue and green quilt, was awake.

Her first instinct was to sit up, pull the edge of the quilt over her nakedness, and shrink away from the man.

"I said come here," he growled. "I bought you. I own you now. You will follow my commands, or I will beat you. I will beat you to death, if necessary."

With a sigh, Dayea pushed the quilt aside, daintily rose to her feet, and walked toward Tajema. This was what she was trained to do.

Sitting in his lap on his cock, facing away from him, on the bench next to the swirling carp in the pond, Tajema had Dayea raise her legs up her chest, The man wrapped his arms around her legs, keeping her jackknifed, and pulled her up and down on his cock. Before he ejaculated, he released her legs, turned her around to facing him, pulled her legs around his hips, pushed her torso down, between his spread, seated-position legs, and, with her shoulder blades rubbing on the stone floor and her straight, jet-black hair streaking behind her, pulled her on and off the cock.

When Tajema had come, they remained in that position. "Now you. Stroke that cute little penis of yours off for me."

32

Dayea reached down and took her boy's cock in one hand. The other hand went to her ripe, hard breasts, which she stroked while she was stroking her cock and gave Tajema the coquettish smile she knew the man would want to see.

"Minobe will be in momentarily," Tajema said, when Dayea had finished himself in a small arc of cum shooting up his belly. "He will prepare you as a Geisha. Clean yourself now—thoroughly. It will be a taxing day for you."

And like that, he was gone. No smile or other sign that he had enjoyed the taking of Dayea. It had been cold, not passionate. Just mechanical, even when, realizing that she was entirely in the man's control, Dayea had tried playing the courtesan within the confines of the straight-up sex of the situation.

The young Japanese man who came to attend to Dayea's makeup and costuming was small and boyish, like Dayea. This presumably was the Minobe who Tajema had said would dress Dayea, but he spoke no Tagalog or English and Dayea spoke no Japanese. Thus, the two couldn't converse, although Dayea felt the other young man to be sympathetic to her and he did, indeed, treat her tenderly and give her encouraging smiles, which made her feel less panicked and confused about her plight.

The nerves flooded back in, though, when Minobe escorted Dayea through shoji-screened corridors to the room where she met up with Tajema again, sitting at a low tea table, in his brown-stripped cotton robe, sashed, but open at the chest to reveal what had been a muscular, firm chest, now given to a bit of middle-aged droop and a slight pot belly. The robe also flared open under the sash where he knelt to reveal he was in angry eruption again, an anger accentuated by his shaft and balls being tinted red.

So had Dayea's been.

What surprised Dayea the most was that behind her, it was all traditional Japanese walls and furnishings. A

33

platform covered in colorful quilts rose further into the Japanese-style room behind where they sat at the tea table. But in front of her, beyond the large prints on the easels—one of which surprised her because the figures were dressed identically to how she and Tajema were now clothed—the rest of the room was stark and was arrayed with arc lights on poles and video cameras on tripods. Men in jeans and T-shirts—four of them—were milling around, playing with the camera equipment—and acting like there was a line drawn across the room, with the nineteenth-century, traditional Japan on one side and the modern commercial world on the other.

"Pay no attention to the cameras," Tajema said as he coaxed Dayea to kneel beside him at the tea table. "They will do what they do and we will do what we do."

While serving Dayea tea as she knelt demurely close beside him, Tajema displayed an affection had hadn't been shown in the previous two takings, murmuring to her how beautiful she was, pulling her loose robe off her shoulder to kiss her there—evidently not wishing to smudge her white face powder—and running a hand into the folds of the robe at her chest to stroke her breasts.

"We are in a traditional Geisha house," Tajema explained to her. "Those blown-up art prints are of ancient Shunga art—the pillow book art of Japan. These are of the homoerotic Shunga, which was nearly as popular as other Shunga in that period. All of the actresses in drama then were played by young men. The young men had their male sexual admirers and clientele."

Dayea started to speak, but Tajema hushed her in a stern voice, "It is not for you to ask questions or to voice any doubts or objections. I am the master here. All you are to do is understand and follow your instructions and to be passive unless or until I instruct you to show that you enjoy it or that you don't. Do you understand?"

"Yes, master," Dayea said, lowering her face and eyelashes submissively.

"You are in the world of Shunga now. That is what the enterprise is—Shunga World. We recreate homoerotic Shunga—in DVD and in still shots. And we sell them to connoisseurs of the art throughout the world. You noticed the print over there where the robes are the same as you and I are wearing, don't you?"

"Yes."

"At some time during this photo shoot, we are going to be in that position. Getting into that position and carrying on from it, though, will be what sells the films and photos. In the final film, the frame will be frozen at that shot, and the original Shunga print will be shown before the film continues. So, you see, the most difficult chore for you and me will be to replicate that exact position at some time during the taking. Now, look at the print. Where does the action take place?"

"On the platform behind us."

"Precisely. So, where do I want you to move now?"

"To the platform behind us."

The pole lights came on as Dayea rose and walked to the platform. Tajema arranged her body artfully along the front edge of the platform and, as the cameras started to roll, he knelt behind her, his robe sash now gone and his cotton robe pulled back to reveal his slight paunch, the nearly drooping pecs on an otherwise muscular body, and his angry red erection. He carefully opened Dayea's robing to reveal just her bare buttocks. Taking her ankle in his hand, he bent her leg forward along the front of the platform and turned her pelvis just enough to reveal that she too had a red-tinted penis and a small set of balls. He buried his face in her crack, and moved a hand up into the folds of her robe to grasp her chest. The camera would not know, at least for now, that he was stroking actual

35

breasts rather than the slightly muscular pecs of a boy man.

Dayea did what she could to depict as the passive Geisha, giving over all pleasure and passion to the male patron. She had difficulty suppressing her surprise, though, when she saw a naked Minobe being escorted into the room at the side by a handsome and powerfully built—and monstrously equipped—man in his late twenties or early thirties. The two of them quickly took a pose at the tea table that was identical to what was happening between Dayea and Tajema on the stage—except they were doing it entirely naked. They continued to be there throughout the photo shoots, mimicking the Shunga poses on the platform.

Tajema rose over Dayea's body, slowly piercing her anal passage with his red-tinted cock and lifting her leg by running an arm under her knee, turning her so that both the act of penetration and her own cock and balls became the focal point of the pose. The jet-black, long and wildly waving hair of his bush, as it did in the Shunga print, gave stark contrast to the smooth, lightly white-powdered curve of Dayea's cheeks.

He turned her face toward his and took her lips in a kiss. The fuck started out slow, sensual, and picked up in intensity and ferocity. Within twelve minutes, Tajema had pulled her up fully on the platform, was up on his knees, using them as leverage to slam his cock home again and again. Her leg was being forced higher, and his other hand was buried in her elaborate headdress, pulling the combs holding it up out, her hair half undone.

By the end of the shoot, she was on her back, with Tajema's knees pushed in far under her buttocks; her legs bent and spread, streaming around his hips; her arms thrown out and up from her body; her straight, black hair fanned out and streaming above her head, her face, the white powder smudged here and there, turned, impassive toward the cameras; her robes open enough at the chest to reveal that she had two firm, melon breasts, both covered and being worked hard by Tajema's hands, as he jerked, pulled out, and ejaculated onto the base of Dayea's small erection and balls.

To get the full effect of the red-tinted cock, Tajema hadn't been wearing a condom. Dayea was checked regularly. She only hoped that Tajema was too.

From time to time Dayea had glance over at the other couple, which continued mimicking everything, but fully naked.

Later, put together again by a Minobe who showed no worse the wear from having been taken by a horse-hung cock from the young, handsome man, who Tajema told Dayea was Uesugi Yasuda and who would be attending all of the sessions, Dayea was wearing more subdued robes. An ochre-colored underrobe in silk rather than brocade, was covered in a simple robe of wide charcoal-colored stripes relieved by narrower ochre stripes. Tajema's robe was the same as Dayea's outer robe.

Tajema explained the art of this, pointing to the print it mimicked.

"The simple color lines make the eyes flow to the center. The robes being of the same material aids this. And what is at the center in that print?" he prompted.

"My buttocks and cock. Your erection. That red sash."

"Precisely. What do you see at your hole and on my cock?"

"Cum."

"Very good. So this print is of what?"

"The withdrawal after coming inside me."

"Yes."

The sequence started with Dayea on her knees, buttocks raised, chest and cheek pressed on ochre-colored quilting with delicate white flowers embroidered on it, her face impassively directed at the cameras. On his knees

37

behind her, his pelvis plastered to her buttocks, Tajema covered her close with his chest from above.

The still shot, replicating one print, but not one with those identical robes, was of his arms embracing her, hands buried under her chest, and just holding there, his cock buried inside her.

Dayea couldn't help looking over at the tea table, which she had thought was overly large in surface when she first saw it but now realized was built to hold the other coupling pair. Minobe's head was turned from her, toward the camera, as hers was, but she couldn't help but notice that the small Japanese man was trembling and straining at having all of Uesugi's cock inside him in this position.

Dayea began to tremble too. Wanting Uesugi in her that deep. Wanting the younger, body-beautiful man with the magnificent cock fucking her.

After fucking Dayea for a while in this position once the action started up, Tajema pulled her down to the floor beside the platform again, causing her to stretch her chest out on the platform and lay her cheek on her upper arm, as it stretched out for the edge of the platform, her hand daintily posed in a raised position, with her fingers curled. Her legs were bent and bound together with a red sash. The robe was pushed up enough off her hips to show the hint of the tip of her cock. Leaning over her body, and kneeling behind her buttocks, Tajema fucked her now-tightened hole.

By command, Dayea was also curling her toes—the curling of fingers and toes being a Shunga art signal, Tajema had told her, of being fucked deep.

The final shot was of him sitting back on his haunches, full frontal, having just withdrawn his cock, and, highlighted a luminous white, cum streaming down his still-angry erection. Cum flowed out of Dayea's anus. Cum puddled on the tatami matting floor between them.

As old and paunchy as Tajema was becoming, nothing had diminished his capability of producing a voluminous ejaculation.

* * * *

After what indeed had been a rough day for Dayea, Minobe guided her back to the room that had been assigned to her, drew a hot bath for her, and sponged off her body as she lay there still moaning softly from what her body had been put through. The whole concept of the Shunga art films appealed to Dayea, though, and it gave her a warm glow. She thought she would glow hotter, though, if she, not Minobe, lay under the big handsome brute, Uesugi.

It surprised her that Minobe was so steeled to it. He was getting the bigger cock, the more vigorous thrust. And here he was ministering to her aches and pains from the day. Of course, he'd probably been here long enough to have adjusted to it all and to have learned to take it. She wondered if it was a progression. If Minobe had once been the submissive for the Shunga art poses—and, if so, could she, Dayea, look forward to moving to coupling with the godlike Uesugi.

In the darkness of the night, Dayea was awakened by the body coming in and stretching out on top of her, trapping her on her belly underneath the heavy weight of him—him, because Dayea could feel his erection at the small of her back.

"Tajema," she murmured. "I am tired and weary. I really can't—"

Her protest was cut off by a sash gagging her mouth and then her arms pulled behind her and tied together at the wrists by another sash and then her ankles likewise tied together. She was brought up to her knees, her chest flat on the tatami mat, and he entered her, slowly, massively, deep. When he was buried inside her, he

39

drew her back into his chest as he crouched over her, reached around her chest, took her breasts in his hands and kneaded them, flicking the nipples with rough-textured thumbs. He began to pump, slowly at first and then frenziedly, as she writhed under him—not from struggling against the assault but from the glorious pain-pleasure of his massive cock working inside her.

This was no Tajema. This undoubtedly was Uesugi. She wanted to be able to tell him that she wouldn't reject him if she were unbound—that she would move better with him, spread her legs further, pull her butt cheeks wide to welcome the maximum depth of him. She would egg him on to fuck her longer, treat her crueler, make her ride on the top of the clouds.

When he was gone, having ejaculated and immediately whipped the bindings off her and melting behind the shoji screen walls, she turned on her back, sobbing in both the glory of the taking and the frustration of having been prevented from raking her nails across his back and challenging him to fuck her harder, to pull all of the pain-pleasure of knowing she was being fucked out of her that had been dulled by her life of prostitution. To make her feel and know that she had been fucked. She lay there, masturbating herself to her own finish, and sobbing quietly, knowing he was just on the other side of the shoji screen, misinterpreting her tears.

The next day she made sure she disabused him of his impression that she hadn't welcomed his visit. That night, they coupled, facing each other, his knees pushed under her buttocks, her torso arched back with his supporting arm around her waist, her head thrown back, her hair swishing on the tatami mat, her arms dangling at her side, while he pulled her on and off his cock with the strength of his embracing arm, dipped his face down occasionally to feast on her nipples, and stroked her small cock to flow after flow with his other hand.

The days were spent under Tajema's body and at his direction as print after homoerotic Shunga print was set on the easels to be replicated in film. The nights were spent with Uesugi taking her in the slightly different poses of the Kama Sutra.

"What does he do with his Geishas when he tires of them?" Dayea whispered to Uesugi after sex. "Do I get to come down to the tea table to couple with you?"

"No, he turns them out on the street. Or he may return you to Joou. I know he told you he bought you from Natsume Yawata, the club manager. But he didn't. He just took you. I know they are looking for you. I could—"

"Shush," Dayea said, placing two slender figures with long fingernails against his lips. "If I am not to stay with you, I don't want to hear anything more of it."

"I could take you away," Uesugi whispered. "I am not long in wanting to leave this myself."

Dayea's heart soared, but she could not dream of this possibility. She had had too many dreams dashed by reality in her life. "Maybe we'll talk of this more," she whispered. "But now I want you to take me in the position of the crab."

* * * *

All hell broke out near dawn, when the light was gray rather than black or yellow. Minobe rushed into Dayea's room; snatched up a robe, which he placed around Dayea's shoulders as she sat up on the mat; and blurted out in broken English, which Dayea had been teaching him, "At the door. Men. From club. Secret place. Behind screen over there. Quick." Minobe held out zoris—rice-straw sandals—for Dayea's feet.

And then Uesugi was in the room too, dressed loosely in a cotton robe and wearing zoris. "Yawata knows you are here. He has come for you. He and Tajema are arguing at the front, but Yawata's men are already fanning out and searching through the rooms. Do you want them to find you?"

"Minobe has shown me where there is a secret compartment. I just don't know what I want," Dayea, full of consternation and indecision, answered.

"Or you could go over that garden wall with me," Uesugi said, with hopeful hesitation.

Running up the alley behind Uesugi, outside the Shunga World Geisha house, Dayea had no idea where they were going, what they would do now, how they would live. But she didn't care. She was with Uesugi.

On the Lam

I don't know how long it took for me to separate out the buzzing of bombs being dropped from a combat plane in my dreams from someone leaning on my door buzzer in the middle of the night. It didn't help that the buzzing stopped when I was awake enough to think about where it was coming from and that it started again as I dozed off.

When I decided it wasn't in my dream, I groaned and rolled over on my side and willed it to go away. When it started again, I rolled out of bed, looked at the time on my alarm clock—4:00 a.m., both too late to be up and too early to be getting up—shrugged into a robe on top of my sleep pants, and padded down the bedroom hall and then down the staircase into the foyer. Whose idea, I wondered, was it for a single man to live in a sprawling twelve-room house?

Turning on the porch light, I peered through window on one side of the double front doors.

Kyle.

I turned the porch light off again and retreated to the kitchen at the back of the house, reasoning that he wouldn't find me there. I automatically switched the "on" switch on the coffeemaker by habit. That's what I did every morning no matter what time I entered the kitchen.

I stood at the sink, peering out of the bay window into the backyard. If I stood real still, I was sure he wouldn't think I was home—not that I was considering that I'd turned the front porch light on and off and that he could see me as well through the window at the side of the door as I'd seen him.

I didn't do sudden wake ups in the middle of the night well. It was not a good time to expect coherence from me.

There was a vehicle on the parking apron at the back of the house. Some sort of blue van. Nondescript. Easily overlooked. It wasn't mine. It must be Kyle's, but that didn't compute either. Kyle was the sports car type, not the nondescript van type. I should know that; I'd bought him a Miata convertible. When I'd done so, he had mentioned being interested in anything but two-seater sports cars.

I hadn't heard any buzzing since I'd come into the kitchen. So, maybe Kyle had left, I thought. The van was still in back. So, maybe the van wasn't his? Whose then?

I padded back to the foyer, turned the porch light on, and looked through the window.

Kyle was sitting on the porch step, looking out into the front yard. This wouldn't do. The neighborhood would start stirring in, what, three hours? I wasn't a morning person. I didn't have any idea, really, when the neighborhood started waking up. I did know that it would be light enough soon for the neighbors to see him sitting out there. And, what? Should I skulk here in the foyer waiting for him to give up and leave?

With a sigh I opened the door. He stood up from stoop—as great looking as ever. The "aw golly gee" mop of blond hair, the "trust me" smile, the mesmerizing blue eyes, the muscular, yet boyish, five-foot-six physique, and the sexy tight T-shirt and scruffy low-rise stone-washed jeans. As he breezed by me, he gave me a brilliant smile and said, "Is that coffee I smell brewing?"

"You can't be here, Kyle," I said to his back, which was retreating toward the kitchen. Kyle knew just where the kitchen was in this house. "This is the last place you should be."

"Which makes it the perfect place to be," he said, as I followed him into the kitchen and watched him take his favorite coffee mug out of the cupboard. "Got any eggs and toast to go with the coffee?"

"I could call the police right now," I said.

"Yes, you could, Dan. I don't see the French vanilla creamer. Ah, here it is." He was rummaging around in the refrigerator. He'd stripped off his T-shirt. He was like a little kid. He'd run around the house naked if he thought the adult in the house—that would be me—would permit it. But it was a tease. He knew the effect his naked torso had on me.

Coming up out of the refrigerator, he turned, smiled at me again, and said, "But you won't, will you?"

"You've got a lot of nerve, Kyle—taking over $60,000 from the company and waltzing off. And where's the Miata I bought you? Is that van in the back yours?"

"I thought it best to park it in back," he said. It didn't escape me that he avoided saying who owned the van.

"And I'm Gus now. Gus McCracken."

"Who the hell names their son Gus McCracken?"

"Yeah, that's kind of a bummer, isn't it?" he said. "I don't see eggs in the frig. You got any donuts to go with the coffee?"

"Just toast or cinnamon buns," I answered, as I moved toward the bread box. But what the hell was I doing? The little bastard who had stolen from me—from my company—flitting in here in the middle of the night, and I was serving him coffee and cinnamon buns.

"You're looking good, Dan. You've kept yourself up real well."

"Where the hell have you been the last eight months?" I asked, pulling a plate out of the cupboard to put two buns on and going to the refrigerator for butter. Kyle liked to butter his buns. He always said that when he'd given me a massage—and it had always made us laugh.

The question was a mistake. He started pattering on about Jamaica and the Cayman Islands and about black bulls until I was just too worn out to keep focused on the problem of him being here. In my defense, it was now 4:30 in the morning, and I hadn't gotten to bed until after 1:00.

"You can't be here, Kyle," I finally broke in to repeat. "I'll give you a half-hour head start before I call the police to say you were here."

"And to tell them you served me coffee and cinnamon buns before waiting a half hour to call them?" He laughed and warm, endearing laugh of us. I could see his point.

"I want to go upstairs with you," he said. "Come here."

I stayed on my side of the kitchen. The knife stand was right next to me. But would I be using one to fend him off or to slit my own wrists? The jury was not just out on that. It was over the hill and half way to Cleveland.

"You are not staying the night, Kyle."

"It's Gus. And we're pretty much past night. It's probably about time for the paperboy or milkman to be coming by to see me leaving your house if I left now."

"There haven't been men delivering milk to the house since the fifties, Kyle. Forty years before you were born."

"Take me upstairs and fuck me, Dan. I've missed your cock."

"That's not going to happen. You can take the guest room at the top of the stairs for a couple of hours of

46

shuteye. But when I get up at eight, I want you gone. If you are, we'll forget you ever were here. If not—"

"I'm not wearing any underwear under these jeans, Dan. I haven't been fucked as well as you can do it in months. Take me upstairs and fuck the shit out of me."

"Don't bother to turn off the light when you go up to the guestroom," I said, trying to keep my voice stern, yet dignified—hiding my trembling hands behind my back. "The cup and plate can go in the sink. I'll put them in the dishwasher tomorrow—like I always did. That guestroom has its own bath. Towels are in there already. The bed's made. Lock your door, as I sure as hell will be locking mine."

Gathering my robe about me, I put my nose in the air and stomped up the stairs.

I didn't, however, lock my bedroom door.

I was barely asleep when I felt Kyle's body stretch out beside mine on the bed. I was enough asleep to mold my body to his before realizing that it was eight tumultuous months since I last did that. I made some effort to push him away, throwing in a, "No, Kyle, we can't be doing this," but the effort was half-hearted and he knew it was.

"You didn't lock your door," he said simply. We both knew he didn't have to say anything more than that. He kissed me on the lips while gliding his hand under the waistband of my sleep pants—he, of course, was fully naked—and grasping my cock. I resisted the kiss for perhaps half a nanosecond before we were playing sucky face. And then I just lay back, sighing and groaning, as he worked his mouth down my torso, opened his lips over my erect cock, and let his tongue glide down the full length of my shaft. He'd always given divine blow jobs. He hadn't forgotten how.

I had my legs bent, feet flat on the surface of the bed for leverage, and my pelvis raised to his buttocks,

47

thrusting hard up inside his passage as he rode my cock to bucking cowboy-perfect position mutual ejaculations.

I don't know how truthful he'd been about the black bulls he'd found in Jamaica and the Cayman Islands, but I'd be in a state of abstemious grief for eight months and was as healthy as they come in cum production. So, not longer than ten minutes after completion in cowboy style, I had Kyle on all fours under me, was fully mounted, and was fucking him again doggy style. He held steady as a statue on the outside while he was all undulating muscles rippling across my thrusting cock on the inside. He talked dirty to me in low, growling tones and I just closed my eyes and pumped and pumped and pumped.

Falling at the side of him afterward, I embraced him, and, with a sigh, drifted off to sleep.

When my alarm went off at 8:00, he was gone. The guestroom hadn't been used—indeed, there had been little time for him to use it as he was in my bed, riding my cock, almost since I'd flounced upstairs. His cup and plate weren't in the sink or the dishwasher.

I was left wondering if he'd really been there at all, or if my lack of him—and of any sex for months—had let my dreams take over reality. One thing was for sure. I'd regretted that, probably in my dreams, I'd told the ghost of Kyle to be gone in the morning before I got up.

* * * *

The day was nearly spent when I came home that evening. Twilight was settling in and the front of the house was bathed in the pastel reflections of sunset. I wasn't thinking about much except the previous night. The thoughts were mixed. I'd had my chance to get Kyle arrested and maybe to have recovered some of the $60,000 he'd walked off with—or, rather, had driven away with in the Miata convertible I'd paid for and with all the clothes and jewelry I'd hung on him—so, make that

$100,000 he'd taken from me. Conversely, I hadn't had a night in the sack with a man like that since he'd left me.

I also couldn't believe that Kyle still had any part of what he'd stolen. I wanted to think that he'd come back just to see—and sleep with—me, but I knew better. He already was out of money again.

Was Kyle worth the loss of $100,000? In many ways he was. But keeping him hadn't been an option. He obviously had been on the lam even when he was living with me, and the police were still actively seeking him. I hadn't been the only one he'd stolen from while he was here—or before I first laid eyes on his beautiful nude body. The police made that perfectly clear to me, as if they had discerned what my relationship with him had been and didn't trust me to give him up. Not that this wasn't justified. He'd been here last night and I hadn't given him up—didn't even call the cops this morning after he'd left.

I poured myself a scotch from the bar in the living room and walked into the kitchen, ready to fix myself some dinner. I looked out of the bay window above the sink. The blue van was parked in back of the house.

Had it been there this morning after Kyle had gone? Had I even looked? I was sure—or sort of sure I had. Of course I wasn't fully sure that last night had happened at all.

I put the glass of scotch down on the counter, turned, and climbed the stairs to my bedroom. Kyle was lying on his back in the center of my bed, naked, legs spread and bent, pillow elevating his buttocks, and his hand holding a dildo half-buried in his passageway.

"I didn't think you'd ever come home," he said as I walked into the room.

"How did you get into the house, Kyle?"

"I have a key."

"The key was taken away from you when you were arrested."

"I'd made duplicates before that."

49

"What is it that you want here, Kyle? If you think I'm going to bankroll you to be able to stay on the loose, you're sadly—"

"You know what I came here for. Come over here."

I had no intention to come under his spell again. I just forgot to tell my feet that. He scooted to the foot of the bed, on his belly, and reached up and unbuckled my belt and unzipped my trousers as I came up to him. He sucked my cock, as I unbuttoned my shirt, pulled it off my back, and then dropped my trousers and briefs. When I had stripped, he turned on his back and let his head drop over the end of the bed, giving me a straight passage for a deep-throated face fuck that had me moaning in remembrance of how good Kyle was at this.

Then I sat on the foot of the bed, as he—much smaller than I was and quite limber—sat in my lap, his channel sheathing my cock, facing me and, using the leverage of his feet planted on either side of my hips, rising and falling on my cock. His passage was tight, which surprised me, as I was sure he slutted around, and he had a thing he did with the muscles of his passage walls that made love to my cock and milked it as no one else had ever done.

"What do you want to drink while I'm fixing supper?" I asked him later when we went downstairs. He was sitting in the living room, facing the fireplace.

"I'll have a Bloody Mary."

"I forgot you liked those. I'm afraid I don't have any mix for that—haven't had it since you were gone."

"I'll have whatever you're drinking then. Who have you had in your bed since I left, Dan?" he called to me where I was puttering around in the kitchen, pulling another steak out of the refrigerator and dumping it in the marinate sauce where I'd put what was to be my steak before I'd gone upstairs.

"Nobody, Kyle. There's been no one since you," I answered as I entered the living room and handed him a glass of scotch.

I expected him to say something about that—something about owning and controlling me—but he didn't say that, and he didn't really need to say that. He'd proved just now, upstairs, that he owned and controlled me. Instead, he jumped the discussion.

"The print over the fireplace. That's new, isn't it? A Chagall?"

"Yes, it's a Chagall. And, yes, it's new. Why is it, though, Kyle, that you won't talk to me about the money you stole from me?"

"You seem to have done all right since I was here. The Chagall, for instance, what did that set you back? $18,000? You're probably worth 25 percent more now than you were when I left."

Yes, the Chagall had cost almost exactly $18,000, and, yes, my worth had gone up significantly in the last eight months. He'd always been good with figures and estimates, but not that good. He'd been alone in the house for who knew how long? Had he been snooping in my papers?

"Have you been snooping in my financial papers, Kyle?"

"You know what I'd like you to do to me after dinner, Dan?" was his response. And then he told me in graphic terms what he wanted me to do to him.

I barely was able to make it through preparing and serving dinner when we were upstairs, on the bed, Kyle flat on his back, with his arms raised and tethered to the two corners at the headboard and his legs spread and bent, as I hunched over him and fucked him missionary style. Then I was under him, holding his waist in my hands, my dick up inside him and punching, as he counterpunched, using his feet planted on either side of my thighs for leverage.

We fucked in various positions throughout most of the night. When I woke the next morning, once again he was gone. He'd cleaned up the dishes from supper the previous night. He still hadn't occupied the guestroom I'd told him he could use the first night.

After breakfast, I called the office to tell them I wouldn't be in that day. I went to the men's store and bought him a new wardrobe of clothes in styles I knew he'd like. Then I went to the grocery store and stocked up on foods I knew were his favorites. I also picked up the mix for the Bloody Marys he drank.

I spent most of the afternoon fixing his favorite dishes, having to go back to the grocery store for ingredients I'd forgotten to get earlier. Then I spent most of the night sitting and watching them molder on the kitchen cabinet top. He didn't show that evening, or that night. I lay in bed going over all of the sex positions we'd used the previous night and the ones he'd whispered in my ear were yet to come.

Eventually, I went to sleep. There were no dreams and there was no Kyle coming into my bed late in the night.

* * * *

I fairly ran to the door from the kitchen the next morning, where I was eating breakfast, when I heard the buzzing of the door. It wasn't the leaning on the buzzer style of Kyle, but I maintained my hopes until I got to the door, threw it open—and found that it wasn't Kyle.

"Detective Taylor," I said, "Please come in. Has there been a development in the case? I haven't seen you in more than a month."

My heart was racing. They'd apprehended Kyle. And not only did they have him back in custody now but he'd somehow also implicated me in everything. The police were here to arrest me for aiding and abetting. Was

52

not turning him in aiding and abetting? And fucking him while I harbored him? The angel on my shoulder was throwing the word "probably" back at me.

"I came to warn you," the detective said as he came into the foyer and I directed him to the living room.

Shit, here it comes, I thought. A lecture and a warning for aiding and abetting.

"Warn me?"

"Yes. The guy who embezzled from your business is in the area. A tourist down in the Virgin Islands was robbed by him and identified him. The guy's name was Gus McCracken. His charge cards were taken and they're being used in this area. So, we think that Kyle Anderson is back in the area. Not too many Gus McCrackens floating around."

That's what Kyle and I thought too was what I almost said. But I didn't. And the Virgin Islands? Kyle hadn't mentioned that. I'd have to check on where they were in relationship to Jamaica and the Cayman Islands. Had Kyle been giving me fake information on that too?

". . . make sure you haven't heard from him—and will tell us if you do."

I only realized then that the detective had continued to talk. And he obviously was still suspicious about the aiding and abetting thing. He was firing a shot across my bow. I was in trouble if I got caught harboring Kyle. But then I looked up as we sat in the living room, and I knew that wasn't an issue. I knew that Kyle wouldn't be back—at least not in the near future.

"Yes, of course, Detective Taylor. I'll let you know immediately if I even get a hint that he's coming around here. Perhaps too you should have some sort of periodic surveillance of this house to see if he does try to come here."

"That's a good idea," Taylor said, sounding a bit surprised. He looked more relaxed, like it wasn't quite as suspicious anymore. Maybe I'd passed some sort of suspicion test by suggesting the stepped-up surveillance.

I felt comfortable doing so, as I was positive that Kyle had gotten what he wanted here and was on the lam, somewhere away from here now. I had looked up, over the fireplace, and had just seen now that the new Chagall was missing. I'd have to check, but I was confident that all of the new clothes I'd bought him were gone too. He'd come and gone during my return visit to the grocery store. There was no question who had taken the Chagall and who wouldn't be back until the money from that had run out.

Not that I'd tell Detective Taylor to add $18,000 to the damage Kyle had done—not to mention whatever else I'd find missing later today.

And, God, I missed Kyle already.

Two-Year Stretch

"I still think you should bring the cops in on this, Logan."

The two young men were sitting in Jan's car outside of the East Jersey State Prison in Rahway. They both worked for the Newark *Star-Ledger*. Jan was an entertainment editor. If he'd been the editor of the news desk, he wouldn't be letting the young city-beat junior editor, Logan Sinclair, go on this undercover assignment at all. But Logan didn't work for him.

"I told you, Jan. Bringing the cops in on it would completely queer the deal. We have a deal with the warden. He wants to pin down the source of the drugs coming into the prison before the cops are brought in. And that's the only reason we're being given this exclusive. I help to identify who's doing it from the inside and I get to write the series. This is my chance."

"This is your chance to get killed, you mean."

"You're getting in too close, Jan. I need to do this. Stop trying to smother me."

Jan could see that Logan meant it—about him getting in too close, being too controlling. It had begun to be a problem in their relationship, and Jan didn't want to lose Logan. He was torn. It was all just too dangerous. He'd done as much as he could to kill the operation, going all the way to the newspaper's editor in chief. But the newspaper was slipping. The publisher had brought in new, bolder management. And Jan had already feared that Logan would hear that Jan was trying to intervene.

Jan didn't want Logan to leave him. It had been the best relationship Jan had ever had. Logan was an angel—a young, blond Adonis who looked years younger than he was. That was Jan's primary fear—the fear of what inmates would do with Logan on the inside. But when he'd finally spoken of his fear to Logan, the younger man had just laughed.

"Of course they'll use me, Jan," he'd said. "I was a rent-boy when you picked me up and got me the training and job in newspaper work. It's precisely why I'm good for this assignment. I can handle myself, and I can blend in better this way. They'll never know I'm a reporter."

"But, you'll be—"

But Logan had gotten angry then, clearly signaling that Jan was pushing too hard. "You use me too, Jan. You used me as a rent-boy and now I give it to you whenever you want it—for free. Don't stand in my way with this."

The best Jan could do under the circumstance, as Logan was getting out of his car, was to say, "I'll visit you as soon as I can, and if there's even a hint that you're being abused, I'll go straight to the cops myself."

"Suit yourself," Logan said, leaning over for a kiss before he climbed out of the car. "But they don't let new inmates have visitors for the first three weeks. They say it helps get the prisoners settled in better."

"That isn't good enough," Jan said, shocked. "I'm going right now—"

"Relax. Just track down a Mrs. Taylor, the prison psychologist. She's my link to the warden in there. I'll have regular meetings with her and she can assure you I'm doing OK or she can pull me out if it gets too hot for me in there. If you go to the cops now, though, you can just pack up all my shit at your apartment and put it out on the street, 'cause I won't be coming back to you."

And that was that. Jan clamped his mouth shut, because the last thing he wanted was Logan not coming back to him. It's just that he'd really prefer that Logan be living when he came back. In any event, Jan would be going right back to the newspaper and filing a memo of disagreement with all of this.

* * * *

"As I understand it, the record says you are in for two years for house burglary. I trust you have the scenario for that down pat? The other inmates always want to know exactly what the others are in for."

"Yes, ma'am," Logan answered. He indeed had the circumstances of why he'd be here drilled into his head—as well as that he no longer was Logan Sinclair, but now was Luke Jameson, and barely nineteen to his real age of twenty-three. His size and baby face would enable him to pass there.

Mrs. Taylor, the prison psychologist, had another coughing fit before she went on, and that, plus that she wasn't looking all that well, made him apprehensive about what she was now saying.

"And you know that not even the guards are in on this. That only Warden Wilson and I know you have been planted here. But you'll have a private meeting with me three times a week—all routine for new inmates—and you know that all you have to do is tell a guard you need to meet with the psychologists and they'll bring you right here."

"Yes, ma'am, I've got all of that."

"And no active sleuthing on this," she continued. "Just listen. We're doing this and using you because you will be able just to drop into the population and no one will think about you listening for anything—you do fully understanding that it will be taxing for you, don't you?"

"Yes, ma'am, I understand," the young man who was now Luke answered. This was probably as close as she was going to get to acknowledging that he had been a rent-boy and that was why he'd been selected—because he could just be there as a toy with no more regard given than the value of his ass.

What he hadn't discussed with anyone in this was that he liked it rough. That's what was really so touchy between him and Jan. Jan was a romantic. Logan wanted to know he'd been fucked. It was part of the prospect of being with randy men behind bars that just hadn't been covered. He wasn't being quite as noble and brave as they thought.

"And you just report to me anything you hear that could connect anyone to the drugs coming in and we'll pull you out just as soon as we get a handle on that. We're bunking you with an older trustee, so you should at least have someplace to retreat when the going gets really rough. And a word of advice on staying safe inside a prison. Find a protector. Make friends with someone others are scared of."

"Yes, ma'am, I understand. And then I get the scoop, right?"

"Right." She was going to say something else, but another coughing fit intervened and she just stood, went to the door, opened it, and waved him out into the arms of a stern-looking muscular guard named Clyde.

The interview had gone OK, but Luke wasn't all that comfortable with how sick the psychologist seemed to be. The prison seemed pretty drafty. He hoped whatever she had wasn't racing around the facility and he'd catch it too.

* * * *

58

Clyde guided Luke down a corridor and into one of the prison blocks. "Guided" was the right word, because he had a hand on one of Luke's butt cheeks from the time they'd cleared the administrative section and were walking through the cell blocks. As they walked, Clyde was leaning into Luke from the rear and making smacking sound with his lips.

As soon as Clyde opened the steel door into Luke's cell block, he called out, "Got a fresh piece of ass for you guys," which brought many of the inmates to the doors of their cells. As Luke was pushed down the corridor between cells, the chant of "Chickee, chickee" and "Got somethin' here for you, kid," and clucking noises reverberated through the block.

"What's the chicken stuff about?" Luke asked Clyde, as they walked long.

"That's for young ass," Clyde answered. "You've the youngest lookin' guy we've had in here in some time, and a real pretty boy. I hope to God you've taken cock before, boy, because if you ain't used to it, you won't last the week in here. You look like you take it, though."

He obviously wanted Luke to say yes, but Luke didn't answer and they now were at the cell he was to share with another prisoner, who turned out to be a thin, bent-over older guy by the name of Horace.

It seemed like Horace was a nice guy, and he spent much of the next three days explaining to Luke what the routines were and advising him on how to negotiate his way through the shoals.

"The time to be most careful is when the guys from this cell block are released into the exercise yard," he said one day. "But I gotta tell you. If you get cornered and you see a screen of inmates forming between you and where the guards are—and they're lookin' the other way, you're screwed and it's best to just go with it. You fight it—call out or anything—you're most likely dead. No reason to call out to the guards anyway. It's not like they won't already know what's coming down. You try to bring them into it and you're the one they'll be pissed with."

On the same day Horace pointed out Big Mike, a big, bald bruiser of a white guy with gang tattoos. "That's Big Mike over there," he said. "If you can, stay out of his way. He rules around here and has the guards in his hands too. He's getting out in a couple of weeks, but he'll be king pin up to the day he leaves."

The fourth day, these two scenarios came together, and it was Horace, standing there with two cartons of cigarettes in his hands, who maneuvered Luke into a shady corner of the exercise yard, where there was a concrete checkers table with embedded concrete stools on either side of them. Big Mike was sitting on the table, and a ring of Big Mike's men was forming as a screen to the rest of the yard.

"Hey, chicken, come over here," Big Mike said. "Yeah, you, pretty boy," he continued when Luke gave him a "who me?" look. "So, what are in here for, kid, and for how long?"

"It's a two-year stretch for burglary," Luke answered.

"Well, I'm just the man to help you with the stretch part," Big Mike said, with a laugh.

Luke didn't even see the fist coming that came up under his chin, snapping his head up, and then buried itself in his belly, taking the wind out of his sails. Big Mike moved real fast for a man that size. He had Luke on his back on the top of the checker's table and his pants stripped off before Luke had his breath back. One of Big Mike's goons had Luke's T-shirt stripped off him and being stuffed in his mouth to gag him, while two others wishboned his legs. There was a little preparation, but not much, before Big Mike was between his legs, pressing down on his sternum with a big fist, working a thick, sheathed cock inside his ass, and pumping him hard.

After Big Mike was finished, the three guys who had helped hold Luke down were given sloppy seconds through fourths.

As Luke hobbled off the exercise field, Horace no longer at his side, Clyde stepped forward to inform him, "There's been a change in cell assignments. You'll be bunking with Big Mike now."

Big Mike must have liked what he got in the exercise yard, because he got it three more times before breakfast the next day, each time slapping Luke around before pushing him down on the lower bunk, painfully immobilizing his arms, thrusting inside him, and riding him hard, pulling out, ripping off his condom, and either shooting up the small of Luke's back or making him take it in the face.

At breakfast the next morning, Luke asked to see the prison psychologist, only to be told that she was in the hospital with pneumonia.

* * * *

If anyone was in for a surprise in Big Mike taking Luke into his cell and fucking him hard a couple of times a day, it was Big Mike. Luke was in his element now. After that first day, when Big Mike let out all the stops and ravished him mercifully, Luke gradually, over the two weeks Big Mike had left in prison, tamed the big man's brutality. Luke showed that he'd take whatever the bruiser had to dish out, but he also showed that if Big Mike gave him some control, it was all for the good in terms of Big Mike's pleasure. Luke showed the man that he gave great head when he let Luke give it rather than Big Mike just brutalizing and force feeding him. And even after Luke had been taken hard, he could impress Big Mike by mounting the bruiser's cock and riding him into the sunset before they both drifted off to sleep—in each other's arms.

What this meant in terms of Luke's mission was that, as it was surmised he'd be able to do, Luke just drifted into the background as part of Big Mike's gang, and he was able to get hints of what he needed to know. Although Big Mike and his gang ended up with some of the drugs filtering into the prison, they weren't part of the delivery chain. They let drop that a single inmate, a Colombian named Gomez, distributed the drugs within the prison. Where he got them, Luke didn't find out. Just this information, though, was enough to pass through channels to the warden.

That was a problem, though. The day Big Mike left the prison and Luke was returned to Horace's cell, saying nothing to Horace about having sold him to Big Mike not only because that suited Luke's purposes but also because you didn't go out of your way to make enemies in prison, Luke asked again to the see the psychologist. If he expected for that to be a problem, it wasn't. But it also wasn't Mrs. Taylor, his contact, he was taken to see.

He was ushered into Mrs. Taylor's office, but a man, introducing himself as Dr. Crawford, was sitting behind her desk.

"Where's Mrs. Taylor?" Luke asked.

"She's in the hospital; I'm sitting in for her. Now, what seems to be—?"

"I have to see the warden. He'll want to see me."

"Now what could there be that you needed to see the warden about? You can tell me. Warden Wilson's away at a conference in Phoenix anyway, so maybe we can work out your problem without him. You're a very good looking young man. I can image—"

Luke did not like the way the psychologist was looking at him. "Um, no matter. Any idea when Mrs. Taylor will be back? I'd really rather be talking to her."

"A few days at least. But maybe there's something I could help you with—and there may be something you can help me with in the process." Crawford stood up from behind the desk and was making to move around it.

Luke couldn't be fast enough in standing up himself and backpeddling toward the door to the corridor. "No, that's fine, thanks. It can wait. I'll talk with Mrs. Taylor when she gets back."

He fairly fell into the arms of the burly guard, Clyde, out in the corridor. Clyde was none too quick either to release him from the embrace he'd put Luke into so the young man wouldn't fall to the floor.

He didn't take Luke back to the cell he now shared with Horace. He guided Luke to what seemed to be some sort of break room for the guards. Six hulking guards in addition to Clyde were waiting, licking their chops and running their hands along their crotches when Clyde pushed Luke into the room.

As one of the guards closed the door to the corridor, locked it, and pulled the blind down on the window of the door, Clyde said, "I guess you can figure out what you're doing here, Chickee." He was taking his baton out of its belt sheath.

"Listen, this isn't—" Luke started to say.

But Clyde broke in. "You can either take this soft or hard. It's your choice." He put his hand into his pocket and came up with a handful of pills. "These will help you take it and to forget it afterward. And there's plenty of them where these come from. Be good to us, and I'll supply all you need. Big Mike said you put out great. We can be partners in this, to mutual benefit, or we can just take it from you. Either way, you're fucked. Now strip, and take your medicine like a good little boy."

As he stripped, Luke reasoned that his work in the prison was done. He knew now who was bringing the drugs in: Clyde, maybe with the help of these other six guards, as none of them had done a double take when he produced the pills and said how easy that were to come by. He just needed to get through whatever time there was between now and when Mrs. Taylor returned to duty and the warden came back from Phoenix.

"Lookin' mighty fine, Chickee," Clyde muttered, giving a low, appreciative whistle. "We're gonna have a ball with you. Climb up on that table and lay on your back."

He had said that if Luke cooperated, they'd go easy on him. Clyde had lied. The first thing Clyde fucked Luke with was with his police baton. Then his cock. Then he let the other six loose for a gang bang. Luke lay back and took it. It wasn't like he'd never been gang banged before. He concentrated on not letting the drugs zone out on him. He wanted to remember everything that happened and to be able to identify every guard who had taken part.

If he ever could get through to the warden. Luke only now was thinking about how tenuous all of this was. And why the hell did the warden just waltz off to a conference knowing that the only link to his prison snitch was in the hospital?

The last door to a possible conduit clanged shut, when a knock at the door marked the entry into the break room of Dr. Crawford, who was the last of the prison establishment to mount Luke's ass and ride him hard.

* * * *

As long as he was in suspension in the cellblock, Luke decided that he might as well keep his eyes and ears open for more conclusive evidence of the drug operation. At the same time he had to stay alive. With Big Mike gone, he now was on the market again within the cellblock—and now there also were the guards to worry about. He remembered what Mrs. Taylor had said about finding a protector. It certainly wouldn't be Horace, but despite having sold him to Big Mike, Horace seemed to like Luke just fine and might help him.

"You want someone like Hakeem," Horace said. "A big black bull, but he has a soft spot."

"Will you help me?" Luke asked. He was holding a carton of cigarettes in his hand. He didn't smoke, but he'd bought his share of the cigarette rations the last shopping day—to use in an instance such as this.

"How do you want me to help you?"

"If I can get him in here during an open cell block period, will you stand watch to see that we're not disturbed?"

That deal set, Luke went wooing Hakeem. This didn't turn out to be hard. The big lunk wasn't all that bright, but he had a soft spot—and a hard on—for small, blond pretty boys.

Luke got up close to Hakeem whenever he could manage it, smiled for him, engaged him in small conversation, and showed interest in the man and his hobbies, which included making figures out of used straws, which he was really good at despite having big mitts, and memorizing the lyrics to rap songs he heard on the radio, which he wasn't that good at because his mind worked slower than the mouths of the rappers did. Luke made himself valuable to Hakeem by memorizing the raps himself and coaching the big black in them. He also was quick to admire Hakeem's straw sculptures.

Luke had to move pretty fast, so almost immediately he was touching Hakeem intimately and making the black bull shudder at the attention and was giving him "come on" looks.

While Horace stood watch during an open cell block period, Luke backed Hakeem up against the wall at the side of the open door, knelt in front of him, and gave him a blow job. Before Hakeem came, though, Luke maneuvered himself between the big black and the wall of the cell, hugged Hakeem's hips with his legs, and made sounds of being taken by the biggest cock he'd ever had—

which might have been close to the truth—while Hakeem fucked him against the wall.

Word went around that Hakeem had taken over from Big Mike in Luke's life, and the threat even by the guards died down. It was only a stopgap arrangement, though, because Hakeem was set to leave prison in another week. That was fine with Luke, as he was sure Mrs. Taylor would be back by then. But he'd made a mistake of telling Hakeem that a deal had been done that would get him out of prison soon too.

"That's great," Hakeem said. "Then I'll be there to pick you up at the gate and we can be together."

The big lug had fallen for Luke, and Luke had let slip that he didn't plan on serving out a two-year stretch. Hakeem hadn't been bright enough to ask how Luke could get out that fast.

"Uh, we'll see," Luke said. "But, yeah, wouldn't that be great? I don't know how you'd know, though—"

"Oh, the grapevine extends outside the prison walls," Hakeem said. "Those on the outside always know when someone's being released."

Just great, Luke thought. It was getting a bit complicated.

But this was when real complication set in. Gomez, the fingered drug dealer, who led a gang of Hispanics, decided he was interested in Luke's services and interested enough to dispute that with Hakeem.

The essential problem was that, when Luke learned that Gomez was interested in him, he regretted he had attached himself to Hakeem. If Luke could gain more direct evidence that Gomez was the inside receiver of the drugs, that would pin this all down. If he could play Gomez like he did Bib Mike, this would be a slam dunk— he could make sure of the connection between the guard, Clyde, and the inmate, Gomez.

Gomez had been nosing around Luke for a couple of days, and Luke did what he could to signal interest.

They were about to settle the arrangement in that shadowed corner of the exercise yard one afternoon when Hakeem came upon them. Before Luke—or Gomez—knew what was happening, Hakeem had decked Gomez, had him down on the ground, and was choking him—with every evidence that he wasn't going to stop until Gomez was dead.

"Hakeem. Stop. Please," Luke cried out throwing himself on Hakeem's back.

"He was going to fuck you," Hakeem declared. "Everyone knows I'm your man."

"Yes, Hakeem, but let him loose, and let's talk about this."

Hakeem left Gomez on the ground, still stunned and fighting for breath. Hakeem stood, placed a foot on Gomez' sternum, and turned to listen to Luke's insistent whispers.

"Please, Hakeem. It's you I want to be with. But you are getting out in a couple of days and I'll be longer. Think. I have to have a protector. First it was Big Mike. And then you. But I need one for the short time I'm still in prison. You want me alive to come out of the prison to you, don't you? It's just for a short time. I need someone like Gomez to protect me. He needn't know it's just for a week or so."

"Well, OK, I see that," Hakeem said reluctantly. "But you'll come with me now."

"Yes, but leave me to talk to Gomez for a moment."

When Hakeem was released from the prison, the pledge was made to Gomez. Servicing him expertly twice a day when Hakeem was out of prison pulled Luke as closely into Gomez' gang and comfort zone as easily and quickly as he had merged into Big Mike's world. The connection between Gomez and Clyde was made, but there was another elusive person in the chain that Luke couldn't reach.

On his last night in Gomez' cell, after Luke had knelt between the Colombian's thighs and worked the man's cock hard with his mouth and then pressed on Gomez' chest to make him lay back on the bed, Luke turned and sat in Gomez' lap, skewering himself on Gomez' cock, and rising and falling as Gomez held his slim waist between his beefy hands and made guttural sounds of deep pleasure.

Afterward, as they lay stretched out against each other, Luke whispered, "I'm worried about you."

"How so?" Gomez asked.

"I know you're receiving drugs through the guards to supply the inmates. That's cool; that's not what's bothering me. I'm worried you're not protected enough. And if you're not protected, I'm not either. There is someone. Someone higher than the guards, I know." Luke was too smart to reveal to Gomez that he knew the specific guard who supplied Gomez. "I don't think it's safe for you not to know who it is. You do know who it is, don't you and are just keeping that to yourself?"

"No, Chickee, I don't know. I think if I knew I'd be a dead man. It's best that I do not know."

Gomez was all South American macho. To acknowledge that he feared anyone—especially an unknown someone—convinced Luke that the Hispanic didn't know the missing link.

So, who did? Luke wondered. Most likely Clyde. Luke had to find a way to be alone with Clyde—to give Clyde the time of his life and somehow to wheedle a name out of him.

But that wasn't to be. The next morning Luke was summoned to the warden's office.

* * * *

"I was surprised you hadn't asked to see me," Warden Wilson said when Luke was brought to him. "I suppose you haven't been able to find anything useful."

"Other than one missing link," Luke answered, "I think I have the information you need. The drugs are coming in through seven of the guards, under the direction of a guard named Clyde—I don't know his last name. And they are going to a Colombian-national inmate named Gomez for distribution in the cellblocks. I think, though, that there is a connection higher than the guards. But, what do you mean I hadn't asked to see you? Mrs. Taylor wasn't here for regular contact. I finally got into see her replacement and asked to see you but you were off in Phoenix?"

"In Phoenix? What do you mean?"

"The temporary psychologist. He said you were at a conference in Phoenix and so I couldn't see you. He wanted me to tell him what I wanted to see you about, but I had been told not to talk about it to anyone but Mrs. Taylor."

"Dr. Crawford? He told you I wasn't here?"

The warden and Luke looked into each other's faces for the longest moment before the warden spoke again. "And not telling him what you wanted to see me about was probably what has saved your life," the warden said. Both of them now knew who the missing link in the chain was.

Later that day, as Luke—now Logan again—walked out of the prison and saw the two cars waiting for him, he knew that what Hakeem told him about news of releases traveling quickly beyond the prison walls had been true.

He tried his best not to make eye contact with Jan, his newspaper compatriot and his lover before he had started his abbreviated two-year stretch, as he walked by the first car. When he reached the second car, he opened

69

the passenger door and slid into the passenger seat. The driver pulled Logan into his chest for a possessive kiss.

When they came up for air, Logan said in a low, guttural voice, "I was afraid that Hakeem would be here for me too, and there'd be trouble."

"I took care of Hakeem," the occupant of the second car said. "He won't be bothering you." A mean look from him was also keeping a frustrated Jan from leaving his car.

"I've missed you big time, Big Mike," Logan whispered. "Take me someplace nearby and fuck the stuffing out of me just like you did in prison."

Big Mike laughed and put the car in gear.

Galician Guitar

[This is the opening chapter of the forthcoming novel, *A Season in Galicia*, by Shabbu, a collaboration of habu's with his cowriter, Sabb.]

The guitarist had been playing flamenco rhythms when I joined Ralph Peters, Sean Madden, and Holland Howard at one of the back tables in the Kennedy Center's small KC Jazz Club hall in Washington, D.C. I'd had a few stops to make after our practice of the Gay Men's Chorus of Washington at its P Street rehearsal hall just west of Dupont Circle. Ralph, who was a State Department cultural affairs officer—and a second tenor in the chorus—had invited us to come by to listen to a cultural exchange musician from Lugo, in Spain, he was herding around the country.

The tickets were free, I needed to stop in someplace warm anyway to get out of this damn interminable snowy winter on the East Coast, and I wasn't anxious to be at home this evening with Sean because we were in a rolling fight that I'd come to believe would lead to a termination of our relationship. I suddenly was glad that we hadn't tied the knot the first chance we'd gotten. I was willing; he less so. I guess he knew better than I did what real commitment required.

Sean was my last real tie to Washington—beyond the men's chorus, of course. And the young and twinky blond was that rare commodity, a first tenor, in the chorus. I was a much more plentiful baritone, so if one of us had to give that up to avoid the other, it really should be me. There wasn't much other reason to hang on. When I'd retired from the law practice early, at fifty-four, I'd said I wanted to travel the world footloose and free. But I hadn't taken my shoes from under the bed Sean and I shared yet. I suspect he had been looking forward to me traveling the world, so that he could put a variety of other shoes under my bed.

I was greeted at the Kennedy Center venue with relief by the second tenor, Ralph, who had the job of trying to make the room look like it was a sell-out crowd. I was waved in with obvious affection by Holland, who had been my colleague and mentor at the international law firm and who rounded out our little men's chorus quartet as a bass. And I was met frostily by Sean, who wanted me to know he was still in a snit, but who didn't want to push it too hard because I was the one keeping him in a luxury apartment just steps away, at the Watergate, and in food and clothes.

It took me some time to unravel all of the layers of clothing I had on in response to the snowfall outside that had continued into March, and I had only started to complain about the weather when both Ralph and Howard held up their hands to stave off my now overly familiar complaint. I made no bones about preferring at least semitropical—or Mediterranean—climates. And yet I continued to live in the Mid-Atlantic states even past retirement and with a financial grounding that could permit me to live anywhere. When I attempted the complaint, Sean just rolled his eyes and gave me a glassy stare.

The atmosphere with Sean became even more icy as the guitarist on stage segued into ballads and, for the first time, drew my attention. He was a handsome man, although perhaps with more character in his face than truly handsome. His features were rugged, dark, and brooding—almost sultry, I would say. His complexion was swarthy, with a two-day growth of beard that he probably kept at that length. I gauged him to be in his late twenties or early thirties. His raven-black hair was wavy and worn long, shoulder length. He was slim, nearly to the point of being gaunt, but he also was muscular. I knew from the program provided that he was Spanish, from Galicia, the northwest quadrant of the country, famous for its vineyards, and I could see him spending as much time working in the vineyard as at his musical craft. He was a strange mix of refinement and roughness, and I was drawn to him by more than his music.

That wasn't to say that he wasn't proficient enough at his musical craft to be sponsored for a trip to the States and small-venue concerts in rooms like this one at the Kennedy Center. The spotlight was on the strong, calloused hands, with the long, sensuous fingers, that he was using to play his guitar, and it was as much that as the beauty I found in him and the sweet ballad music he was playing that captivated my attention—and, yes, my arousal.

The Galicia region of Spain, I thought. I hadn't considered going there. I had considered Portugal, though, which also was on the Atlantic coast just south of Galicia. I decided I would consider that part of Spain now, especially after I'd leaned over to Ralph and said, "Are all the men in Galicia that sexy?"

"All of them under forty," Ralph had answered, with a laugh.

I looked over at Sean, who was pouting, which, of course, on his Byronesque blond visage, looked cute, and I realized that it was, indeed, over with him. I no longer was that interested in "cute"—and certainly not in brooding.

I had retired in a pique. It wasn't Howard who had asked me if my coming out would hurt the business of the law firm, but it might as well have been him. He knew I was gay. He had initiated me—years and years ago when I was clerking for him. But he wasn't surfacing this question among the other senior partners of the firm. He was too powerful. They only brought it up when I paraded Sean out and joined the gay men's chorus. Howard hadn't come out; I had. And it wasn't Howard who took the consequences.

So, I retired early; took my assets, which were considerable, out of the firm; and started a new, carefree life. But had I really? I was still here in Washington, still with Sean in my bed—but not enjoying that nearly as much as I had when it was all hush hush.

"And what do you think of our Spanish guitarist? I mean his music, not his sultry beauty," Ralph whispered to me while the musician was taking a short break. Ralph was the nervous type, and for some reason he always wanted to know what I thought about one of his State Department cultural projects. Maybe he kept asking because I was always honest with him and he often made adjustments from my suggestions.

"He's beautiful," I answered. "I'd like to take him home with me."

"I meant the music, I said," Ralph shot back, with a laugh. "You're always ready to take a good-looking man home."

I heard a huff from the other side of the table. I thought that Ralph and I were conversing at low enough volume, but perhaps not. That was at the base of our rolling fight. Sean had dragged me to an art gallery opening—he was a curator at the Smithsonian—and had left me to flutter around with a group of his friends, so I'd taken one of the artists home for the night. Sean somehow had expected me to just stand around and be his presentable meal ticket, I guess. But if he thought I

74

was going to let him control me like that simply because I was moving up in age, he was sadly mistaken.

Besides, I'd taken the artist home because I sensed that Sean was going to go off with one of his friends. And, indeed, he didn't return home that night. I had done what I did, I now thought, to bring the roundabout arguing we'd been doing to a boil.

"The music is beautiful too," I said. "I very much like how his hands were spotlighted. I suggest you keep that in future concerts."

"Will do. Thanks. I'm glad you liked that. I'm taking him to Vinoteca for a late dinner, and he's agreed to play a few sets in their upstairs lounge. Would you like to go with us?"

"Yes," I shot back immediately.

"And would Sean—?"

"No. We drove separately, and I know Sean has an exhibit to put together and needs to be at work early tomorrow. We'll just not mention Vinoteca."

Vinoteca was a small, exclusive restaurant in northwest D.C. that included trendy jazz and specialty music in its upstairs lounge. Ralph often took the exchange musicians there for more intimate gigs.

It was in the upstairs lounge at Vinoteca that I learned that the Spanish guitarist, who Ralph introduced me to as Xavier Franco and who had a firm handshake and a divine, speculative smile, also had a heavenly tenor voice and I became totally smitten with the man.

And if I had to guess, I would have said he was smitten with me too. We sat near him at a table, and all the time he was playing and singing, he seemed to be playing just for me—to me. When he'd asked how I liked his concert at the Kennedy Center, I had been honest— that the flamenco music very good, but what really caught my interest were the ballads. And here, at Vinoteca, he played mostly ballads. He played them and he sang them to me.

He started off one by explaining that it was an Irish Celtic song but that his region of Spain had once been Celtic too and retained the influence of the Celts in its music. Thus, he was going to sing "Star of County Down," which I joined in applauding as I knew that ballad well—we'd sung it in the gay men's chorus—but he was going to alternate the verses in the languages of his home—Galego, Castilian, and the musical-heritage Celtic language. He would sing the chorus in English.

Somehow Ralph must have told him I sang too and knew that ballad, because when he came to the first singing of the chorus, he paused and motioned to me.

"From Bantry Bay up to Derry quay and from Galway to Dublin town . . ." he sang in a clear, high tenor. On the next line, "No maid I've seen like the brown colleen that I met in the County Down," I tentatively came in under him in a baritone harmony with the melody he was singing.

I came in stronger on the next chorus, after he'd sung verse two: "As she onward sped . . ." in Castilian Spanish, and here, as he guided me, I took over the melody of the chorus, with him soaring above me in a tenor harmony.

I was smitten, and the decibel rating of the applause indicated that others had been smitten too.

A beaming Ralph put his hand on my forearm amid the hearty applause and said, "I have Xavier booked into the Georgetown Suites Harbor Hotel, which should be on your way home to the Watergate. It's getting very late and I have to check in at State before I go home—and Randy's been complaining a lot lately on how late I've been getting home. Would you mind terribly . . . ?"

No, I wouldn't mind at all.

* * * *

I'm sure we both knew we were going to fuck when Xavier took my car keys from me, handed them over to the valet, and invited me up to his hotel room. But it was still a surprise to me that, when I came up to his room from the bar downstairs with the bottle of whiskey he wanted and two glasses, I found him stripped down to his briefs and sitting on the side of the bed, strumming his guitar.

He spoke better English than I spoke Spanish, so that's what we spoke. I was impressed that although he had all of the rugged looks of a farm laborer—belied as they were by the sensitive way he stroked his guitar strings—he spoke so many languages, as he had demonstrated by singing in Spanish and Galician as well as Celtic and English. And I was nonplused that we did talk, sitting there side by side on the hotel bed, sipping whiskey, and talking about Spain and music and his impressions of the States, when we both knew what we were working up to, especially since he settled that off the top.

"Ralph told me he knows you from some sort of gay men's choir—that you both go with men."

"That's right," I answered. "Does that make you uncomfortable?"

"No, not in the least. I find you very attractive. Ralph tells me that you are very well equipped, as well."

"Does he now?"

"He says you are a top."

"Mostly. I have gone both ways, but, yes, I prefer to top. I hope that—"

"Is convenient? Yes it is. I knew as soon as I saw you that we were going to fuck. I do like to have some form of release after playing concerts as tonight. That cultural palace on the river is quite intimidating to someone who comes from rural Galicia."

"Cultural palace on the river? Oh, you mean the Kennedy Center. Yes, it's imposing, I suppose, but we

77

have arts centers like that in most of our big cities. I thought the jazz club setting was just right for your performance. It was very intimate—sensual even—and I thought it suited you. You're a very sexy young man, you know."

I was confused. I was used to working up to it. He had initially been very direct—and matter of fact. It was as if having established we would fuck—and, indeed, I could see that he was as hard inside his briefs as I knew I was—he now wanted to revert to some cultural form of foreplay.

We had spoken of getting it on—making sure we were a fit, which, I was pleased to learn, we were. But he now was talking of his experiences on his tour. I almost laughed. I was sitting beside him, still fully clothed, the two of us nursing a bottle of whiskey, and nearly nude he had approached getting down to the sex I assumed we would have—we both knew I could tell he was hard; I certainly was—and were now having a civil conversation on his impressions of his musical program.

"I have played in Madrid and Barcelona, of course. They are more festive than here. They chatter through the music, but somehow still absorb it completely. The audiences I've played to here so far are so serious. I wonder if they really like—"

"Your audiences at both the Kennedy Center and the restaurant this evening were mesmerized by your playing, Xavier. You understand what mesmerized means?"

Xavier nodded that he did. I continued. "They listened so silently out of respect and because they didn't want to miss a single chord of what you were playing or lose the tune of what you were singing. You didn't like this reaction?"

"No, I did like that I wasn't just background music. But it put so much responsibility on me—I felt like I had to work so much harder to make it sound right. I'm afraid

I made many mistakes. In Spain, I play at the outdoor restaurants at night and just sit in the shadows, giving a foundation to the dinner conversation."

"You made no mistakes that I or, I'm sure, anyone else heard, Xavier. Your playing was divine. And you know what else is divine?"

"No, what?"

"Your body is divine. The curve of your hard cock that I'm tracing inside your briefs is divine. And the whiskey bottle is empty. And it's getting late. I want to make love to you now."

"No, I wish to make love to your body first," he said, as he laid his guitar aside, sank to his knees in front of me, gently parted my knees to put my legs into a wide-open stance, unzipped my trousers, fished my cock out, and opened his lips over it. As I sighed and leaned back, burying my elbows into the surface of the bedspread behind me, he moved a hand up my belly to my chest, opening buttons on my shirt and spreading the shirt open as he moved.

The abruptness and baldness with which he went about it embarrassed me and actually made me start to go soft, so I pulled him up to beside me on the bed, embraced him with one arm, and my hand went to his dick through the material of his briefs as his hand encased my cock. I moved us back to panting foreplay. That helped return me to getting hard and I was able to get him going in that direction too. I tried to kiss him on the lips, but he turned his face from me. It was obvious he wasn't interested in that sort of intimacy. He did, however allow me to kiss him elsewhere on the face, in the hollow of his neck, and down to his nipples.

He came quickly with just that much attention. I had managed to move my hand under the waistband of his briefs and grasp and stroke his cock a few times before he came, but not much more. It was as if he hadn't really done this before and had no control over building up his arousal.

After he came, he pushed me off him, stood and stripped his briefs off, mounted the bed, and immediately went on all fours, with his legs spread and his tail turned to me. He was signaling that he wanted to get on with it—that he was offering his ass for me.

It was a very nice ass. His thighs and buttocks were covered with a curly black down and even his asshole was rimmed with black fuzz. Aroused by his lean, sinewy body, much more of the man of the outdoors and hard work than I was used to encountering in the cultural circles I traveled in, I moved behind him, working my tongue over the down on his thighs and buttocks and then smoothing down that encircling his rim before moving my tongue inside him. I grasped his cock, pulled it back between his legs, and divided my efforts and attention between his asshole and his cock and balls.

He moaned, trembled, and moved languidly under my embrace. It took time for me to open him to the point that I thought he could take me and then more time, with him grunting and groaning but holding in place like a bitch dog wanting it, before I could finally work my thickness inside. But then he just stoically took it until I had pumped him to an ejaculation.

Afterward, we stretched out against each other on the bed, naked, and he let me embrace him and slow stroke his cock as we both dozed off. I made another move to kiss him on the lips, but this obviously wasn't something he liked, so I desisted. He still left me with the impression—even though there was no holding back from him in letting me fuck him—that he hadn't been with that many men before.

When I woke sometime in the middle of the night, it was with an aching pain in the arm that I had under him, encasing his waist at this point. His back was propped up on pillows against the headboard, and he was smoking a cigarette, a little frown on his face, his face highlighted by the only illumination in the room, the lamp on the nightstand.

"Do you regret—?" I started to say, but he didn't let me finish the sentence.

"No, of course not."

I moved my left arm from under him while moving my right arm over his belly and turning toward him. I lowered my mouth to his right nipple and licked and sucked it. He was breathing more heavily than when I woke and I could feel his dick start to harden under the attentions of my right hand. But his cigarette apparently was important enough to him not to respond otherwise.

"I don't think you're supposed to be smoking in this hotel," I murmured, "especially not in bed."

"If they want to chase me down for it, they'll have to follow me to Spain," he said, his voice a low growl—not angry, more disinterested in what anyone thought about him smoking.

"So, even from what you've seen in the States, you want to go back to Spain?" It was a pertinent question. He looked like he came from rough, somewhat primitive circumstances in Spain—although I'll have to admit that this was a large part of his turn-on factor for me—and from what I heard from Ralph on these cultural exchange programs, it was a problem often to return musicians like him to their home circumstances after they'd gotten a taste of the amenities and appreciative paying audiences in the States. The program was meant to seed pro-American sentiment in countries abroad, not to skim off the cultural cream of other societies, but often the effect was the latter.

"I can't wait to go home. I am enjoying this tour, yes, but I would wither and die if I was away from Galicia for long. That is heaven on earth."

He spent considerable time then, as I was working his nipple with my mouth and his cock with my hand

81

telling me of how much a paradise that region of Spain was. And, though I was concentrating in preparing him for sex again, I was listening to him too, and he had me convinced of the glories of the region he came from.

My preparation had a surprising end though—one I didn't take into consideration and never would have thought I would enjoy, but that made me lost to him. His cigarette and sales job on Galicia finished, he stubbed the butt out on the corner of the nightstand—which I'm sure was viewed with alarm the next day by the hotel maid—reversed himself on me and stretched over me. We sixty-nined for several minutes until—and past the time that—I was craving release, Xavier refusing to stop working me when I said I was ready to come.

When I did come, spouting off on his throat and chest, and was then in a moment of weakness and vulnerability, he quickly moved off me, reversed his body again, and turned me belly to bed. Slipping his arms under my arm pits, he put me in a full Nelson, arched my torso off the surface of the bed, and, as I screamed bloody loud in surprise and initial pain, he skewered me to great with his long, thin, hard cock, and pumped me hard and fast to his own ejaculation. Only as he came, did I realize he wasn't sheathed. I had been fucked before but not for some time—and certainly bareback. He wasn't thick, but he was long and a total surprise—not only that he'd do it but also that he'd do it with such cruel, powerful thrusts. Shocking as it was, it totally aroused me, and I came again before he did.

Without a word, he rolled off me, turned out the light on the nightstand, and was snoring within minutes. I took that as a signal that we were to sleep then. It might have been a signal for me to leave him and go home, but I found I didn't want to. He was such a change for me, had such an arousing body, gave me something I hadn't had for some time—excitement, surprise, and variety.

He also had fucked me; I had forgotten that I once could be satisfactorily completed with a man inside me. And what a man he was.

I was disconcerted and slightly unfulfilled by his complete noninterest in kissing or exploring each other's bodies with hands and tongues. I never quite reached satisfactory intimacy with him either that night or later. But it occurred to me that this was part of the heightened arousal with him—continually wanting more—and that perhaps what took me to higher levels of arousal and prolonged the mystery of having sex with him rather than Sean, who was all touchy feely, was the raw lust he evoked, stripped of any attempts at affection.

I was awakened by the sound of the telephone ringing on the nightstand next to Xavier. Drapes were pulled over the window, but the sunlight that was fighting to get into the room at the edges of the window and at the slit where the drapes were pulled together told me that it was way past dawn. Still early for me. Since I'd retired, I'd gotten up when I woke up—which was usually a lot closer to noon than to dawn.

Xavier was laying beside me, on his back, propped up against the headboard, and smoking another cigarette. He picked up the phone and then handed it over to me. "It's for you," he said.

"For me?" Who the fuck knew I was here, in Xavier's hotel room? I hadn't even known I'd be here this morning. It was Ralph Peters.

"Paul," I heard him say. "I trust you had an interesting night."

"You could say so," I answered. "How the fuck did you—?"

"I hope Xavier was satisfactory."

"One hell of a surprise," I answered. "But how the fuck did—?"

"Listen, I'm in a bind, and you're retired. And if you are hitting it off with Xavier and all, I was wondering .

83

. . and you have been saying that you were antsy in retirement and were looking for a little excitement. Well, I was wondering. Xavier's on a three-week tour. Chicago from here and then San Francisco and L.A. Back to Austin and then Atlanta before going back to Spain. I'm really swamped here. I'm wondering if you'll travel with him. Be his handler for State. I know I can get it approved. All expenses paid."

"Me, travel around the country with Xavier? I don't know how I can . . . or if he'd want to . . ."

I had to take a breath. Xavier had smiled and wagged his head to signal he was happy with that and then had leaned over my body and taken my cock in his mouth to seal his approval.

"You don't have that many responsibilities here," Ralph said. "We both know that. And I know you're writing gay novels now, but you can do that anywhere— and I think that Xavier could give you a plotline to purse anyway. Besides, it's been a hard winter here in D.C. and you've made it harder by continuously complaining of the cold and the snow. Granted Chicago will be colder, but the rest of the trip will be in warmer climes, and it will almost be spring by the time you return to D.C."

I couldn't argue with that. And so I didn't, arranging to visit him in State later in the afternoon to start the process of taking over from him as Xavier's handler on this tour.

Handler. Which was rather funny, because Xavier was working on giving me a blow job and was handling my ass with a finger stroking my prostate when I placed the receiver back on the telephone.

"I'm glad you will be my guide," Xavier said, with a deep growl in his voice. "Now I want to fuck. But who takes who first?" I opted to side-split him languidly for starters and I ended up with my shoulders bearing my weight on the hotel room carpet next to the bed and him standing and holding my legs spread wide in the air as he jack hammered down into my ass.

There was more of the same as we traveled around the States. As he practiced in the afternoons, I wrote to a novel draft inspired by our arrangement. The novel was finished and snarfed up by my publisher before we reached Atlanta. I would accompany him to his concerts in the evenings, doing all of the managerial work, and then we'd flip-flop fuck much of the night away in hotel rooms—leaving a swath of first-class hotels with burn marks on the corners of the nightstands all across the country. Most of the mornings were for sleeping to recover from exhaustion and more sex to recover a modicum of exhaustion.

By the time we reached Hartsfield-Jackson Atlanta International Airport in Atlanta and I was waving him toward the departure ramp, I was smitten, totally adjusted to an exciting new life that I knew now would be cut off in an instant, and was ruminating over what I could do to keep the wet dream from ending.

The stake of this was driven through my heart and I was spurred to unthinking action when I arrived back in Washington, D.C., to find that Sean had cleared out of my apartment in the Watergate and was now living with Ralph Peters, displacing the last man he had in his bed, Randy, apparently. It was like musical beds in Ralph's place.

I didn't discover they were now a pair until I went to the next practice of the gay men's chorus and found them wrapped up in each other. It took Howard to explain the obvious to me. Ralph had used the time that I was floating around the States doing his job to take Sean from me. It didn't matter that before I left I was trying to think of ways to pry Sean out of my bed. I certainly didn't want it to be a matter of someone taking him away from me.

My ego bruised, and seeing myself as a laughingstock, I skipped the next men's chorus practice, not wanting to come face to face with the pair. The day after I'd done that, I realized that there really wasn't anything keeping me tied to my current location and life at all. And I was finding myself dreaming of Xavier and missing his shocking and surprising ways.

Focused, off kilter, and completely frustrated, I went on the Internet and began researching houses in the Lugo region of Spain's Galicia—where Xavier was from. Xavier hadn't given me his address—in truth he hadn't given me any means of contacting him, although, as I now remembered it, I'd tried to get that from him—until I realized he didn't have to tell me. All of his contact information in Spain was in the paperwork I held as we traveled around the States on his cultural tour.

He came from a village called Guntin to the southwest of the larger town of Lugo. Within forty-eight hours of looking, I'd contracted and sent a deposit on a partially renovated nineteenth-century stone country villa outside of the village of Friol, twenty-two kilometers northwest of Lugo.

I had tasted the surprise and variety of Xavier— and of the flip-flop, which I'd had no idea would send me so far up into the clouds of arousal and completion. There was nothing to hold me in Washington, D.C.—or in the States, for that matter. I was going off for an adventure in retirement and for rejuvenation in rural Spain.

The Madison

It was quite a step up, from senior waiter in the formal dining room to senior evening desk clerk. All of the lower-end staffers at The Madison were careful to congratulate Philip—perhaps a bit too careful, formally, and perfunctory on the part of many of them. Philip knew it was a leap-frog advancement, although he thought he'd done a fine job in the dining room. He knew that many would ascribe the advancement to a special "in" with Old Man Stewart.

Mr. Stewart was the head porter at the posh hotel in Richmond, Virginia, on West Grove Street, at the top of the Fan District. It was just a couple of blocks away from the even more posh Jefferson Hotel, on West Franklin. These were perpetual steps away, though. The Madison was always running to catch up with The Jefferson in style and services but never quite catching it.

The position of head porter was much more responsible and powerful than it sounded. Mr. Stewart's job was to stand in the lobby and make sure that everything ran smoothly. In doing that, he was in charge of everything—well, everything but Housekeeping, but, as the head housekeeper was a woman and this was 1920, you could just as well assume that Mr. Stewart was the day-to-day top dog at The Madison. The hotel manager did most of his managing from the golf links.

It wasn't Philip's fault that Mr. Stewart favored him. It wasn't Philip's fault, but it was his fate, that he had started at The Madison just before the Great War and at the same time Mr. Stewart's only son, Ron, started there, or that Philip and Ron had shipped off to France together, or that only Philip had returned from France and had been with Ron when he died. It wasn't Philip's fault that all of the hopes and dreams that Mr. Stewart had had for his son were thereby transferred to Philip.

But many on staff at The Madison saw all of this differently and watched Philip like a hawk for any chinks in the armor Mr. Stewart covered him in. That's why Philip felt he had to be perfect and exemplary in everything he did at The Madison, with the result that he did everything extremely well. But it also meant that Philip had to internalize all of his own feelings about anything.

And that was why, on the second evening of Philip's move to the reception desk, he nervously looked away from the theatrical appearance of the not young, but not too old man just inside the entrance to the hotel, looking expectantly about with enough authority and arrogance that Mr. Stewart was quickly at his side.

He was dressed to the nines in a gray suit with matching gray cape, top hat, and gloves. The cane he carried was burnished wood with a gold lion's head handle and gold tip. He was tall and well, if large, built. He had the face of a leading actor, albeit one of the previous decade, and a perfectly styled head of gray hair. Philip decided that his eyes were gray too in the moment that he'd frozen at the sight of the man and been able to gather his wits and look away.

In the moment, though, the man's eyes, after scanning the lobby, had returned to the reception desk and had captured Philip's eyes.

Mr. Stewart was signaling behind his back, holding two fingers extended. Philip knew the signal was both for him and for the two junior porters who materialized from behind potted plants and rushed to take possession of the man's trunk.

On each reception desk shift, the five most-important guests who were expected to check into the hotel were identified. Mr. Stewart, who knew all of the repeat guests of any import, would signal which guest had entered the hotel so that the staff could greet the guest by name—and so they also knew the five most-important guests to be extra differential to. The same system was used at The Jefferson—but to include more than the top five guests. Mr. Stewart's goal in life was to have to use both of his hands for this maneuver as the head porter at The Jefferson did. To do that, though, there had to be more than five extraordinarily worthy guests each night to rank, and although there were at The Jefferson, there weren't, as yet, at The Madison.

Philip knew he had to look up and make eye contact with the man Mr. Stewart had identified as the second most important guest to check in on the evening shift as said guest approached the reception desk. He did so, only to be fully captivated by the knowing gray eyes again—and the slight smirk of a smile.

"Good evening, Mr. Bell," Philip said as evenly as he could, even though he felt his heart had risen to lodge itself in the back of his throat. "Thank you for choosing The Madison for your visit to Richmond. Per your request, the Jackson Suite is ready for you." And, indeed, it was ready for Jack Bell's arrival, complete with chilled champagne and an hors-d'oeuvre cart.

Jack Bell inclined his head slightly and broadened his smile, also slightly, to acknowledge his appreciation for being recognized by name. Of course he considered it his due. Anyone who went to the theater regularly, which Philip didn't, would recognize Jack Bell on sight. He had been the leading stage actor of his day, primarily on the New York and London stages. Now he was an impresario, staging his own plays and operas.

He was in Richmond for the start of the season at the Lyric Opera House on Theater Row, over on the 100 block of Broad Street. Bell was in Richmond for only a few days this time, attending a season-opening concert of Brahms' *Four Serious Songs*, being introduced to America, under Bell's sponsorship, by the British baritone David Bispham, in his farewell tour of America.

The impresario would be coming back to Richmond for an extended stay later, though. For some reason he hadn't been able to book into The Jefferson, which, Mr. Stewart knew, wouldn't making him favorably inclined toward the competing hotel where he normally stayed. Mr. Stewart wanted him back at The Madison later in the season, and he had prepared the hotel staff to do everything it could do to make this happen.

Philip couldn't avoid eye contact with the man as he checked in and received his key. Bell's scrutiny was quite open and Philip was wilting under it. How could he tell? Philip wondered. And *could* he tell? Was Philip just imagining the extra bit of interest?

"Let me take you to your suite," Mr. Stewart said smoothly, coming up beside Bell. "Your luggage is already up there."

"Perhaps you can show me to the bar instead," Bell said, turning to speak to Stewart, but holding the hand that Philip had proffered with the key for perhaps a fraction of a moment longer than necessary. "A drink and then I'll be going out for a bit. You can have my luggage sent straight up to the suite." He looked at the key. "Room 140."

"Yes," Philip said. "The Jackson Suite, room 140. Please don't hesitate to call the desk if there is anything we can do for you."

"Oh, I will. You'll be the first one I contact," he said. "Room 140. Remember that."

The head barman, Robert, came up to the desk with a stack of receipts as Stewart was ushering Bell across the vast lobby toward the hotel bar.

"Might expect mincing steps of that one, or twinkle toeing a foot off the ground," Robert said as he leaned an elbow on top of the reception desk.

"Excuse me?" Philip said.

"You can tell what a man like that is into," Robert said. "You can always tell. Of course, in his case, other men—mostly jilted ones—have already told."

"*Can* you tell?" Philip asked. He was aware of the porter, Bernie Irons, who was standing at the other end of the desk turning away. He well knew why Bernie would do that. He was an attractive young man. He also roomed with Philip on the attic floor of the hotel. Much of the large staff of the hotel lived in the hotel—and worked there most of their waking hours. Philip was well aware of Bernie's proclivities—and that he had turned his affections on Philip. Philip just hadn't done anything like that—not since returning from the war, at least. He had come home resolved not to be like that, to recast his life. And he thought he'd been successful at that. Bernie, he knew, pined in silence and isolation, not having a clue of what could, at another time, be between the two of them.

His belief that he had successfully made a transformation made Philip wonder even more why the impresario, Jack Bell, had made the immediate assumption he apparently had made when their eyes had locked.

Later that night—much later, as Philip was close to coming off his shift—Jack Bell entered the hotel again, walking not too steadily, with a sloppy grin on his face, and with a much younger man supporting him a bit. The younger man—younger by a couple of years than Philip's twenty-four—looked more pretty than handsome. But quite good-looking he was. He was blond and willowy

91

and, though his suit wasn't as expensive-looking and well tailored as Bell's was, he wasn't a street urchin either. Philip guessed that he might be a student at the recently opened and nearby Richmond Professional Institute or maybe a shop clerk Bell had picked up at a bar—there was one, the Docks Club, down by the river in Shockoe Bottom—where such men skulked around, or so Philip had heard. Whatever was going in this line, like the consumption of alcohol, was still well underground in the staid Richmond of the 1920s.

Supporting each other, the two slowly worked their way up the grand staircase.

Philip was closing out his records behind the desk. Mr. Stewart was leaning on the other side of the desk watching the two men climb the stairs, his face a set mask that Philip knew was one of disapproval and distaste. Robert, the barman, appeared, bringing his close-out receipts. His eyes too went to the stairs.

"Would you look at that," he said. "How brazen. Right out in the open. There's only one booked in that suite, I would reckon, Mr. Stewart. Is that so?"

"Aye, that's so," Stewart answered, his voice hard.

"Well, are you going to let that be? That nonsense is against the law. The hotel could lose its license."

Stewart turned and gave Robert a steady look. "There is nothing that either of us saw. I don't like it any more than you do. But there is certain business you don't turn down in this town. Not with The Jefferson just a couple of blocks over. I have seen nothing, and neither have you, Robert . . . or you, Philip, son," he said, turning to him.

"Yes, Mr. Stewart," Robert said, and edge to his voice. "I hear you."

Philip just nodded. This tore him apart. They were right, of course. It was against the law, and hotels were especially scrutinized, although rarely ones as high class as The Madison. But what really tore him up—and it was, to

92

Philip's surprise, just tearing at him this evening and had been in his mind since Jack Bell had arrived that afternoon—was knowing Mr. Stewart's attitude on the subject as well as what else he knew that he could never say. It ripped at him when Stewart called him "son." He knew that he was being a surrogate in the old man's eyes for the son he lost. Philip knew the basis for that was that he'd left for France with Ron and had been there when Ron died. What he never could tell the old man, though, was how close he and Ron were—as close as two people could be—closer than most men would admit they could be—that Ron had died in his arms but had been no stranger to being in Philip's embrace.

And, on top of that, he had to watch Jack Bell and the young man he'd brought back to the hotel walking up the stairs—up the stairs to the Jackson Suite, room 140, to the king-sized bed in the Jackson Suite.

Never before, since he'd returned from France, had Philip felt so conflicted and frustrated—and aroused. Not before this moment, though, did he admit to himself that he lusted for Jack Bell.

* * * *

Philip woke the next evening about 10:00 p.m. in his bed in the small attic room he shared with the porter Bernie Irons to the feeling that he was being watched. The gas lamp on the wall was dimmed down but let off enough light for him to make out in the murky light Bernie in the other bed, just a few feet away from him. He was being watched. Bernie had his eyes open. He was staring at Philip. The expression of ache on his face made Philip want to cringe. He realized that one of his hands was cupping his cock under the covers. He hoped that Bernie didn't realize that—although from the movement of the sheets at Bernie's groin, it was evident that Bernie was following a fantasy of his own.

With a groan, Philip turned over in the bed to face the wall. On top of all the other feelings that were accosting him that he'd thought he'd managed to sublimate in his mind, he really didn't want to add the obvious want of Bernie for him to the list. It wasn't that Bernie wasn't desirable. It, rather, was that he *was* desirable—and obtainable. A relationship with another hotel employee like Bernie wouldn't be long in reaching the awareness of others on the hotel staff either. Philip had managed to force the natural interest in Bernie out of his mind up until Jack Bell had arrived at the hotel the previous day.

This was supposed to be Philip's day off, but they'd been shorthanded in the dining room and he'd volunteered to do the afternoon shift there. He needed to build all the goodwill among the hotel staff that he could muster. He'd hit the sack coming off that duty and had fallen right to sleep. That had been a mistake, because now he was awake and might sleep fretfully in the night, if at all. His thoughts went back to the previous night when Bell had returned to the hotel with the young man. At the time, especially since both of them were at least slightly inebriated, he thought of that men's bar in Shockoe Bottom, the old dockside section of the city on the James River, he'd heard about. He couldn't see Jack Bell going to a place like that.

But he himself had had fantasies of going to a place like that. Some days he thought he should check out if there really was such a bar—not to go in, of course, but to know that something like that existed in Richmond. On other days he wanted to forget the name of this phantom bar altogether.

If it was a phantom bar.

Restlessly, he turned over again. Bernie was still looking at him, but as if in embarrassment at having been caught doing so, he gave an audible sigh and turned over in the bed himself.

Thirty minutes later, unable to sleep and reasoning with himself that a walk in the night air might make him sleepy, Philip found himself walking out of The Madison. Without giving it any thought at all, he let his feet move him toward the river—the James and the part of the city known as Shockoe Bottom.

* * * *

He had just meant to see if there really was a Docks Club in Shockoe Bottom. He didn't really believe there could be—not being the type of bar he heard it was. That was illegal in Virginia. He had to look pretty hard for it and then only found it, in a basement walk down on a cobblestoned alley running up from the docks on the James, by following a couple of young male drunks staggering by arm in arm who had stopped in the shadows near Philip to kiss.

Once he'd seen where it was and the couple thump down the steps, bang on the door, and be let in, he still didn't really believe it was that kind of bar—more of a speakeasy—and he thought he'd probably been mistaken that it was two men he'd followed.

When he rapped on the door, a big bruiser of a guy who looked like he'd just walked off the docks gave him a close up-and-down scrutiny, smiled, and accorded him entrance.

"You be new offerings here," the doorkeep said.

"Just checking what's here," Philip mumbled.

"Well, the likes of you will be real welcome here now that you be here; there will be a lot ready to just check what you got," the man said, with a snort, gesturing in the direction Philip was to go.

The room was smoky and dimly lit. It was fairly crowded and noisy. All Philip could see were men, and snatches of racy conversation from a mix of deep and tenor voices cutting through the noise. He almost turned to leave, but the guy at entrance to the bar room said, "Haven't seen you here before. Guys are really gonna like you. Belly yourself up to the bar over there. I'll bet you won't have to pay for your drinks."

Such affirmation from the greeters were just making Philip more nervous about being here. He had assumed—and hoped—that he could just observe on the fringe.

Alcoholic drinks, free or otherwise, were as illegal as homosexuality in the States at the moment, although access to them flourished under the surface. The Prohibition Era had set in in the previous year. Philip wouldn't mind having a drink or two himself, despite the ban. Alcohol had been a staple on in the trenches he'd so recently escaped from. For that matter, so was men turning to men for affirmation, affection, and forget.

He moved in the direction the doorman indicated and found himself standing in a just-vacated space at the bar. The men on both sides of where he had landed turned and smiled to him. Both offered to buy him a drink. As nervous as he was, he suddenly felt freer than he'd felt in years. At least here maybe he could be unguarded and honest with himself. He didn't have to do more than just talk. He didn't have to do anything about his desires. One of the men, younger than he was, quite good looking, slender, and a bit limp wristed, placed a hand on his forearm, letting his fingers ruffle up the matting of hair there, and gave Philip a brilliant smile.

Philip felt a chill go up from his spine and his cock begin to harden.

Less than fifteen minutes later and after a beer, a whiskey chaser, and some very explicit talk from the young blond, who lisped a name of Chad, no doubt a false name, but receiving a false name and profession in response, Philip was in a back corridor of the club. His shoulder blades were pressed into a black-painted rock wall, his hips were angled out from the wall, his trousers and underdrawers were down around his ankles, his fingers were buried in blond curls, and he was receiving a divine blow job. It was the first such attention he had received since Ron had gone down on him in France the night before Ron was blown out of the trenches by a hand grenade.

Philip was left in the dark corridor, trousers still around his ankles, pelvis still jutting out, and now going soft after he'd ejaculated and the blond, having gotten what he'd come for, having evaporated. Mixed emotions were coursing through Philip's mind—disappointment in his resolve and weakness, euphoria of experiencing a long-denied pleasure, resignation that he was what he was, railing against what he was, frustration that it hadn't gone beyond a blow job. He didn't plan to fall into this ever again, and there was a disappointment that, if it was his last, he didn't get more.

As he pulled the trousers up and was buckling his belt, he rationalized that it was some sort of check on how well he was fighting his nature. It was only a blow job— and it had been performed on him. Perfectly straight soldiers had accepted blow jobs from other soldiers in the trenches during the war. It didn't mean they were queer. It was to receive a natural release. This didn't mean Philip had slipped—not really. It had only been a blow job, and it had been performed on him. He hadn't fucked the young blond. Sure, he'd thought about doing so, and he couldn't positively say he wouldn't have done so if it had been asked. But he didn't initiate it. That's what was important.

He could go back to The Madison and his new life now, and know that the thoughts that the sensual and assuming impresario hotel guest Jack Bell had sickened his mind with had been dissipated.

And then, while he was still buckling his trousers and coming through the beaded curtains from the dark corridor and into the not-much-lighter barroom, he heard a laugh separating itself from the crowd noise and his attention was drawn to a nearby table. The laugh had come from Jack Bell, who was sitting there with yet another young man—and who was staring, and smugly smiling, directly at Philip. Philip's mind went back to the encounter in the darkened corridor. A vague figure had appeared briefly at the other end of the corridor and the, with a laugh—a laugh very similar to Jack Bell's—had withdrawn.

* * * *

The next evening Philip looked up from his station at the reception desk of The Madison and into the eyes of Jack Bell. Mr. Stewart was standing a few steps away, turned to observe the entrance of the hotel, but Philip had no question that the head porter was tuned into everything going on in the hotel's lobby. Bell was as handsome as ever and was elegantly dressed, in white shirt, vest, and matching trousers, his eyes sparkling and an amused smile on his face.

"I will be staying in this evening, room 140," he said to Philip, maintaining his smile.

"Yes, sir. Very good, sir," Philip answered, quite properly but a bit stiffly. He was determined to act like the man knew nothing, had seen nothing. But Jack Bell wasn't going to let him go.

"I don't think I've caught your name. I want to remember you for giving good service."

"Thank you, sir. My name if Philip, sir." He dare not give a false name. Mr. Stewart was standing just there, listening to everything. The staff had been told to be extra solicitous of Jack Bell to win his future business. But Mr. Stewart surely had no idea at all what this dance at the desk was about. Philip knew, though, and Jack Bell most assuredly knew.

"That's room 140."

"The Jackson Suite, yes, sir. Room 140."

"I'll be there, alone, all evening."

"Yes sir, I'll see that you're not disturbed."

"It could be that I want to be disturbed," Jack Bell said. And then he gave that laugh Philip remembered from the gay bar, turned, and floated up the grand staircase.

Of course Philip had no intention of going to room 140—not tonight. Not any night that Jack Bell was booked into this hotel.

The last thing he had to do when he was on shift was to walk the halls of the top two guest room stories of the hotel to ensure that all was quiet and in order.

"I'll take your floor as well tonight, Bernie," he told the porter who shared his room in the attic. "You look beat. Go to bed."

"I'm fine," Bernie said, giving Philip a searching look—a knowing look, in Philip's estimation. And a false assumption, Philip said. Bernie's hall check assignment was for the two lower floors. Philip's view, though, was that he only was offering because Bernie looked worn out. He was doing it as a favor. It was no big deal.

But Bernie had been behind the desk when Jack Bell had come by, and Bernie was more aware of what was oppressing the atmosphere than Mr. Stewart was—or that Philip would admit, even to himself.

Philip did the upper floors first and worked his way down, until, without really intending to, he was standing at the door of the Jackson Suite, room 140, with his hand raised.

He would not knock. He would come this far to show himself that he could resist.

He didn't have to knock. Jack Bell had sensed that he was at the door—or had been watching for him through the eyehole—because the door opened of its own volition, and Bell was standing on the other side, in a silk dressing gown, but unsashed, so that it parted down his

99

sternum and belly, and was parted at his belly by a hard, jutting, upcurved cock.

No words were spoken. No words needed to be spoken, and there was no question who was in charge. Maintaining the half-amused smile that the theater impresario had turned to Philip the day Bell had arrived at The Madison, that he'd shown to Philip in the Docks Club encounter, and that he had flashed that very evening at the reception desk, Bell merely took hold of one of Philip's arms, pulled him into the room, reached beyond him to close the door, and pressed down on Philip's shoulders, guiding Philip down to his knees in front of him. Philip took the hard cock in his mouth and made slow love to it.

Bell fucked Philip on the bed, with Philip's wrists bound to the headboard above his head with his own leather belt. Philip started on his knees, his chest flat on the surface of the bed, and Bell's face plastered between his butt cheeks. Bell fucked him doggy style then. Philip had always been the top with Ron, but he made no effort to resist Bell doing whatever he wanted with him. The younger man came fairly quickly and collapsed flat onto the bed after ejaculating, with Bell riding him down and continuing to pump to his own climax.

There was nothing tender and passionate about it—just Jack Bell putting another notch on his own belt. Still, for Philip, it was as if all the barriers of suppressed need and desire were being exploded and he was being born again into the life he was meant to have. He ached for more—for Bell to suck him off as the young blond had hurriedly done in the dark corridor behind the Docks Club, or for the two of them to explore each other's bodies with their hands and tongues, or for Philip to be inside Bell.

But it didn't go that far. After Bell had come, he withdrew from Philip's ass, rolled off the bed, and padded toward the bathroom. "There's a ten-spot on the nightstand," he called out over his shoulder. "The service is good, very good indeed. You may leave while I am in the shower."

Bell stayed at the hotel for two more nights. The next evening, the first time after having been in his room that Philip came face to face with him, Bell returned to the hotel in the late evening with another young man in tow.

When he came to the desk for his room key, he moved to the side of the desk where Bernie was standing and asked him for the key to room 140. He gave Bernie the amused smile he'd once given Philip. He didn't look at Philip at all.

In frustration and anger, that night, in the room Philip and Bernie shared, Philip slipped into Bernie's bed and fucked Bernie half the night away, roughly and with as much passion as Philip could muster. In the morning, as they both drifted back into awareness, Bernie made Philip fuck him again.

This coupling became a near nightly ritual. Neither man made a single complaint about what he was receiving from the other.

Jack Bell checked out a day later, during the dayshift when Philip was still pumping Bernie in their attic bedroom. To Philip's knowledge, Bell never booked in The Madison again.

But as unsatisfying as sex with Bell had, in retrospect, been for Philip, the part of bringing him to accept who and what he was something Philip was grateful for. It did complicate his life, however. He and Bernie had to be very discreet about their relationship. It was still against the law, not to mention against the code of decorum for The Madison staff. And there was Mr. Stewart's attitude on top of that. Philip wouldn't be at the hotel, wouldn't have had a job to come home from the war to, if it weren't for Mr. Stewart. And now, if it weren't for the loyalty he felt he owed to Mr. Stewart, Philip would move away from the memories of The Madison, if he could.

This all put him in a dangerously balanced sense of limbo.

* * * *

The days and weeks went on, and both Philip and Bernie became adjusted to their life and their secret. Although there had been whispers among the staff of their new relationship, nothing concrete had been said. Normally, Philip's rise to Mr. Stewart's de facto assistant, the head porter's favoritism evident and marked by all on staff, would merit him a private bedroom of his own in the attic. But neither Philip nor Bernie welcomed a change that would make their liaison more dangerous. They became adept at hiding the relationship when working the reception desk, but having to creep around in the staff area at night would not have gone unnoticed for long. They were in luck here, though, at least for now.

"I'm sorry, I tried to replan the staff rooms, but I just can't free a single bedroom for you yet," Stewart told Philip one afternoon.

Trying to look at least a little disappointment, Philip answered, "That's fine. It's probably best, even, as I already hear mumblings about favoritism toward me. Bernie doesn't snore too badly."

Bernie didn't have much of a chance to snore at all, with Philip fucking him through most of the night. The problem that was slowly creeping up on them was to get enough sleep to be able to function in their jobs at all.

The delicate balance was destroyed one evening, though, when a middle-aged guest entered the hotel lobby, walked up to the desk, and asked for Philip. He was a salesman for the type of construction material that went into stage set designs, and he was quick to declare that

The Madison had been recommended to him by the stage impresario, Jack Bell.

"Mr. Bell tells me that you, in particular, give very good service, Philip." He was giving Philip a hard look and a cold smile and held Philip's hand for a moment longer than was necessary when he took his room key. He took a look at the key and noted the room number aloud in a very deliberate tone, "Room 328. You may wish to take note of that room number, Philip. I don't plan to go out this evening. I expect the same good service Mr. Bell told me that you provide."

"I'm sorry, but—" Philip answered. He had no intention of doing this again. The city regulations on hotels were very strict—it didn't take much to get a hotel shut down as a business of ill repute. For that reason, unaccompanied women were not permitted in the hotel bar and were closely attended in all public areas. It would be far worse on a hotel if a staff member were found providing the sorts of services Philip knew this Preston Alexander was suggesting. And if it were males only involved—well, Philip thought the five-story dome over the lobby area would come crashing down.

"It would be very sorry indeed for the hotel if it became known . . . but there's no reason it should become known, should it, Philip? Perhaps you could show me to my room."

Philip looked around in panic for Mr. Stewart, to try to turn the trip to the room over to him, which would be natural and would be enough of a privilege to a guest like Alexander that he couldn't deny accepting the honor. But the head usher was standing over near the entrance to the dining room, conversing with a truly important couple.

In resignation, Philip turned the desk over to Bernie. "I'll be showing Mr. Alexander to his room," he said. Then he added, his eyes on Alexander, who gave Philip a slight smile, "Then, if you can handle the desk alone, I believe I'll take my evening break. I shouldn't be more than a half hour."

At this, Alexander's head inclined and his smile broadened.

Alexander stood in the middle of room 328, while the junior porter brought the suitcase in and placed it on the luggage rack and Philip slowly made the transit of the room, adjusting the drapes and checking the bathroom to ensure it was properly stocked.

As the door to the room closed behind the porter, Alexander was unbuttoning his trouser fly and Philip was kneeling in front of him.

The salesman was quick about it, putting Philip on all fours on the carpet in the center of the room; covering the young man's body from above, Philip's trousers and undergarments down around his ankles; mounting Philip; and fucking him to a quick ejaculation. A ten-dollar bill floated to the carpet next to Philip when the salesman was done. The full import of the business Philip was now end was sealed.

The kicker came when the salesman demanded that Philip return for a couple of hours that night. Philip had to manufacture the need to make a night deposit for the hotel at the hotel's somewhat distant bank before the morning to explain an absence from his room to Bernie. Such was Stewart's reliance on and favoritism toward Philip that Bernie had no reason to question that an important errand like this had been assigned to Philip. And, if nothing else, it gave Bernie a couple of extra hours of needed sleep.

Alexander took Philip more slowly and completely in his hotel room bed that night, not giving Philip a chance to leave until the salesman had dozed off to sleep. Philip quickly cleaned himself up in the bathroom, trying to make sure that there would be no hint to the maid the next day that more than one man had been in the room, and looked both ways to the ends of the corridors when he left. He was in luck that there were no lurking staff members to see him leave Alexander's room at the hour of the morning.

Philip tried to tell himself that this was a one-time happening. The salesman admitted that he'd given Bell a deep discount on stage supplies for information on how he could get his itch scratched in Richmond. Surely, Philip thought, it would be just that one time.

But of course it wasn't. There was the Broadway actor taking the lead in one of Bell's plays and a financier from Charleston who Bell needed to back one of his productions. And, although, it didn't happen often, what Philip was now blackmailed into providing constituted running a male brothel—no matter how high class it was—and could get the hotel closed down. Philip was part of the hotel's receptive staff and the extent of his receptiveness was undeniably illegal.

As the only out Philip could think of, he started to explore where he could get a similar job far away from Richmond—one where he could avoid the extra services. He started to discuss his desire to leave with Bernie, without telling him the real reason why he would do this. Bernie expressed the desire to go with him, and such was their relationship—the only stable and satisfactory aspect to the life Philip had fallen into—that Philip started looking for both of them.

The kicker, of course, was Mr. Stewart. Philip was a surrogate son for the head porter, and Stewart was grooming Philip to take over from him at The Madison. He even told Philip that the reason why he was training Philip so hard and was ignoring the mumblings of the rest of the staff about favoritism was that his doctor had warned him that he needed to slow down with his work and turn much of the responsibility over to someone else.

If Philip just cut and left, it was quite possible that it would kill Mr. Stewart. Certainly it would crush him. Philip couldn't bring himself to do this.

But then that was taken out of his hands. One morning Mr. Stewart didn't appear in the lobby. He had died in his bed in the night.

The staff started to buzz loudly and to give Philip dirty looks when they thought he wasn't looking. But Bernie could see them doing that, of course, and reported it all to Philip.

"They have a right to resent me," Philip said. "I have risen too fast and been moved by too many men who had more right to the training for the job."

When he was called into the hotel manager's office, he knew what he was being summoned for, but he was prepared.

"I thank you, Mr. Taylor, but I'm afraid it would be disruptive to the staff. If you think about it, I'm sure you'll realize that the disgruntlement will disrupt the service the hotel has been known for and will put it at a disadvantage to The Jefferson. Randolph Peyton is your man for the job. He's been here for many years and is respected by the staff. They will accept him where they won't me."

"Yes, I can see your point. But I respect Mr. Stewart's judgment and I must honor his memory. Perhaps the position of head waiter in the main dining room so that everyone's dignity is maintained."

I'm trying to save the dignity of the hotel here, Philip thought in frustration. I'm trying to save The Madison from being judged to be a male brothel. I could as easily be called on to provide the extra services in the position of dining room head waiter as at reception. What he said, though, was, "I don't see how it would save Andre's dignity. He is nowhere close to retiring from that position. No, I have seen this coming. I don't wish to take a position that is in competition with The Madison. If you will give me a good letter of recommendation, I have found another position a good distance from here—at The Homestead, up in Hot Springs, in the mountains. I ask only one thing."

"Yes, what is that?"

"I ask that the staff be instructed not to tell any guest who asks where I have gone. I don't wish anywhere I go to be put into comparison with The Madison."

As Philip left the hotel manager's office, secure in the belief that he had shut down on Jack Bell's recommendation service on his own terms, he knew there was another stipulation for his leaving The Madison. Bernie would be going with him. He'd already bought a cottage in Hot Springs from the inheritance Mr. Stewart was leaving him, and he'd found a position for Bernie in an inn that was separate from The Homestead resort. Neither the hotel nor the inn need know that Philip and Bernie were living together—and living in the way they chose to.

He almost laughed out loud. He had seen a reservation for Jack Bell registered for three weeks hence. By then he and Bernie would be gone, and Jack Bell would have to start all over again if he wanted to compromise the reputation of The Madison.

Covered

"You know I would give you money if you wanted—for anything but what you've said you need money for."

"I know how you feel about my plans to marry Missy Vanderhof, Anton. I wouldn't ask you for the money I need for a honeymoon. In fact, I don't know why you've been willing to set this arrangement up for me."

"I owe a favor to Luigi too."

I felt it was more than this. Some days I felt that Anton was possessive and jealous of my relationship with a woman and other days I felt that he was tired of me. At one time I thought we were moving to a deeper commitment, but now I wasn't sure. I had not been the one who was vacillating, but this needed to be brought to a head.

We were on a balcony of Villa Sebastian overlooking Italy's Lake Como, the town of Bellagio on the far shore, and the Grigna Mountains in the Italian Alps beyond. You couldn't ask for a more idyllic backdrop for what we were doing. I was lying on my back on a chaise lounge, my silk robe parted and flowing away from me on either side. Anton's knees were buried far up the small of my back, his dick already two inches inside me, waiting for me to open fully to him. He was bent nearly in two and had just lifted his mouth from my cock. I had already sucked his cock to throbbing. There was no question that he was going to fuck me.

I had known that this was what the owner of the prestigious New York art gallery had brought me on the business trip to Rome for, although I was surprised he did as he hadn't appreciated at all learning that I planned to marry into the superwealthy Vanderhof family of the Hamptons on Long Island. My cajoling that being married into the Vanderhofs would make me all the more effective in selling the art in his gallery didn't seem to impress Anton much.

To make that momentous move, I also had to declare that I was going fully straight. No more sitting on that fence, going with men and women alike. The Vanderhofs were just too conservative and too much in the public eye. Anton hadn't taken it well that I wouldn't continue with him on the sly in spite of what I told others I associated with.

I owed him everything. He'd pulled me out of a Chippendales lineup in Las Vegas, saying I had just what he wanted in an art salesman—and in his bed. Knowing artists of all kinds, he had diplomas forged for me at the prestigious Potomac School college prep institution in Virginia and the University of Pennsylvania, not wanting to use schools closer to New York, where clients of the gallery might ask "do you know?" questions. He also had completely outfitted me for the part of a well-heeled New York patrician and had schooled me well in the type of art he handled.

In my defense, I learned quickly and didn't flaunt my "degrees."

When I thought he would kick me out for going "straight," he surprised me by offering me the chance to go to Rome with him on a buying trip. He made no bones about where I'd be sleeping during the trip, and I didn't kick up a fuss. I may have pledged (to myself—of course

Missy and her family had no idea I swung both ways. To them, I was just fetching and harmless eye candy) to go one way for something much more comfortable than just security, but the ceremony wasn't for a couple of months and I saw no reason to start early.

Anton was a good lover. He wasn't young—he was in his early fifties—but he was trim and handsome. And he was equipped like a horse and knew how to use his equipment.

I had told him before he'd offered to bring me on this trip that I needed to do some side art deals to earn enough money for the sort of honeymoon Missy and her family would expect. Anton turned me down flat on that—and also said even then he wouldn't give me money to pay for what he said would be the biggest mistake in my life—but he did say, although he didn't want to hear of me making any side art deals, that he'd help me earn the money myself in another way.

He was secretive on how that would happen beyond saying we could combine the trip he already had planned with a money-making venture for me. He really was being too generous about all that—suspiciously so, I thought, knowing how he had railed behind my back about me selling out to the Vanderhofs. For the life of me, though, I couldn't figure out the angle he would be using to stick it to me. Not even after he laid out the plan he'd worked out—which was after he fucked me that morning on the balcony of Villa Sebastian overlooking Lake Como, Belagio, and the Grigna Mountains, could I figure out what his stake in this was—beyond that favor he said he owed Luigi.

We both felt the head of his cock breaching my sphincter muscle. Having done that, he plunged for the depths with that long, thick cock of his, making me arch my back, encase the small of his back with my legs, cry out to the heavens, and hold on for dear life as he pumped me hard and deep. It was a rough fuck, but then that was Anton's style—refined in public demeanor; cruel in bed. It didn't leave me with the impression that he was demonstrating his anger at my decision to leave his bed when we returned to New York.

After he had finished me, making sure that I came before he did, he held for a few minutes, his forehead plastered to mine and watching the fire in my eyes die down to embers of fulfillment and satisfaction. When we'd both cooled—although I knew it wasn't really over; it rarely was over with Anton with just one fuck—he rose off me, pulled me up from the chaise lounge, and guided me over to the marble balustrade overlooking the ground that sloped down to the lake. A stone terrace descended in different levels to the lake and a stone pier and boat house. A swimming pool took up most of the terrace two levels down from the house. Two young men—as young as I was, mid twenties, and in as good a physical shape as I was in, which was very good indeed—were walking around the pool. I had been here a day and a half but I hadn't seen them before—just Luigi, the fashion photographer whose villa this was and his somewhat elderly house staff.

"See the young men down there?" Anton asked.

"Yes. Are they pool boys?" One of them was using a long-handled skimmer to take leaves out of the pool.

"No. They are male models. They are here for Luigi to photograph. If you wish to earn money for your honeymoon, you will get to know those men intimately. And Luigi will be photographing you as well."

I suddenly understood what this money-making plan was. I still was suspicious about Anton's motives, and it may have been that he thought this would embarrass me or that I wouldn't sign off permission to be photographed with those two for someone's private collection. But, if so, Anton didn't fully understand what my short life as a Chippendales dancer had entailed. He should have understood; he fucked me the first night he saw me perform on stage.

I could do this.

* * * *

I was at a disadvantage all during the photo shoots. I spoke a little French, so I could converse to a limited extent with the French model, Jacques, a tall, slender and willowy, androgynous beauty with dark, sultry looks. Luigi, the photographer, a hirsute middle-aged man, who was stocky but heavily muscled, and the other model, an Italian, Paulo, also of dark complexion, but more swarthy than sultry, and strongly muscular, spoke only Italian.

Anton, who, I think, fluently spoke every language known to man, had returned to Rome to buy more paintings, saying that I would know what I needed to do when it arose and that what I needed to do wouldn't have much to do with talking.

What I needed to do was to pay attention and to let Luigi—and the other two models, as needed—manipulate my body as if I was a manikin. And I had to let them pose fashion clothing or remove clothing as they willed. The three of them jabbered like magpies over the scene being shot, and I just did their bidding. Being the blond among dark and sultry Mediterranean men, I always seemed to be in the middle of whatever shoot there was.

Luigi would click off still shots while two assistants walked around with video cameras. We used the full facilities of the villa, from the lakefront to the swimming pool and balcony, and even the various sumptuously appointed bedrooms.

Anton had warned me that the photos included fashion shots but would continue on into three-way sex sessions, with the latter material being sold at high prices to private collectors.

"You'll see clothing shots in international fashion magazines," Anton had said, "But the collector material at the other end of the spectrum will remain in private collector hands."

I made the mistake of not asking him what happened to the material in the middle of the spectrum. I don't know if he would have truthfully told me how some of the fuck scenes would be handled even if I'd asked him. The money being offered, though, was so good that I didn't ask him.

I had never done double penetration before, but I did it now. Typically, the posed clothed shots would move on to me—the Nordic blond—between the two dark-complexioned men, with them undressing me while the three of us kissed and groped one another. More often than not, the first fucking, after I had been on my knees, working their exposed cocks with my mouth, was the two of them taking me separately with the other one still embracing us and both of them clothed. Anton told me later that there was a special market for shots and vids of two clothed men fucking a naked one.

After a break, Jacques and Paulo would get naked too, and we would wrestle around on the given set, with me flat on my back, one of the other models sucking my cock and ass while, my head flung back, I sucked off the other model. They would take turns fucking me then, as I sucked the other one, until the climax came with various positions of both of them with their cocks inside me.

As enjoyable as these two young studs were—in addition to making a lot of money out of letting them have their way with me—the attentions of Luigi were even more arousing. I'd had no idea he would get into the act too, but he did, running the whole gamut from posing with me in clothes for fashion layouts to fucking me hard on lounge beds by the pool and in his own bed, both for the cameras to roll and, at night, between his sheets.

Luigi was well versed in the poses of models, obviously having been one himself earlier in life, and he was very well preserved—a Mediterranean Zeus.

He surprised me the first time he fucked me on the chaise lounge on the villa's balcony where Anton last had nailed me. The surprises were threefold: he manipulated me in such inventive positions; he was horse hung, having a bigger and thicker cock than either of the other models—and of Anton, as well—and I discovered he knew a little English.

"Give me it, give me it, givemeit, baby," he cried out as I was rolled up onto my shoulder blades on the surface of the chaise lounge; Luigi crouched over me, covering me close; my legs stretched out, my ankles fisted in his hands; and his cock driving deep inside me.

I was doing some yelling too and moaning at the thickness of him; the feel of his curly, salt-and-pepper chest hair rubbing on my chest; and the big cock of his penetrating and corkscrewing down into me. All the time the cameras were running and an assistant was clicking off still shots.

"Oh god, yes, fuck me, Fuck me, FUCK ME!" I responded with genuine passion.

"Fuck you, fuck you, fuck you, right, baby," he answered in heavily accented English, as he drove harder and faster.

"Fuck, yeah, fuck yeah. Give it to me," I answered in English, involuntarily, not knowing or caring if he understood me. Just wanting him to continue pounding me.

And then, as he settled down into a rhythm, "Lax, baby. Daddy take good care you."

Presuming he was telling me to relax, I did so, going limp, allowing him to penetrate deeper. And he indeed was taking good care of me—very good care indeed.

* * * *

I was lying on my belly on Anton's bed back in Manhattan, and he was stretched out on top of me, his cock still buried inside me, both of us, no doubt, concentrating all of our sensations on his cock going flaccid inside me. I thought of it as a farewell fuck. I hadn't told him, but I'd found a small apartment of my own. There had been no change in our relationship since we'd come back to New York from Rome. And I was slightly irritated that he had so easily given me over to the type of modeling job on Lake Como that he had. Surely he knew what it would entail. He couldn't think much of our relationship if he'd let me fall into that.

I half wondered if he'd gotten a kickback from Luigi for bringing me to the Italian photographer. Or maybe this was his passive aggressive way of getting back at me for my plan to marry and then be faithful to a woman.

We were getting closer and closer to a wedding date, so I had decided that I might as well just leave Anton's bed—and his employment if he fired me—sooner rather than right before moving out to Long Island to the Vanderhof estate.

"Anton, I think—" I started to say to begin the transition.

"I want you to see something I bought today," he said, interrupting me as if he hadn't heard me say anything, He pulled out of me and bounced out of the bed. He left the room. When he came back, he was holding a paperback book in his hands. "I think you'll find this interesting."

I took it from him, looked at the cover of the book, and then back at him, in surprise.

"That's me on the cover of the book—with Luigi. Not a fashion shot. An image of us embracing, half naked." The title on the cover was "Taken at Lake Como." The author's name was habu.

"Yes. Isn't it a scintillating photo? Now I wish I'd been able to stay at Lake Como for that week. Luigi told me that you were quite enjoyable—quite good. Go ahead, read a few paragraphs."

Half in shock, I opened the book and started to read:

> "Give me it, give me it, givemeit, baby," the count cried out as the American rent-boy, Jon, was rolled up onto his shoulder blades on the surface of the chaise lounge; Count Benito crouched over the beautifully formed body of the blond prostitute, covering him close; stretching his flexible legs out, gripping the young man's ankles with his strong, patrician hands; and driving his thick cock deep inside the well-used anal passage.
>
> The American writhed under the horse-hung count, crying out for the fuck and moaning at the thickness of him; the feel of his curly, salt-and-pepper chest hair rubbing on the American's heaving chest; and the big cock of his penetrating and corkscrewing down into the depths of the throbbing channel.
>
> "Oh god, yes, fuck me, Fuck me, FUCK ME!" the rent-boy answered.
>
> "Fuck you, fuck you, fuck you, right, baby," the count answered in heavily accented English, as he drove harder and faster.
>
> "Fuck, yeah, fuck yeah. Give it to me," Jon answered in English, involuntarily, not knowing or carrying if the count

116

understood him. Just wanting him to continue pounding away with his cock.

And then, as he settled down into a rhythm, the count whispered, "Relax, baby. Daddy will take good care of you." Having given the Italian aristocrat the arousal that got him hard and saddled, Jon relaxed and went limp, his arms dangling off the sides of the chaise lounge on the balcony of the count's lakeside villa, and arching his head over the end of the divan for his mouth to receive the cock of the count's son, Guido, as the young man moved into place and his hands slid down to the American rent-boy's nipples.

"That's me," I said, now in deeper shock. "Not just the cover image but the text as well. And whereas Luigi's name was changed, mine wasn't. Anyone I know reading this will know it's me."

"Precisely," Anton said, with a smile on his face. "I thought using your real name was a nice touch. I think I forgot to tell you that, in addition to fashion photographs and private porn clients, Luigi runs a gay male image photo service. Your image is going to be plastered over quite a few erotica and porn books, I'll bet—a lot of them with gay content. This one is as connected to you personally as it can get."

"I don't understand. Why—?"

"It would be tragic, I think if this were to fall into the hands of the Vanderhofs. I doubt they'd want you to marry into their family with book covers like this floating around."

"You would—?"

"I've thought of everything I could to keep you with me, to keep you from making the mistake of trying to act straight. It would be a miserable life for you. And I

117

want you so much. You don't have to marry Missy Vanderhof. You could marry me."

"Marry you? You'd go to these lengths to keep me with you?"

Beyond what I was saying, I was searching my mind for evidence that he, as he said, had tried everything he could to keep me with him. I certainly hadn't seen that. I thought I'd done everything I could to open his eyes to committing to me, without effect. What had he just said? That I could marry him?

"Yes, you must know I want you to stay with me."

"Well, if you want it that badly . . ." I tried to hide my euphoria. This was all I wanted. Bringing in the possibility of marrying Missy Vanderhof had all been a Hail Mary ploy to try to make him commit. And it had worked. Not in the way I had anticipated, but it nevertheless had worked.

"Let me show you how badly I want to keep you," he whispered, as, having gotten hard again, his cock once more was beginning to move inside me.

I relaxed. "Oh, Daddy, give it to me," I whispered, determined to read the rest of that book as soon as I could to see just how much sex I had enjoyed between its covers.

Mountain Memory

We both were wearing our fatigues and bundled up against the fall night air at the edge of the woods behind the mess hall. So far there was no reason to adjust our warm clothing beyond my fly being unbuttoned. My cock was out as I leaned back against a tree trunk, but it was being kept warm by Corporal Hart's mouth enveloping it.

Corporal Hart was just one of my willing boys. We'd come a long way together to Berlin and beyond from the landing at Anzio, and many of us had become as close and comforting and interested in and willing for mutual release as men could be who were on the move on their feet for two years and subject to being shot on the spot for finding their relief in women encountered along the trek across Europe. Not that it wasn't equally dangerous to be caught engaging in the release we did.

Hart looked up into my eyes, his with a pleading expression on them, asking, I knew, if I was ready to belly him against the tree, cover his back, and give him the full length and girth of my cock.

I was, and would have done so, if it hadn't been for the commotion coming from the back door of the mess hall, by the trashcans, where Cook was speaking gruffly to someone in the shadows.

"Hey, what yer doin' there? And who are you? You're not from the camp, are you? A local. A Kraut, I think."

With a sigh, I gently pushed Ted Hart back on his haunches, folded my cock back into my pants, and buttoned up as I walked toward the mess hall. Duty called. It already was nearly pitch black here below a cliff of Kehlstein Mountain in the German Alps, in the most remote southeast corner of Bavaria. Only the light from the mess hall kitchen windows, cast across the shadows of two men, one rather small and struggling and the other tall and heavy and grasping the smaller figure close, provided any context to Cook's gruff voice and answering whimpers in German. My immediate thought as I approached this tableau was that there would be some sentry I'd have to dress down. German nationals weren't allowed in the camp without escort—and not at night at all.

In fact, we had license to shoot them on sight. There were signs, in German, explaining that plastered on the compound fences.

"I found this Kraut rummaging around in the trashcans," Cook said as I walked up. "I told you that I thought there was a wild animal at the cans for the last week. Turns out it's only this little guy."

"Well, let me see what we have here," I said, as I reached them. "He doesn't look so dangerous."

And, indeed, he didn't look dangerous at all. He looked so weak and emaciated that he might be on his last legs. Pity that, I thought. He was quite a good-looking young man. Not young, young, of course. Maybe his late twenties or early thirties, but life obviously was being cruel to him. It hadn't been all that rewarding to any of us as World War II was winding down across Europe. And some of us had to walk here from the toe of the boot that was Italy.

I had taken my guys all the way to Berlin to help cut off the head of the snake there the previous May, not losing one soldier in the process. For our reward, we were sent up here into the far reaches of Bavaria to sit in a temporary camp between the mountain town of Obersalzberg, up against the lower cliffs of the Kehlstein Mountain and in the shadow of the third highest peak in the German Alps, Watzman Mountain. I don't wish to sneer at the assignment we received as we waited to be shipped home—nearly all of us to wives and children no matter what we'd gotten into for solace and relief during the last two years marching from Italy to here. We actually had a plum assignment. Obersalzberg had been the winter retreat for Adolf Hitler himself and his sycophants, built up here on the lower slopes of the Kehlstein as a retreat for the führer during the 1936 Olympics in nearby Garmish-Partenkircher.

Hitler had spent more and more time up here in the waning years of the war, and he'd stashed a lot of the loot up here that he and his cronies had pulled out of art museums all across Europe during the German occupation. My unit's job was to guard and inventory this stash until it could be properly dispersed again. We were not far from the end of accomplishing this, which was a good thing, because the winter of 1945-46 was pressing in on us, and this place would be one snow-covered iceberg come December.

And a look at the obviously starving young man in the tattered clothing and overcoat who Cook was holding by the scruff of the neck told me that it was unlikely he could survive the winter.

His eyes showed a mixture of fear and resignation. My heart turned over. I'd seen far too much of the suffering among civilians in this war. There was nothing about him that spoke soldier. He fit the bill of starving artist more. The complete look of surrender and vulnerability in his eyes moved me—and not just my heart. Cleaned up and fed he would have been almost irresistible to me and my appetites.

"Who are you and how did you get into the camp?" I asked. He looked at me with a complete lack of comprehension. So, a German refugee no doubt. Certainly not American and most certainly not belonging in this camp. I knew all of my men—more than a few of them I knew biblically.

"Are you hungry. Were you looking in the trashcans for food?"

There was a flash of recognition in his eyes, but still he said nothing. He probably knew that rummaging for food here was inviting a death bullet. He had to have been totally desperate to even contemplate risking it. At that point the assistant cook, Private Green came to the kitchen door.

"Kyle," I said to him. "Is anything left over from the night's mess?"

"We have a bit ham left and there's bread," the private answered.

"Can you make a sandwich with that please—a big one—and give it to this man, and then escort him back to the main gate, please? I'm too tired tonight to write up an incident report. But on your way back, please make a round of the sentries, let them know a civilian got into the camp. Tell them to look at every inch of fencing for a breach and report to me tomorrow. And tell them that, despite the breach, I haven't released any orders permitting target practice."

"Yes, sir," Kyle answered. When he came back with the sandwich, wrapped in a newspaper, and handed it to the young man, Cook let loose of him and I drew both Cook's attention and that of Kyle to me to ask them just not to say anything to anyone about this. We were not supposed to offer any help at all to German civilians. In the moment it took for me to do that, though, the young German had disappeared.

I sighed. I'd have to write up some sort of report after all. "I still want you to go to the sentries, Kyle, I said. I hope to God one of them doesn't shoot the young man while he's trying to get back out of the camp. But there's a breach in the fencing someplace. The only side not covered is the cliff below the Kehlstein, and that's a sheer rock wall."

A little sad now—at what war does to us all—and slightly irritated that I'd have to write up an incident report, I returned to the edge of the forest where Corporal Hart was waiting for me in the dark. Reverting to an earlier stage of our preparation, we engaged in a bit of lip play and groping before he sucked me off again. It was with weary thoughts of all we'd been through and the toll it had taken on people like that young man at the mess hall, whose hands I'd seen—the hands of a professional or artisan, not of a farmer of soldier—that I embraced Ted Hart from behind as he leaned into a tree and spread his legs, entered him deep to his moans and groans, and worked him hard to give both of us release and something more pleasant to think of than what we'd been through in the last two years.

I was finishing with Ted, holding him close in my embrace, his head turned to me, our lips meeting, and the last short spurts of my cum ejaculating into the quick of his passage when I floated up out of our "transported elsewhere" time separated from the present and slowly became aware of our surroundings again.

As I drifted back into reality, I sensed that the two of us weren't alone—that we were being observed. I slowly rotated my head around, not wanting to spook off whoever it was. But just that slight turn was enough for me to hear the crackle of pine needles underfoot deeper into the forested area. Just the glimpse I saw was of tattered clothes in browns and grays and black, and I instantaneously thought of the young German who had been caught at the trashcans.

I released Ted, who slumped against the tree trunk, and, after an affectionate stroke of his cheek, strode out in the direction in which I sensed we had been watched. But of course when I got to the tree I had marked as the figure's hiding place, no one was there.

* * * *

Cook approached me in the mess hall two evenings later as the dinner hour was drawing down and men were leaving the hall. We were in a state of unaccustomed limbo here at the base of the German Alps. The men had been warily trudging through fields, avoiding roads, where ambushes could be set, and being ever aware of their environment for years before landing here in the small camp near Obersalzberg below the Eagle's Nest, Hitler's famous mountaintop tea house that was carved out of the rock of the Kehlstein. Here, the march was over. The war was over. Presumably the danger was over, although there continued to be whispers of "lost cause" partisan cells that kept the Americans close to their camps and bases. There was little for the men to do in the evening after dinner and before night when they could surreptitiously move about their barracks into each other's beds. They lingered in the mess hall, but it was dark and growing late.

I habitually ate late, walking around to the tables earlier in the meal, coffee in hand, checking on the well-being of the men—and frequently making assignations with one or two of them for meetings in my separate room in the night.

"Excuse me, Captain," Cook said, his voice hesitant.

"Yes? Is there a problem? I saw the supply truck come in today. We were shortchanged in some rations?"

"No, Captain, that is all good. It's the German refugee from the other night."

"The young man who somehow got into and out of the camp without alerting one of the sentries?" I was still chaffing over that happening. I had doubled the sentries. I also was chaffing a bit from having gone soft and giving him something to eat. I was somewhat surprised that I didn't have half the population of Obersalzberg at the front gate the next morning begging to receive what he had.

"Yes, the same," Cook said. "He returned. I caught him going through the trash again."

"And did he run off when you found him—like the other night? I can call out the men to search the camp for him. We need to know how he's getting in."

"No, sir. I have detained him."

"Detained him?" A chill went up my spine. The regulations were to summarily shoot any German invading a camp to steal anything, especially food. I thought it was barbaric, but I had been assured that it was the only way to keep the starving population from trying to overrun the camps. An example ran through my mind that had been spread around the country and, I had been assured by high command, was true and was repeated as a deterrent. The story went that a young German boy earned scraps of food at a U.S. base near Heidelberg shortly after the fall of Berlin by shining the shoes of the base commander. He was seen running out of the commander's tent with a pair of shoes in his hand and was shot by a sentry who didn't know of the arrangement. Just beyond where he fell was a rock on which the shoe polish and brush were neatly arranged. He had just decided to shine them outside rather than inside the tent that day.

Deterrent perhaps, but it choked me up each time I thought of the cruelty of war. I knew I could have shot the young German scavenger two nights previously—and that perhaps some of the men would have expected me to do so and would think it weakness that I didn't. That was probably why I only told who I had to about the incident. So, part of me was relieved that he had escaped.

But now he was back, and under control, if I understood Cook correctly.

"Yes, sir, I have him locked in the storage room."

"Well, I guess we'd better attend to him, then," I said, with a deep sigh. "Let's not let the whole camp hear about this, though." I had absolutely no resolve to shoot the young man. After trying to discern how he was getting into the camp, I'd send him on his way. I was still struggling in my mind whether to send him away with food or not. If I fed him again, I knew he'd be back. If I didn't feed him, maybe he would realize this was a blind alley for him. What I was really struggling with in my mind, I knew, was whether I wanted him to come back again—and where that might lead. I hadn't been able to get him out of my mind.

When the storage door was open, I was torn between crying and laughing. The young man was sitting on the floor, in the dark, and had found and torn into a sack of raw potatoes. He was munching on one. He looked up at me in the doorway with a panicked look on his face, but he was holding onto to half a raw potato as if his life depended on it. I didn't think he was going to give up the rest of the sack without a fight to the death either. And, as he looked even more emaciated than he had two nights previously, it's possible that his life did depend on it.

There was nothing else I could do. I turned to Cook. "Is there still stew in the pot from the evening's meal?"

"Yes, sir."

"Dish up a bowl of it—and a chunk of bread and some coffee. And bring it to our guest in the mess hall. And, Private Green," I said, turning to the assistant cook, "See if you can rustle up some civilian clothes that will fit this young man. Put them in my room."

I went into the storage room and bent down, and pulled the young man up to his feet. He was as light as a feather. "Kommen mit mir, bitte," I said, hoping my tortured German was understandable. "*Sie mussen essen.*"

He looked at me with glazed eyes, but he allowed me to guide him into the now-empty mess hall. He was still clutching the sack of potatoes under his arm and I made no move to take it away from him.

After he'd polished off the second bowl of stew and I motioned that any more would probably make him sick and he'd lose it all, I attempted to communicate with him again. "*Konnen Sie sagen mir—?*"

"Perhaps we should speak English," he suddenly said. "I appreciate your attempts at German, but ..."

I was too shocked to speak in any language for a few seconds. "You speak English. And I mean English English, and your accent is impeccable."

"Thank you. I have lived in both London and Paris."

This just made it all the more tragic for me. He was educated and spoke with a refined accent. And he'd been brought this low.

"What are you doing here then? And are you English?"

"I'm German. I was painting abroad when the war started. But I had to come back ... for my family."

Ah, I was right. An artist. He was a painter. "And did you find your family?"

"No," he said softly. "I'm Jewish. My family was gone by the time I returned."

"Oh. My name is Trent. Yours is—?"

"You can call me Jake. But I see that you are a captain. So I must call you captain."

"OK, then, Jake. You can call me Captain Carter. I've asked that some cleaner clothes be found for you and you can come back to my room. I have a bath. You can shower there. I take it where you live doesn't have

127

washing facilities?" Of course I wanted him to tell me where he lived and how he was able to get in the camp without being seen by a sentry—and possibly shot.

"I couldn't possibly . . . but thank you for the meal. I should go now."

We both rose from the table. "Are you going to leave that sack of potatoes here?" I asked. And when he looked lovingly at it, I said, "You can have the potatoes, Jake. But you have to stop coming into the camp. We are supposed to shoot anyone who does that."

"Being shot is not the worst thing that can happen here in this time," he said simply, his eyes downcast. But he picked up the sack of potatoes.

"Winter is going to be bad here," I said. "We should only be here for another month or so, but if you promise not to come into camp to go through the trashcans again—and if you don't tell others of it—I will see to it that you can have some food left for you every evening."

He stood there stolidly, with down-cast eyes, although I discerned a slight tremble in his body that might have be caused by emotion. I was struck with how beautiful he was, even in this condition, and my body was stirring.

"The food must be left outside the camp, though. Do you know of the track up the mountain from here, and the religious shrine about a 100 yards beyond the main gate at the side of the road—the one with a closed wooden container at its base?"

He merely nodded.

"You will fine food there for as long as we're camped here."

I told myself I wasn't doing this because he moved me to desire—and certainly not because he was German—but because he was Jewish and had been in freedom and had returned despite the danger to find his family. And because he hadn't found them. The war in

Europe was over now—justice and humanity needed to be brought back into the world. Even if only in small ways at the beginning.

"But I have a condition for leaving you food periodically."

"What?"

"You must get cleaned up tonight and take a new set of clothes. Those are in tatters."

When he had showered in the bathroom attached to my room—having my own facilities being the privilege of rank and command even if my unit was a small one—he padded out into my room in the nude. His body was perfectly formed and even as thin as he'd become, he retained muscle tone. He was beautifully equipped.

"Are you going to take me to your bed now?" he asked simply, in a low voice, his eyes, with the long, curly dark eyelashes fluttering.

"Excuse me?" I said. I had taken an overcoat I had replaced out of a closet, and I held it between him and me defensively, wondering wildly how he'd know that I'd developed a hard on from the knowledge that he was naked, in my shower.

"I saw you the other night, with the young man, in the forest. I saw that you made sex with men. If you want me clean, it must be because you wish to use me. You may to do. I will lie under you. I am sorry that I am too thin to be desirable now, but you are being kind to me, and—"

"No, please. That's not necessary," I said, embarrassed—embarrassed mostly because all the time he'd been in the shower I'd been fantasizing about fucking him, thoughts that only ran rampant when he came into the room naked. "I assure you that I have no designs on you. Just put on these clothes and go, please. I'll have someone escort you to the main gate. And take the food from the shrine; don't try coming in to go through the trash. You may be shot for trying."

"I am sorry if I have presumed—or if I have displeased you," he said with downcast eyes.

"Not at all," I answered. "I would not dream of taking advantage of you, though."

"It would not be taking advantage," he murmured. "I do lie under men."

This was my opening, but I was too shocked and obsessed with my responsibility to answer. And not having responded at once became the answer.

I stood, quaking, after he'd left. I wanted him even more now than I had before he'd offered himself to me and I had turned him away. It was only after he'd gone that I considered that what I'd told him meant that, under other circumstances, I would want to fuck him.

I hadn't done what I had for him to get my cock inside him. Surely I hadn't. I didn't want to believe that this might have been a motive, even subconsciously. I wasn't that much of a using predator. Thinking on that made me think beyond that. All that time walking from Italy to here. I was in command. I fucked what, five or six of my men regularly. Was that because they wanted it as much as I did? Had I been fooling myself? Taking advantage of my position. Surely the army would see it that way.

It snowed steadily although lightly for the next two days, accumulating maybe three inches of snow, but promising a blizzard in the not-too-far-distant future. I was under the covers—a pile of covers—reaching "warm" for the first time that day in this indifferently constructed group of temporary camp buildings. I was nearly asleep, when I felt the draft of the covers being raised and a body slipping in under the covers.

Earlier, Corporal Hart—Ted—has been with me in my bed. We had writhed against each other on top of the sheets, as we often did, not being able to be satiated enough with the touch, and smell, and taste of each other. As was also often the case, I had speared him in a side split and moved in and out of him deeply until he was putty in my embrace—relaxed and completely open so that he took me to the root, murmuring his surrender to me. I turned onto my back, pulling him with me so that he was full length on top of me, both of us bending our legs so that we could get leverage off the surface of the bed with the balls or heels of our feet for me to thrust up into him and him to rear back into my pelvis to meet the thrusts.

I embraced his chest with one arm, latched onto the lobe of an ear with my teeth, and fisted and jacked off his cock as I pounded his ass. We came almost simultaneously, Ted first spouting toward the ceiling and splashing on his belly and chest, and me creaming his channel deep.

As we lay there, panting, the cold of the room crept in to push away the heat of our sex, and, reluctantly, he said, he left me.

I hadn't called for Ted to attend me; he had come to me on his own in the night. I had felt so guilty about the possibility that the men I fucked only allowed me to do so because of my rank that I hadn't been with any of them for two days. Concerned when yet another body burrowed under the covers with me several minutes after the corporal had left my bed, I moved my hand toward the nightstand where I had laced my service revolver, but a hand gripped my wrist.

"Please, Captain Carter, you said I'd only be shot for entering the camp again if I was going through the trashcans. I came for you, not the trash. I meant what I said when I said it wouldn't be taking advantage."

"I told you . . . you don't need to—" I didn't finish that sentence as I was overtaken by a moan as the mouth of the young German who had told me to call him Jake found and enveloped my cock.

When he had subdued me into an irrevocable want of him, which didn't take long, he lifted his head and said,

"Although I am grateful, I'm not here because of that; I'm here because I want you inside me. I have lusted for you since I watched you fuck that young soldier against the tree—and then again just now, as I watched you two through your window. I want your cock. I want what you gave that young soldier just now." He slid his lips over my cock again and, with a sigh, I gave in to his ministrations.

With me on my back, he rode my cock for what seemed to be hours. We lay and murmured to each other as we rested between fuckings.

"You do this like a pro," I whispered. "I thought you said you had a family here you'd come back for. I had assumed a wife . . . and children."

"One does what one has to to survive in wartime. All I had for the last year that was marketable was what the guards of the führer's winter house craved. I acquired, first an expertise and then a taste, and then a need for it myself. Yes, I had a wife and children," he answered. "I think of you as having a wife and children too back in your country. You do have a family, don't you?"

"Yes," I admitted, "I do."

"It's the war. It's the same for both of us, I think. It's just the war. A man has his needs, no matter the circumstances he finds himself in."

"Yes, it's just the war," I answered, as he brought his face down to mine for a kiss. But it wasn't just the war. Not with this man. It was more than that. I couldn't fool myself about that. "We'll be leaving in four more weeks," I said, not knowing why I'd brought it up. But, in fact, knowing why. And then, many minutes later, when the panting and rhythm of the fuck had abated into a mutual flow and we were lying there, recovering, knowing we weren't done, only taking a rest to recover, I whispered, "I will miss these mountains." I couldn't tell him what I'd now discovered I'd really miss.

"You don't have mountains where you come from?"

"Yes," I answered, with a laugh. "I come from the Rocky Mountains, running down the middle of America."

"I've heard about those. Like our alps, but not as tall."

"Yes. I'll miss the tallness of these mountains."

"And I'll miss the longness and thickness of you— the vigor and musky scent of you," he said, after a hesitating. "But we'll have these four weeks, if you'll let me come again."

"Yes, we'll have these four weeks. But then we'll be gone and it will be the middle of the winter. There'll be no more food to put out for you."

"There wasn't food before you came. Afterward I don't think it will be the food I miss from your going."

We fucked again then, tenderly, me holding him under me on his belly, and languidly mining his ass passage.

He thought I was asleep when he slipped out of the bed, dressed, and left. But I wasn't. I still needed to learn how he was getting into the camp past the fences and guards. I quickly pulled on my fatigues and followed him at a distance, aided by watching for his tracks in the recently fallen snow. I followed his footsteps up to the base of the Kehlstein Mountain towering over the camp to the south, but then lost the track where the rock started. Still, it all looked like a sheer rock wall to me. That's why we hadn't bothered to fence it in.

Three weeks and five visits from him later, I discovered where he went and how he got there. I managed that by staking out the shrine where the food was left for him and following him from there. His trek took him up a rocky incline at the base of the Kehlstein and then descending by a circuitous channel with rock walls on each side into the back of the camp. Another, nearly invisible, crevice in the rock was accessible by moving sideways. This passage opened up and ascended the mountainside to a glade of trees. A shack close to collapse was hidden in the trees.

I stood at the door as he mussed with the food over a small table, turned away from me so that he didn't see me for the longest time. The room contained the table, a rickety straight chair, and a cot. The rest of the room was taken up with painting supplies. An unfinished oil painting sat on an easel.

The painting was of the nearby Zugspitz, the tallest mountain in the German Alps. The mountain commanded the distance. Nearly centered in the foreground was a ravine leading down toward the base of the mountain and rising on either side of the canvas. Mist enveloped the floor of the ravine. On the left, rising out of a rock outcropping on the side of the ravine, roots clinging to hard-won crevices in the rock, was a lone pine tree. The branches of the tree were nearly barren, although there was a hint that it was still fighting for life even though its only grounding was solid rock.

Although the painting obviously was of the Zugspitz, upon closer inspection, I knew the painting really was about that lone pine, clinging to the last vestiges of life by tenacious and hopeful roots buried in the crevices of hard, unforgiving rock. The mountain of the painting reminded me so much of the mountain rising above my family ranch in Colorado that it choked me up and I briefly entertained the thought that he'd been to the Rockies. That must have made an audible sound, as Jake turned in surprise.

I expected him to be angry. I had ferreted out his lair, which he obviously had wanted to keep as a secret.

He merely smiled a sad smile though, and started to undress and move to the cot, where I fucked him like the end of the world was at hand.

And for us, it was. I had to inform him that it would be too dangerous for him to visit the camp again, and that I'd now be too busy to break away to visit him here. The orders to pack out had arrived and the last week in the camp would be chaos.

He let me go with a tender kiss at the door of his shack. He said nothing about what this departure meant for him—either in the lost sex or the end to his food supply. And I said nothing either. I didn't want to think about it, and there didn't seem to be anything to say about it. But in subsequent years I was haunted by not having found some way to protect him.

The night before the transport convoy arrived to take us away for the flight home, one of my men came to my office.

"This parcel was left for you at the gate, Captain," he said.

"Who—?"

"It was a German guy, but he didn't give a name. But he's the guy who has been coming into camp at your order." The soldier knew what Jake and I had been doing, of course. All of the men probably knew.

When I unfolded the yellowed, German-language newspaper print away from the parcel, it was revealed to be the painting of the Zugspitz I'd seen on the easel in Jake's shack. It had been finished. In my melancholy at parting from Jake, the lone pine stood out of the painting even more now than it ever had done.

Regardless of what else had to be done, I left my office immediately and, after some fruitless searching, finally found the entrance of the ravine at the back of the camp that led me to the doorstep of Jake's shack. The shack was deserted. I decided that he probably was right—that good-bye was inevitable and prolonging it would only add to the grief.

Since he wasn't there, I told myself that he had gone into the town and would find shelter and sustenance there. I kept telling myself that for some time. I don't think I ever convinced myself that he'd done so, though.

Like many a soldier before me, I returned to the States, to my lucrative cattle ranch, and to my wife and two children. I fell immediately into a normal, straight life. Like so many others—the lucky ones—I was able to compartment off my war years from the home life I had gone to war to preserve. And like so many others, I wasn't quick to respond to my children's innocent questions of "What did you do in the war, Daddy?" because I had gone to war to save them from knowing what one has to do in war and the totally different person it demands you be.

It was only when I was feeling vulnerable or nostalgic that I thought back on what I had done with men during the war—and inevitably my thoughts at these times went to Jake.

I shouldn't have rewrapped the painting in the yellowed German-language newspaper print. In shipping it had clotted with what must have been still-damp paint on a hip of stone on the side of the Zugspitz and took the top layer of paint away, leaving an impression of the printing on the newspaper. For a year or more I searched for an artist who would touch the painting up for me. All of them in the Denver and even the Los Angeles area said that the work was too fine for them to touch.

They all asked me where I'd gotten it. I, of course, was vague with my answer. After a while, considering the interest the painting evoked from other artists, I began to fear that someone would think that I had raided the art stash in Bavaria that my unit had been assigned to protect and I hid the painting away. I could not forget it, though, and each time I took it out to look at and my eyes went to the lone pine, I remembered—and I felt myself go hard. The painting kept pulling me back to it and, nearly a year later, when I had occasion to go to New York City on business, I decided to make another effort to have the damage to the painting repaired.

A prestigious gallery in New York said they had an artist who could attempt a touchup. "But I doubt that anyone can match the delicacy and tone of the original artist. You'll be able to tell the difference."

"Do the best you can," I said. "It pains me to see it like it is now. It looks wounded, and I don't want to think of it that way."

"By the way, do you have any idea what you have here?" the gallery official asked.

"Yes, it's of the Zugspitz in the German Alps. I served near there at the end of the war. It looks just like the real thing. It was given to me by a refugee, in exchange for food."

"Yes, it would look like the real thing," she said. "You have here a Jacob Gelmen painting. There's his mark down in the corner. This painting is worth a big fortune, even with the flaw. Very few Gelmens survived the war, although he was the toast of London galleries when the war started. It was ironic, but the London studio where he worked and where most of his paintings were stored was bombed out by a German rocket during the London blitz."

"A famous artist?"

"Absolutely," she said. "A real tragedy. He was Jewish, you know. He was safely away in London—well, as safe as London was under rocketing conditions. But his family was in Germany. He left London to go find them long after everyone knew that would be suicide—he was Jewish, you know. Yes, I already told you that. Sometime in 1943, I think. Yes, indeed. Should you ever want to sell this, Sothbys would be delighted to handle an auction for you."

"Thank you, but I don't think I could ever bear to part with it," had been my answer. I was so choked up that I barely could get the words out. Besides the fact that if I did try to sell it, the question of how I got it when I was in charge of protecting an art stash would crop up again, there's no way I would ever give it up.

I almost didn't ask, but I couldn't bear not to. "The artist, Gelmen. Did he stop painting?"

"He must have been killed in the war when he returned to Germany," she answered. "Nothing has been reported of him since the war. This looks like the paintings of his later work. It may have been one of the last pieces he painted."

The gallery's artist did a decent job of touching the painting up—at least it was better than the mar of the paint removed by the newsprint—but the real benefit of having it retouched was that the touchup only highlighted how much finer the original artwork was.

And, even more than before, it no longer offered a "marred" focal point to take away from the centrality of that lone pine, clinging to life on its rock.

Before the end of the decade, I found an excuse to fly back to Germany—and to Bavaria—on my own. On the ruse of wanting to hike in the German Alps, I went back to Obersalzberg, being able to stay in the U.S. Army's General Walker Hotel thanks to having maintained reserve status and risen to the rank of major. I found where our camp had been, now, I was happy to see, returned to productive farmland. And I found the opening in the rock wall at the base of the Kehlstein.

I found the shack, but the roof had caved in and there was no sign that anyone had been there for years. The winter of 1945-46 had been a rough one in Germany. It was hard to conceive that Jacob Gelmen could have survived if he had remained here. I almost poked around in the ruins of the shack but decided not to, being very afraid of what I might find.

But if he had survived, there would have been no reason for him not to have resurfaced in the art world and taken his rightful place and enjoyed his international reputation.

I both didn't want to think about it and wanted to cherish the memory of the short time we'd had together—in what now was a world that was closed to me and taboo to mention to anyone.

The painting, though—and the art gallery official had shown me on the back where it had been titled as "Mountain Memory"—was mounted over the fireplace in the living room of the ranch house.

There was a fire in that section of the rambling, log-sided ranch house in 1952. The only object I was able to save in addition to getting the family out before the roof collapsed was "Mountain Memory."

I had saved from that fire all that was precious to me, though.

H003

The plane was, Conner estimated, four hours out of Frankfurt when it started its descent. He couldn't be precise on the time, because they had taken away his wristwatch. In fact, in a men's room in the Frankfurt airport, they had taken all of his clothes away. He'd also been given an intrusive cavity search in a stall, while one of them, armed with a mop bucket and mop stood at the door behind a "closed for cleaning" sign. Then he'd been given a new set of clothes. Somehow they'd gotten the sizes right.

They hadn't denied him a window seat, though, and he knew they were landing on a remote runway of the U.S. Air Force base at Incirlik, on the underbelly of Turkey. His handlers hadn't anticipated this—at least not in the instructions they'd given him—and he only knew it was Incirlik because the others had prepared him so much better so much longer. It didn't matter, though. Taking all of his clothes from him hadn't made a difference; neither did the consensus of his handlers that the destination would be somewhere in eastern Europe. Of course they could just be zigzagging him around Europe and the Middle East to totally mix up his sense of direction.

They certainly would do whatever they could to hide the ultimate destination. The whereabouts of ultimate destination was a large part of what he sought in his assignment.

The apparent military officer who was the only other passenger on the plane was wearing a U.S. Air Force uniform with the insignia of a lieutenant. He'd made no effort to hide an identity with the U.S. military, so Conner assumed he wasn't really U.S. military. Conner's handlers—who also claimed they were U.S. military, had prepared him for that subterfuge. They'd told him those who were transporting him were CIA. But Conner didn't care about those games. It didn't mean shit to him who they represented, or who his handlers were doing this for. The cause was fine; the money was better; the adventure of it was arousing to him.

It beat the monotony of what he had been doing. And he'd been waiting for an opportunity like this for some time.

The escorting officer hadn't bothered to cover up his nametag, which said "Preston." So, Conner assumed he wasn't really named Preston. That didn't bother him either, because he wasn't really named Conner.

He was, however, exactly what he had been contracted to be—a male escort . . . prostitute . . . rent-boy . . . male whore. Whatever they wanted to call him. And he understood that where he'd be going it would be to service dozens of men who hadn't had any for some time—men in top physical condition whose demands would be rigorous.

But, at the same time, he was more than just a male prostitute and was on this journey to accomplish more than satiating a lineup of randy and fit men.

Before he deplaned, Lieutenant Preston placed a blindfold over Conner's eyes and guided him down the stairs to a waiting jeep. Conner had seen the jeep parked where the plane had come to a stop, and he thought it just a tad late for Preston to be blindfolding him. But then Preston wouldn't have known that Conner had been schooled on identifying possible landing ports from the air, aided in this case by the approach from the direction of the setting sun that had been taken when coming in over the Mediterranean Sea.

When the blindfold was taken off, Conner found himself in a small room that must be a medical room of some sort—a doctor's examination room. The coloring was stark white and the furniture was limited to a metal desk with a straight metal chair facing it and another one beside it; a dominating green enamel medical examination table, complete with stirrups; a standing scales; and a clothes horse. A full set of clothes down to briefs, socks, and shoes was hanging on the clothes horse. There were two doors, but no windows. One door, closed—and Conner had heard the lock turn—evidently led to the corridor they had entered from. The other, Conner could see, led through an open door into a bathroom with a small shower, again looking very sterile and medical.

Preston was leaning back on the desk top and giving Conner a hard stare. The man could do scary quite well. He wasn't what Conner thought of as an Air Force officer—someone on the thin side to fit more readily in the confined spaces of a jet cockpit—and with refined features. Conner had always thought of the smarter and more patrician military men as going to the Air Force, with the grunts going to the Army and the truly thuggish going to the Navy. Conner preferred being fucked by the latter—and by Marines whenever possible.

Preston looked like a Marine—thus, to Conner, a thuggish grunt with superior intelligence and great bulk. That's mainly why Conner hadn't thought Air Force. Preston was built large, not as in fat, but as in tall; rugged facial features; broad chested, tapering down to a relative thin waist; heavily muscled; buzz cut; and a demeanor of power, authority, and no nonsense. Definitely not Air Force in Conner's mind. He assumed former Marine or Naval Seal turned CIA.

Conner knew it would be folly and useless to oppose the man; he had no intention of doing so. Nor had he been instructed to try to resist anyone at this phase of the trip. His job was to get to where these men, whoever they represented, wanted to take him. Just that, nothing more, that was the basic mission. Anything else he could find out was gravy.

"You know they will want to fully test you before they take you to the secret base, don't you?" he had been told. "You will have to prove yourself at this point—a point much before we want you to reach. All you have to do is reach the secret base and try to accomplish certain identifications. You must make them want to complete the journey. They will test you for capability and endurance."

"Yes, sir, I understand," Conner had answered, wondering, of course, how taxing or distasteful this testing would be, but such an assignment not being out of line with what he'd had to do in the Las Vegas male brothel at a desert ranch he'd be recruited from.

Happily, from the moment he'd seen the pseudo Air Force lieutenant approaching him in the business lounge at the Frankfurt airport, Conner had been looking forward to the moment he knew they had reached here in this medical examination room somewhere in the Incirlik Airbase complex.

"Strip, please," Preston said in a commanding voice. "Do it slowly, the way you would do it for a client—the way you'll do it for any of the men who want you to do it. The clothes can just be tossed in the corner over there. You won't be wearing them again."

Conner did as he was told, slowly and teasingly removing the clothes, all the time giving Preston sultry looks. When Conner unbuttoned his shirt, Preston unbuttoned his as well and let the sides flare away from his body. He wasn't wearing an undershirt. His chest was as massive as Conner had perceived it would be, with bulging pecs, rimmed on the underside with a matting of blond, curly hair, which then trailed down his sternum, washboard abs, and hard, flat belly.

There were some well-built cowboy types who came to the ranch outside Las Vegas, but not many who looked as good as this guy did. Conner liked having sex; he even liked it rough; he liked it better with a well-built dude. He'd loved being fucked by every Marine who had fucked him.

As Conner unbuckled his belt, Preston unzipped his trousers and fished out a half-hard cock that, in its length and girth, complimented the rest of his manly, Marine's body.

"Stop," he commanded before Conner unbuttoned and unzipped his trousers. "Come here, go on your knees, and give me a blow job first. Make me like it."

Conner knelt in front of Preston, as the officer leaned his buttocks back into the edge of the desk and palmed the desk top with stiffened arms extending out from his body. Conner took the cock in his mouth and gave the man deep head. Preston grunted and groaned in a low, bass voice as Conner sucked him off expertly.

"The balls. Suck the balls," Preston growled, and Conner complied. After he'd licked and sucked them briefly, Preston growled again. "I want to face fuck you." He took control of Conner's head with his hands, and Conner returned his attentions to the cock, more or less just holding his mouth in a big O and providing straight passage to the back of his throat, while Preston manipulated Conner's head with his hands and pumped the young man's face with his cock.

With an, "Oh Fuck, oh shit, I'm gonna come," Preston jerked Conner's head off his cock and creamed the young man's face. The officer released Conner's head, and the young man swallowed the cock again and cleaned it with his mouth. He looked up into Preston's face and grinned to show that it hadn't been a chore for him.

Taking the size of the cock *had* been a bit of a chore, but not one that Conner couldn't handle. Size did make a difference in Conner's enjoyment.

Nothing that was happening now was taxing or distasteful to Conner, and he was trying his best to convey that to Preston.

"OK, back to the center of the room and take the rest of it off," Preston said in a deep, trembling voice.

Conner didn't have to be told that he'd done well. He knew he'd passed that part of the test.

After he'd put on a striptease for Preston, he was told to go into the bathroom and take a shower.

"Clean yourself out well. There's a douche bottle in the shower to help with that."

When he started to close the bathroom door, out of habit, Preston growled, pushed it open, and stood in the doorway, leaning on the frame. "I will watch you soaping up and showering. Make me want to fuck you."

A half hour later, Conner was bound to the examination table, on his back, his legs raised and spread in the stirrups, and his wrists bound to the side of the table on each side, as Preston proceeded with another cavity search, this time with his greased fist up to the knuckles in Conner's ass—and eventually beyond. Conner had already sucked him hard again, with his head flopped over the top of the examination table, giving Preston a straight shot for his cock in Conner's mouth as Preston leaned over Conner's chest, chewed on the young man's nipples and ran his tongue down Conner's belly before swallowing his cock in a sixty-nine position.

The cavity search ended with Preston mining Conner's passage with his cock.

Eventually, showered again and dressed, Conner was led out of the room and into a small waiting room—again windowless and, he presumed, with the exit door locked. A young muscle man, with a blank look on his face, and reading a girlie magazine sat so close to that door that Conner knew he couldn't have left by the route without permission if he wanted to. Conner wasn't built for muscle work; he was built to please muscle work.

He wasn't the only one in the room, however. There were two slim, but busty, young women—one blonde and one brunette, sitting very close together on a waiting room-style couch across the room from him. They were whispering to each other. Conner couldn't decide what the language was, but it certainly seemed east European to him. Not as guttural as Russian, but close.

In their dress and their demeanor, it was clear to Conner what they were. He'd been told there would be female prostitutes too—obviously more than one, given the probable mix of interests of the soldiers Conner and the women would be servicing at whatever secret base they were being taken to. Conner was a little miffed. They looked more like whores than he thought he did. He'd come from a high-class brothel. They looked almost scaggy.

Preston walked over to the women and pointed to the brunette, reaching down and grabbing her forearm roughly and pulling her up from the couch when she didn't respond immediately.

There was a knock on the door, and the doorkeeper let in a scruffy looking Turk, swarthy and hirsute and scowling slightly. Conner wondered how Preston and his people wouldn't have realized that Conner would know a Turk when he saw one. But then, he'd been pulled out of a Las Vegas brothel at a desert ranch. They probably hadn't done any sort of a background check on him at all to find out that he'd been around the world a couple of times before landing out in the desert.

If they'd done a half-way thorough background check, they wouldn't have hired him at all.

"This is the pilot for the next leg," Preston said to Conner. "There's a deal going with him, and I want to make sure you have the stamina for what's ahead anyway.

146

You are to take any man I send to you before I clear you for the next leg of the trip."

Preston then took the brunette into a different examination room than Connor had been in—and that Conner hadn't noticed before—and slammed the door behind them. Ah, he swings both ways, Conner thought. He tucked that away in the back of his mind in case it would be useful later.

In the meantime, the Turk—the pilot for the next flight—herded Conner into the first examination room and fucked him doggy style on the examination table. While he was doing so, Conner tried to make enough conversation to unobtrusively fold in subtle questions about where they were going with telling the hirsute Turk that he was a magnificent swordsmen, but the pilot was tight lipped—at least until he decided he wanted to suck Conner's cock to an ejaculation.

Standing at the door as he left was his copilot, the pilot said in broken English. Conner wasn't told that he had privileges next, but he didn't really have to be told.

The copilot was both more inventive in positions and a bit looser lipped with information, especially after Conner demonstrated, with loud cries in the man's own language, that he was being taken expertly—better than the pilot, which the copilot seemed to appreciate hearing. The copilot used the examination table stirrups for Conner's arms and knelt on the end of the examination table, with Conner's ankles locked at the back of the copilot's neck, while the copilot fucked him and beat Conner's cock off with his fist. The copilot inadvertently dropped that they would be flying northeast and that the land would be desert. He also dropped the term, H zero zero three. H003. It seemed to be a place. And it gave Conner his first concrete piece of intelligence to pass back when he was able. His handlers had other ways to follow and locate him, but he now had a possible installation name.

A younger, willowy man, who wanted to be fucked rather than to fuck, was next. He later proved to be the steward on the very private flight of the C-130 Hercules cargo plane that flew Conner northeast from there. Conner, of course, had been schooled in identify the various transports and cargo planes flying.

Conner had no idea who the next to last guy was. He was a Turk and had a bigger cock than his body size promised, but Conner didn't see him anywhere after that. He was older—but not less vigorous in his fucking—so Conner surmised he must have been management level in this operation. The last one to appear and fuck him was the young man who had been guarding the door. He was American, by accent, and kept saying how much tighter and more enjoyable Conner's hole was than that of the blonde. Conner assumed he was talking about the blonde prostitute who had been sitting out in the reception room.

In all Conner had been fucked by six men. Not much different from a Friday or Saturday at the Las Vegas brothel. He decided he must have passed the endurance test, as it wasn't long after he'd showered the cheap-smelling perfume of the blonde off his body that Preston had returned, told him to dress in the new set of clothes provided, and he was led, blindfolded, out to what turned out to be a C-130—with just bucket seats and various-sized boxes of supplies in the fuselage portion he was in and no windows.

He tried to figure out how many hours the flight was, but the coffee the steward gave him must have been drugged, because he dozed off and had to be awakened as they were landing. Before he went to sleep, though, he saw Preston roughly pull the blonde up from where she was sitting and take her farther to the back of the plane and beyond a wall with a door in it. She was making a lot of noise over the rumbling of the engines before Conner drifted off to sleep, so Conner thought Preston probably had some special needs when he went with a woman.

148

* * * *

No one bothered to blindfold Conner and the two women when they staggered off the C-130. The women were more disheveled and staggering than Conner was. He touted up his wobbliness to both the flight conditions and the drug he undoubtedly had been given. He suspected that the women's condition was at least partially the result of having been roughly used during the flight while the plane was bumping along through turbulence. They both looked bruised. The two clung close together and cast suspicious and hard looks at the world around them. That they instinctively withdrew from Preston when he came close to them spoke to how roughly Preston had used them.

Conner smiled inwardly in thinking of how Preston had used him. At no time had he thought of shrinking away from the man and his monster cock.

The reality of the world around the three prostitutes explained why they weren't blindfolded. There was nothing but scrub plain to what Conner judged from the angle of the sun to be the west, north, and south, and barren mountains to the east. His geographic training and the piecing together where they'd started and what the copilot had revealed about their flight direction, Conner reasoned they were in one of the "Stans"—Kazakhstan, Uzbekistan, or Turkmenistan. Probably not Tajikistan or Kyrgyzstan, or there would be mountains rising on all sides.

There wasn't really nothing. They had landed on a short airstrip, which is probably why a C-130 was required, and in the near distance stood an anomaly for the otherwise deserted plain they were on—a compound that had all of the characteristics of a state-of-the-art maximum-security prison.

Which, if everything his handlers had worked to achieve, was exactly what he had expected to find at the end of his journey. Conner was sent to locate a suspected—by one foreign policy agency of the U.S. Government—an unacknowledged private prison—by another foreign policy agency of the U.S. Government. Putting two and two together, this was the installation that shouldn't exist and it was designated H003. That designation made Conner wonder if there were other prisons in the series—an H001 and H002, at least.

It stood to be determined whether what Conner was learning would ever make it back into the hands of those he was serving. Despite the multiple changes of clothing and the full-body searches, his handlers should be beamed into much of what he now knew. At the thought of this, Conner worried the molar that wasn't a real molar with his tongue. But there was the question of whether he'd make it out of here alive to serve his own interests. All he could do was to roll with the punches—and, in this context, the thrusts—and struggle for survival. In the meantime there was more he needed to learn.

They were met by a contingent of Marine-looking soldiers dressed in fatigues without insignia of any sort. All of the guards looked like they could break Conner in two, if they wanted to—and more than a few of them gave him surreptitious looks indicating they anticipated having a go at him. The three of them—Conner and the two women—were separated, the woman having to be pried from each other's arms—and marched to the compound, where they were taken in two separate directions—the women down one corridor and Conner down another. Conner was never to see either of the women again. He had no doubt how they would be used, but he had no knowledge of how and where they ended up.

He was marched to a room much like the one where he received clients at the Las Vegas ranch, except that it was larger to accommodate all that was there. Also, although there was a long window on the outer wall, it ran above standing height and was studded with thick bars.

Other than that, there was a double bed, a desk, with two straight chairs, a small sofa and upholstered chair, a chest of drawers, and a few ominous touches. There was a smaller version of the medical examination table, complete with stirrups and restraints, that he had been strapped to in the room at the Incirlik airbase. In the corner of the room a sling was hanging from the ceiling on chains. In the center of the room, other chains with restraints dangling from them hung from the ceiling, and there were hooks in the side walls, some with chains and restraints hanging from them. The room was fully carpeted, except for a circular cut-out area underneath the hanging chains in the center of the room. This was concrete and sloped into a drain from all sides. One door led to an efficient and sparkling clean bathroom, with a shower; and another door was to a closet, where the back wall was covered with all the whips, restraints, gags, and sex toys that Conner assumed would be involved in what he was doing here.

Although there were torture rooms at the Las Vegas ranch to be used at premium prices and with particular, masochistic and willing, prostitutes, there was nothing this sophisticated or merged with the other outfittings for male-on-male sex. If this was designed to impress and scare Conner, it accomplished its goal.

He was to find there were no street clothes in the bureau doors or closets—just various bits of provocative temporary-use wear—and he was made to strip and his clothes taken away by the men who had escorted him to the room and who closed and locked the door to the outer corridor when they departed. Except when he was told to dress in something provided, Conner was naked for the next eight weeks.

His next and subsequent meals were slipped in to him through a slot in the door. There was a well-appointed countertop refrigerator, he found, in one corner of the room by the bureau, though. He had all of the drinks, including liquor, and snacks he—or his guests—could want. And the meals he was served were good, the food plentiful. They obviously wanted to keep him fit. The closet contained workout equipment, and he learned to used the various sex paraphernalia dangling from the ceiling to aid improvised workouts.

And there was the other vigorous working out he got over the next eight weeks.

His first visitor was, he decided, the installation commandant. He was middle-aged, maybe even late fifties, but he was as fit as any of the younger prison guards there. And he was just as much in the need of sexual release. He was a particularly cruel man. Conner thought "former Marine" again.

Just as Lieutenant Preston had, the commandant leaned back into the desk and asked a naked Conner to pose for him and then to kneel in front of him, with only the commandant's dick exposed, and suck him off. That's where the experience with him parted from what Preston had done, though.

The commandant was more sadism inclined. He hung Conner from the chains in the middle of the room and flogged and zapped him with an electric prod and squeezed his balls and edged him in rounds of frustration in jacking him off before stripping fully—he'd already taken his shirt off, revealing a barrel chest and an abundance of salt-and-pepper chest hair—and fucking Conner from the rear.

He left the young man hanging until two guards arrived a half hour later to release him and help him hobble to the shower.

After he'd done Conner and the young prostitute was still hanging, the commandant said, "You know what you're here for, don't you? What you were contracted to do."

"Yes, sir," Conner answered through swollen lips, as the older man had been free about punching Conner while he was using him.

"You're known as a relief contractor. The men out here get cranky if they don't get enough relief. And they like fresh tail. You do well by my men, and you'll be going home in two months as contracted. Otherwise . . . well, let's just say you don't want to not do well by my men."

Conner was left for two days to recover. After that he fell into a regular routine. He averaged thirty visits a week and discerned, he thought, sixteen different men who used him, including Preston and the commandant. Since they'd brought in two women, Conner judged that more men were using them than were using him. Monday through Thursday, he serviced six or seven men each day—and it wasn't always Conner as a bottom; a good third of his visitors wanted him to fuck them. Some of them wanted to be abused as well. Fridays were for threesomes and gang bangs. Saturday morning Conner was given over to sadists, using the full range of toys in the room. Saturday afternoon was for one session of double penetration. And then he was given a day and a half to recover before Monday rolled around again.

It was a tough schedule, but it didn't prevent Conner from learning what else he needed to learn while he was there.

By standing on the desk, Conner could bring the window on the outside wall to eye level. He found he was looking down from a third story into some sort of exercise yard. Over several days, he was able to put together a schedule for the use of that yard. He also could identify some of the prisoners they were housing, and, no doubt, interrogating here. All suspected international terrorists. Some thought by the public to be dead. None of them,

153

Conner was sure, were men those running this prison would know he had learned to identify.

There were the Yemeni terrorist organization leaders, Ali Abdullah Mansour, Abd-Rabbu al-Hiajiri, and Samir Saleh, who had been claimed to have been evaporated by a drone missile at a meeting outside Sanaa six months earlier. There was the former physicist and Russian separatist, Stefan Belur, thought to have gone effectively to ground. The Turkish separatist leader, Arif Aghan. Even an American, Jason Kowl, who had dropped out of sight after a failed attempt to bomb an airliner. All of the men were released into the courtyard separately and alone. All hobbled about, indicating that their incarceration and interrogation weren't a picnic. The Yemenis—including verification of rumors they were alive—had been Conner's principle concern.

Conner had all he needed to gather. Now it was just a matter of surviving the eight weeks and trusting that he would be let free, as agreed—a difficult and iffy proposition. But there was more than the money he'd been paid involved.

* * * *

When the fallout came, it came quickly and later than Conner thought it might. Conner was sitting with Lieutenant Preston in the Istanbul airport, where they were to part at last at the conclusion of Conner's contract, when Conner saw his handler standing off from the departure area and looking at him intently. As soon as it was obvious Conner saw him, almost doing a double take, the handler gestured toward a men's room. Conner's gaze turned to the men's room to see that another man he recognized was standing by the door to the john, dressed as a cleaner. It seemed this was a ploy all U.S. intelligence agencies like to employ. He had a mop and bucket beside him, and Conner caught on that the man would close off the rest room as soon as Conner and his handler entered it.

"I'm going to the men's room before we board," Conner said, standing.

"Good idea. I was about to suggest that. I'll go with you," Preston answered, also standing.

"It's OK, I can go alone," Conner countered. But then it was obvious that Preston wouldn't let him go alone. It was equally obvious then too that Preston and his people weren't going to let Conner simply fly away from here. He was ticketed for Frankfurt, although after they'd cleared through airport security, Preston had taken Conner's ticket back from him. He wasn't going anywhere until and unless Preston let him. They were close to calling boarding. There was no reason for Preston to stick close to him now. Preston had said he was ticketed for a later flight going someplace else. He didn't say where.

Preston reiterated that he was going to the men's room too. And, despite Conner saying he wanted to go alone, Preston was closely following him.

As they entered the men's room, Conner's handler having preceded them, Conner sensed the agent posed as a cleaner blocking off the door in their wake.

Preston didn't know what hit him. He was down on the ground, a bullet from a silencer having made a third eye for him, and the handler was dragging the body into a stall.

"You didn't have to do that. They were letting me go," Conner said, angrily when the handler came out of the stall.

"Of course I had to do that. They weren't going to let you go. Preston was going to kill you before you got on that plane. Probably was going to bring you in here and off you while everyone else was boarding."

Conner decided to let it go. "You managed to locate the site? They call it H003."

"Yes. The transmitter in your tooth filling worked a charm. The installation is in Kazakhstan, near a village called Chelor. We're already well on our way to tracing the secret agreements back to the Agency. Did you manage to find out anything else? Anything on the prisoners?"

Conner hesitated just a few seconds too long in answering and the indecision in his face showed. The handler's face set hard and he lifted the gun he'd used to kill Preston and pointed it at Conner. "You know who some of the inmates are, don't you? Tell me who you saw there."

"Shouldn't we leave first?" Conner asked. "Are you booked on the flight to Frankfurt too? I could talk to you on the flight."

"You could talk to me now," the handler said, his voice menacing. Then a surprised look shot across his face and he toppled to the floor, a knife sticking out of his back.

"Jamal," Conner exclaimed, seeing the figure of the man materializing behind the falling handler.

"Shhh, there's a back door to the restroom," Jamal hissed. "Come away with me, we can be gone from here before the others come looking for their man. This man wasn't going to let you leave here alive. They just didn't want to kill you any closer to their operations. Did you find any of our comrades where you were taken?"

"Yes," Conner answered the man from the Mideast terrorist unit Conner had been secretly working with as a sleeper in the States for years. "Some of the Yemeni leaders are still alive; the prison is near a village called Chelor in Kazakhstan. But I will tell you all when we're away from here."

He would tell them all, of course. Their cause was his as well. But he would dribble the information out slowly to maximize his chances of survival. If he'd learned anything from this operation, it was to trust no one fully.

Who's Afraid of Stan Snodgrass?

"I thought I asked you to wear the tighter shirt under your jacket, Dillon—the one with the V neck that shows off the line between your pecs so well."

"Gunther Strang is the chair of the English Department, Madge. And isn't his wife the daughter of Montebello's president? I didn't think you'd want me to look like your boy toy."

"Of course I want you to look like my boy toy, Dillon," Madge said, as she rose from her dressing table, turned, and came in close to her young husband. "There's no hiding the difference in our ages, so we might as well make the most of it. And it's because Gunther Strang is chair of the English Department that I want you to look your most fetching. You know I'm up for tenure at the college this year and this is a one-on-one dinner for Strang to hone his assessment of me. I want you to look like a boy toy to him too. We've been over all of this before. I told you about Gunther."

"Yes, I understand—which is why I didn't think you'd want me to look like an Italian rent-boy. That wouldn't be too subtle."

"We've discussed Gunther before, Dillion. He's not exactly the subtle kind himself. there's a time-honored way of going about these things at this college. I've tried to make as clear as possible that you might have to help me with this. It's not as if you haven't—"

"You know I don't like to discuss any of what has happened in the past, Madge."

"Just humor me here, Dillon—and help me with this tenure thing with whatever it takes. The other shirt, I think . . . please?"

"Oh, OK," Dillon said as he went back into the closet.

Madge and Dillon had been the scandal of the fall at the small, sleepy—somewhat moldy, even—private university, with the esoteric study programs, that was tucked away in the Great Smokey Mountains. She was an associate history professor, and Dillion, eight years her junior, was finishing out his fifth year of eligibility as captain of the tennis team by taking graduate classes at the university in history.

It wasn't just the age difference that had fueled a scandal that was just one in a long line of scandals going back to the Strangs' own marriage and beyond. Sondra McMillan Strang—the emphasis always put on the "McMillan" because Sondra's father, Clifton McMillan, was Montebello's iron-fisted president—had robbed the cradle herself when she lassoed the young, then-married history associate professor, Gunther. Over the ensuing years, Sondra, who had been born and raised at the university, had been in many a scandal with men attached to Montebello, with the joke being that a male faculty member couldn't get tenure without laying the president's daughter first. The most recent buzz was her rumored liaison with a math professor, being ultra juicy because the math professor was a twenty-eight-year-old woman.

The rumors that Dillon's marriage to Madge had largely spiked, encompassed questions of the genders of his relationships at college. As well as being a first-class tennis player, he was one of the university's premier blond, blue-eyed, championship smile hunks.

Montebello might be a small, sleepy private southern institution hiding in the foothills of the mountains, but it had more than its share of spice.

Dillon was trying to cut down on the spice when the hot redheaded English professor came on to him and even showed interest in marriage. He'd always figured in the back of his mind that she had some reason of her own for this marriage. Now he thought he was figuring out what it was. She'd never made any bones about how important getting tenure at Montebello was.

* * * *

Dillon pulled to a stop in front of the Strang cottage on the Montebello campus. The garden setting was impressive, but the house appeared just to be a small wooden outbuilding on a tree-lined cul-de-sac, with larger houses of other senior faculty surrounding it. Initially, Dillon thought it was someone's garage.

"You sure this is the place? He's chair of the English Department, isn't he?"

"This is it," Madge answered. "It's bigger than it looks. It rambles back away from the street in a couple of later additions. But it originally was a caretaker's cottage for the president's house that abuts it at the back. The garden actually goes with the president's house. The professor's wife acts as her father's housekeeper and hostess, so she has to live close. The Strangs have the run of the president's house as well. Let's go in. We're fashionably late now."

"You sure you want me to do this?" Dillon asked as Madge opened her door. She gave a heavy sigh and sank back into her seat, but she didn't close the car door.

"I'm not really afraid of the other one they're looking at for tenure, Stan Snodgrass, but this is my last chance at tenure. I'll take any extra edge I can get."

"Don't you mean I'll take any edge you can get?" Dillon said.

"This is important to both of us. Remember what I did for you. I saved your reputation. And remember who puts the food on the table and provides both the table and the roof over the table. You may be a high-paid tennis pro sometime in the future, but not this week, and you have to eat this week."

"And now you want me to sully my reputation again."

"You're in no danger of that. The Strangs are married, but they live entirely separate lives. You know how Gunther swings, and I'm sure you've heard that his wife bonks all male faculty members. Which means you don't have much to worry about on that score. She's a snob about who she fucks. I wouldn't even be surprised if Sondra was being done by her father. The two of them are practically inseparable, and she won't let anyone forget that she's the university president's daughter. She has no life beyond him. Well, other than the bottle. The woman is a lush. Strang has to carry her home early from almost every faculty party. No one says anything, though. She's the president's daughter."

"So, why are you worried about this Snodgrass guy? Will I have competition from him with the professor?"

"Hardly. He's in his forties and is an ugly beanpole. His wife is younger and quite the siren, but I can't see Strang having any interest in him—and certainly not her. But it's Stan's last chance at tenure too, and he's been walking around with an 'I've got a secret' expression on his face the last couple of weeks. I'm sure it's just bluff to put me off."

"And it is putting you off?" Dillon asked.

Madge's expression turned ugly. "Of course not," she snapped. "Let's just go in and get this over with. Just charm the pants off the man—literally."

160

Sondra McMillan Strang met them at the door of the cottage. Dillon got the reference to being a lush right off the bat. She was a bit slack mouthed, was using the frame of the door for support, and had a large, half-full glass of amber liquid, swirling a couple of ice cubes, in her hand.

Dillon had never met her before. Now that he saw her—a faded beauty in her late forties who was closer to Rubenesque than trim—he realized that he'd seen her many times before—always in the background, in the shadow of the university president when he made his formal appearances. Until now, she had just been part of the wallpaper to Dillon.

He instantly felt sorry for her, especially when they entered the bookcase-lined living room, with its study-like atmosphere and Dillon was introduced to Professor Strang. He obviously was a good bit younger than his wife was, perhaps about forty, and had been a real hunk in his day. He was a Germanic blond, with pale blue eyes and a classic, square-cut face. He came across as all vitality to Sondra's fading beauty. Dillon didn't know why he had the impression he did—that once she'd been the driving force in the marriage but that now she was pathetic and that her trysts with male faculty members, doing her to curry favor with her father, were a last-ditch effort to reel her husband back in. But this thought made him pity the woman all the more.

Madge had told him that the two were amicable but hardly a dedicated couple—but when he saw the two together he realized that President McMillan had bought Gunther Strang for his daughter with favoritism, which was a very strong motivator in the small world of a university campus. This so obviously was a case of a father keeping his daughter in thrall by keeping her close and nearly smothering her with entanglements.

Dillon hated to think it, but he would have guessed that her happy hour had started in her bedroom as she was getting ready for the evening. Her auburn hair, with its lacing of gray strands was not quite in order, and her lipstick had overshot the corner of her mouth when she'd applied it. Her shirtdress had been indifferently ironed and the buttons on the top were one off, causing the bodice to gape a bit unfortunately, as she was buxom, and, as she lurched more than moved about, she evoked the worry that one of the puppies might escape at any moment.

It was all a pity, as she really had a strikingly fine-featured face under the badly applied makeup and the most engaging violet eyes. If her attempts at a smile could only reach her eyes, Dillon thought, what a temptress she would be. Her body was curvy enough to be an asset still if only she made the effort to carry herself better.

From long familiarity with the ritual of such evenings, the four settled in. Guiding Madge to a sofa in the middle of the room, the two women sat, and Sondra conversed in standard faculty-night formula with Madge. Meanwhile, with a hand and head gesture and a smile, Gunther pulled Dillon over to a bookcase, where he'd been standing, leafing through a book, when the guests arrived. Checking on the two women from the corner of his eye, Dillon sensed Sondra coming to life more and growing more attractive with each passing moment as she leaned into Madge and freely used arm gestures in her conversation. The two had found a topic they could work over and both at least could pretend to be interested in.

"Have you found an interesting book?" Dillon asked the professor, working to engage the scholar's interest. Madge had told him that Gunther's specialty was nineteenth-century German literature. Dillon had no interest in, or knowledge of, the subject.

"Yes, I often find myself stopping when I pass one of the bookcases and pulling a book out at random. As you notice, our little abode here is a firetrap with cases stuffed with books lining all of the walls, but what it lacks in safety, it makes up for in good insulation."

162

"Is that a German novel?" Dillon asked.

"But of course—by August, the duke of Saxony-Gotha in the early nineteenth century. It's *Ein Jahr in Arkadia*. Do you know it? Are you a literature scholar like Madge?"

"No, not really. I'm studying history—Chinese history. And I couldn't even begin to catch up with what Madge knows about American literature." Might as well work in a plug, Dillon thought.

Strang was standing near him, very close. He cut a fine figure and was dressed in an almost medieval billowy cotton shirt that was buttoned only half way up and loose-fitting cotton trousers. The shirt was gauzy and Dillon was able to ascertain that the man's torso was well-muscled and his chest was matted with curly-blond hair. Dillon guessed he was playing Renaissance man tonight.

"You didn't say anything when I told you what book this was," Strang said. He was holding the book nearly under Dillon's nose with one hand and was palming the young man's shoulder blade with the other.

"I'm afraid I don't speak German," Dillon said. "I took Latin as an undergraduate. And I'm struggling with Mandarin now—and losing that battle, I'm afraid."

"Ah. The title translates as *A Year in Arkadia*. It's a rather famous—infamous to some—homosexual text, as was August—homosexual, not a text. It's a love story between two military men in the duke's service, although there are those who believe the duke himself was one of the men he wrote about. The German intellectual movement in those days was so much more open than in later years, you know. There was Heinrich Zschokke's *Der Eros oder Uber der Liebe*, or *Eros or Concerning Love*, from the same period, not to mention Alexander Von Sternberg's later Jena and Leipzig, and the even later *Fridolin's Secret Marriage* by Adolf von Wilbrandt. Really, Uranien love, the love, what they called Heavenly Love—intimate relations between an older man and a younger was quite openly written about then, and in quite open language. It was only later that—"

"Let's not forget the distaff side, darling," Sondra chimed in from across the room. "Lesbians had their day during the Gründerzeit Movement era too. Don't forget Frank Wedekind's *Die Büchse der Pandora—Pandora's Box* or, even later, Aimée Duc's *Are These Women?* But perhaps you're boring the young man with your fetishes—excuse me, your enthusiasms. I think you're overwhelming the young man."

Indeed, Dillon did feel a bit overwhelmed. The man was coming on strong. In addition to the obvious enthusiasm for the subject, the professor seemed to be aroused by it as well. His hand had dropped to one of Dillon's butt cheeks, and Dillon could clearly see that the man was hard. His trousers weren't constructed to conceal. Dillon suspected that was wholly on purpose.

"I'm sorry," Strang said. "Am I boring you?" His voice sounded like he was concerned, but he didn't take his hand away from Dillon's butt.

I get it that you want to be boring me, Dillion thought. But that's not what he said. "No, not at all," he answered dutifully. He was actually relieved. He'd thought he'd have to do the work to get the dance started, but Strang had started it as soon as they'd entered the house. It almost was as if Sondra would know how this would go and was aiding it. She had Madge shepherded off to a corner of the sofa and, sitting turned in the sofa herself with her back to the men, she seemed almost to be running interference for her husband.

"German literature may be a bit heavy for the boy, Gunther," she said. "Perhaps he would like to see the greenhouse. Your orchid collection may be much more interesting to him."

"Am I embarrassing you by talking about homosexual novels?" Gunther asked Dillon.

"No, not at all," Dillon answered, looking into Gunther's eyes and fluttering his own eyelashes.

"Well, I'm delighted to hear that. I'd gotten the impression from scuttlebutt around the college that it wouldn't be an uncomfortable topic. But the orchids. Would you like to see them?" Gunther asked, looking deep into Dillon's eyes. "Would you like to see the orchids? Cook won't have dinner ready for a half hour or more yet. I know Madge's love is English literature, and Sondra majored in that as well. The women would best be rid of us for a while anyway. It will be just the two of us in the greenhouse for the interim."

"Yes, of course, I'd love to see your orchids," Dillon answered. And Madge wanted me to get you alone for as long as it took to win you over to her cause anyway, he thought. This was proving to be easier than he had feared it would be, although the next fifteen minutes or so might be dicey.

But it was going surprisingly smoothly.

* * * *

There was a reason Dillon's assignment was going smoothly, which was revealed to him as soon as they entered the greenhouse, a Victorian confection attached to the side of the vehicle garage for the president's house and jutting out into a garden illuminated by well-placed and – disguised lights to give the impression of a fairyland. The lights were blazing on the first floor of the president's house and the tinkling conversation from a cocktail party in progress could be heard across the expanse of the garden. Dillon knew from Madge's instructions for the evening that President McMillan was in Atlanta to give a speech, so he reasoned that the party must be one of the many that was booked for a college organization and that didn't require McMillan's presence.

Still, the nearby party across a firefly-sparkled garden, with the swirl of heads, torsos, and raised glasses visible through the wide expanse of greenhouse glass and the hanging orchids, lent a surrealistic effect to the straightforward talk of Professor Strang now that the two were alone.

"We don't have long, and I sometimes need a good buildup, so we might as well get right down to it," he said as he and Dillon drew into the humid atmosphere of the orchid display.

"Excuse me?" Dillon answered, not so smart that he could flip that fast into a new, fast scene.

"Tonight is about Madge's tenure prospects. You are here to plead her case with your body, are you not? I don't need the preliminaries. I knew of your past reputation on campus before Madge came to me and told me you'd take cock if I'd treat her favorably in the tenure deliberations. I made no promises but said I'd give you a whirl. Now that I see you in person, I'll be quite willing to give you that whirl."

Dillon could have feigned that he didn't know what this was all about, but he did, and the professor was right. A half hour—twenty-five minutes now—wasn't long for him to make the case that Madge had insisted that he do.

Besides, Strang's cock was already out of his trousers, he was fisting it, and it already was hard. With a sigh, Dillon knelt down in front of him and took the cock—a rather nice one—in his mouth.

The surrealism continued for Dillon as, with his trousers and briefs bunched around his ankles, he was bent over a cleared-off ledge with his nose nearly plastered to the glass of the greenhouse wall. His eyes watched the swirl of the party in the president's house through the large windows looking out on the lit garden and Gunther Strang stood close behind him, hands grasping Dillon's hips, and cock working in and out of Dillon's ass channel.

Gunther was muttering in guttural German, so Dillon decided the professor must be enjoying himself. So, assignment completed as far as Dillon was concerned; he'd done what Madge had pressured him to do. It was up to Strang now to decide whether this favored Madge's candidacy for tenure. Dillon felt a little guilty, though, because he was enjoying the working of Gunther's cock inside him. Despite all of the rumblings on campus during his earlier life at Montebello, Dillon did enjoy having a man's plump cock inside him rubbing against his prostate. And he did enjoy soaring on a high and releasing his seed from a man's attention. He even, tonight, enjoyed the surreal effect and danger of doing it here in the greenhouse where anyone who decided to get a smoke or a secret grope in the garden could come away from the party in the president's house and discover Gunther and him going at it.

It took more than the half hour, and Dillon didn't make any effort to bring it to an earlier climax. When the two men returned to the cottage living room, though, the women said nothing about the extra time and dinner was still not on the table.

"Has Sondra been chewing your ear off about women's literature in nineteenth-century Germany?" Gunther asked Madge jovially as they strode, all smiles, into the living room.

"Something like that," Madge mumbled, but she was looking a bit distracted and nonplused. Dillon hoped she was having remorse about what she had pressed him to do—and that he'd carried through and done for her. He felt a little pleased with himself that she was in this disconcerted mood.

In contrast, Sondra had become more aware and was moving more self-confidently—more erect and more in command and, yes, looking more lovely—than she had looked when the men had departed the house.

Dinner was an anticlimax. The Strangs prattled on almost solely between themselves through the meal, being clever and witty in their choices of comment, both all smiles and vivacious, while Madge was somber and noticeably withdrawn, and Dillon was icy with her, shooting her "Aren't you proud of what you made me do?" glances when he got the chance. There were points to be won by playing the martyr here; he didn't have to reveal that he'd enjoyed Gunther's cocking.

He also played up to Gunther. This only partially was as punishment to Madge. He, in fact, wanted Gunther to know he could have him again. What Gunther had done had brought back memories to Dillon of a time of greater sexual fulfillment than he had gotten from Madge in the short time they'd been married. Sex with her had been better—enhanced by being forbidden—when they were having their affair, than it was afterward, when they were married.

Madge maintained her distant mood and downcast eyes after they'd entered the car for the short drive back to their house.

"Aren't you going to ask me whether—?" Dillon started to ask as he pulled the car away from the curb.

"No," she fairly spat out, turning her head to the passenger window. "I could see that you managed."

"And you don't have anything to say? No word of thanks?"

"Yes, of course, thanks," she shot back. "Now, if you don't mind, I have a splitting headache and I'd rather not engage in silly chit-chat on the way home."

Dillon shrugged and turned his attention to the road. He actually thought the evening had gone quite well. Madge's behavior now only enhanced the glow he still felt from Gunther Strang's attentions. This just added to his resolve to see Gunther privately again when the chance arose. He was pleased that Gunther had suggested it, and he hadn't hesitated to agree to it.

And he didn't really give a fuck if Madge got tenure or not. He had the distinct feeling that they wouldn't last much longer as a couple regardless and then he didn't give a shit where she went. She was just a user.

* * * *

Sondra and Gunther Strang stood at one of the cottage's living room windows looking out onto the street and watched Dillon and Madge drive away. Gunther had an arm around Sondra's waist, which is as close as he'd gotten to her in several days and was as close as he would get to her for several more. Both were smiling, their eyes were blazing, and they were humming the same tune softly.

"Did you enjoy him?" Sondra asked.

"Yes, of course. He's quite a luscious piece. And he must have enjoyed it too. He said he'd be happy to do it again anytime we could arrange it. And you. Did you get into Madge's panties?"

"You know I did. Probably not as enjoyable an encounter as you had—she was stiff at first and held back until I spelled out the tenure issue with her. Then she was fine. Moody afterward, as you could see when you returned."

"So, are you going to support her for tenure with your father? It continues to amaze me that these faculty people don't understand the control you have over your father—and that neither Madge nor Stan Snodgrass seem to realize that the route to currying favor for tenure here doesn't arrive at me—that it's in the hands of Clifton McMillan and goes through you."

"I don't know yet whether or not I'll support her over Stan Snodgrass. Madge is ambitious and has a great body, but she's a grasping bitch—and a cold one at that, during the act. Stan and his wife are coming for dinner on Thursday night. I know it will be a dull evening for you, being forced to discuss French Romanticism with that blowhard Stan all evening, but his wife is quite a sweet little thing. If she is as accessible to another woman as campus rumor has it, Thursday might just be Stan Snodgrass' lucky day."

Come the White Stallions

The familiar, ominous image materializes before him of a narrow track in the woods opening toward him from a convergence of stark, bare-branched trees in the distance with a swirl of choking ground mist. Derek feels his heart racing and the essences inside him rising as, from the far end of the track, where the trees converge, the whirling figures form—white and muscular—and start pounding toward him. The figures solidify, separate, and take on the visage of stallions—magnificent, pure-white beasts—pounding toward him, coming closer and closer. Two of them. As they soar toward him, hooves barely touching the ground, black smudges above the stallions begin to form into riders. The gleam of whirling steel overhead.

The stallions peel off in both directions as they roar past him on either side. His body jerks and lurches from the centrifugal force of their passing, and . . .

. . . his hands clutched to the sides of Michel, saddled on and riding his cock. He arched his back up from the bed and cried out as he ejaculated deep inside the Frenchman's passage. Michel fell off to the side of Derek, stretched along his body, moved a thigh over Derek's, and searched for and found Derek's lips with his.

As they cooled down, Michel whispered, "You cried out at the climax. Something like 'They're coming.' Is that what you exclaimed? What were you thinking?

What did you see? You were looking intensely at the ceiling. And I've never known you to writhe like that—to come that much—before."

"Horses. White stallions. They were magnificent and monstrous at the same time. They were going to run me down. The expressions on their face were a mixture of malevolence and sheer terror. And then I came, and they had passed by me."

"Ah, *la petite mort*. Oo la la." Michel smiled, kissed Derek on the lips again, and gave him a smile when he'd pulled away.

"La what?" Derek asked. "It wasn't funny. It was . . . frightful." Derek's irritation showed in his voice.

"*La petite mort*. A little death. In France we equate it with orgasm. As close to a glorious death as one can get, we say. And the white horses. They are associated with death too. You must have had a special ejaculation."

"Yes, I did," Derek answered. But his voice was a bit distant. He was thinking of something else, something more sinister in relation to the white horses. He had another idea why they had intruded into this last fuck with Michel.

"Just the horses?" Michel asked. "No riders . . . dressed in black? Swinging swords? That would be a different matter altogether."

Not wanting to answer or for Michel to see the expression on his face, Derek looked beyond the French doors of his father's hunting lodge. As if on cue, the figures appeared in the distance, at the opening of the tree line, where the drive from the lodge entered the forest. Two white horses. Stallions. Both with black-clad riders. The two men his father employed to handle worker disputes at his factories.

The hoofbeats of the horses as they raced for the lodge hammered in Derek's brain. Michel didn't seem to be able to hear them. But they were so loud in Derek's head that he couldn't understand why Michel remained oblivious—still taking and giving pleasure with his hand roaming on Derek's naked body.

He looked into the handsome face of his French lover in panic. Michel's return look was only one of satiated lust and complete devotion. To avoid frightening Michel until the very last moment of inevitability, Derek grabbed the sides of the Frenchmen's curly haired head and pulled their faces together for a passionate, hungry kiss. One last kiss.

The men were at the door in the lodge's great room beyond, and then forcing their way in, reaching for a now-shocked and struggling Michel.

* * * *

Derek Hoffman first saw Michel Picault standing with one foot on a bench and the other one on a table top in a biergarten at the foot of the cobblestone street from the university that also surrounded the base of the castle. His high tenor was floating out over the chorus that surrounded him in singing the rousing drinking songs of the university. He didn't appear to have a care in the world, and there didn't appear to be a reason why he should.

He was a gorgeous young man—just having arrived at the university when Derek was near time of leaving and sinking into the staid, but dull, life of his father's manufacturing empire. Derek already had been engaged—in absentia, by his father—to the daughter of a rival business prince. Watching the boisterous, full-of-life Michel leading the drinking songs made him reconsider having dutifully fallen into plodding along to the fate his father had carved out for him. Michel was small and slim of stature, all smiles and bravado that belied his small stature, and dark and sultry, a man of the Mediterranean south. He was dressed in silks elegantly enough, if not up to Derek's father's standards. That he was not up to

Derek's father's standards weighed heavily in Derek being drawn to him.

Derek had dabbled in man love before—usually in small, otherwise hidden rebellions to the demands from his father—as, indeed, had nearly all at the university, where students were expected to unfurl their wings and curiosity for a short time before settling down to responsibility and mind-numbing mediocrity. There was nothing deemed unmanly in letting a man fellate you or even allowing you to pin his buttocks to a mattress in mere mechanical release, all being explained away by a deeper explorations of the meanings and workings of Greek philosophy.

But Michel was like a beckoning flame, a soaring phoenix—almost literally that night, as he rose up from the table top, his voice and beer stein held higher than all the rest—and Derek instantaneously had the desire to rise to the heights with him, if only for one more brief burst into the sun before joining his father's life and plan for his future existence in the senior Hoffman's "exciting" ball bearing factory world.

Whatever the appeal of Michel, representing a world that Derek was about to lose forever, he was mercurial, charismatic, attracted to Derek's blond, muscular good looks, highly experienced in lying under and fellating a man, malleable, and willing. And that night he was drunk when Derek followed behind him as he staggered out of the biergarten, caught up with him as he struggled up the steep and narrow cobblestone street toward the university grounds, pulled him into an alley and up against a stone wall, and fucked him hard and deep.

Michel laughed, spread his arms and pressed them against the slimy and grimy stone wall of the alley, as he jutted his buttocks back, into Derek's pelvis. There was no struggle. Just burning need and quick acceptance, as Derek unbuckled, first Michel, and then himself. Michel turned his head, his lips finding Derek's, as he jerked a bit and moaned deeply at the penetration and then full, pumping possession.

For Derek, it was an act of desperation, an attempt to both reject the world he inevitably was sinking into and to steal from Michel and share the blazing light that made the young French student's seemingly carefree and heinous world so glittering. For Michel, it was just another encounter of being ridden hard with a man's dick inside him—of being wanted so badly that the man took what Michel was more than willing to give.

So steeped in Michel's light was Derek that he wanted to prolong the experience as long as possible, and when he asked Michel to come back to his university lodgings with him, Michel readily agreed. Once there, Michel could clearly see that Derek's lodging circumstances were so much more desirable than Michel's were and Derek's attentions were flattering and satisfying enough that Michel remained in Derek's rooms and in his bed for the rest of the university term.

Derek's father didn't learn of Derek's definite turn toward men—and one man, in particular—until the end of the term, when Derek returned to the fold and moved Michel to the family's Black Forest hunting lodge. The lodge was in use by his father only during hunting season, so even then Derek's father only was keyed into the waywardness of the son because of Derek's unseasonal visits to the forest and his increasingly somewhat rebellious and nonpliable attitudes on the match that had been set up for Derek and on how privileged he was to be entering the world of ball bearings.

In these brief months, Derek couldn't get enough of the enticing and malleable young man, who met him at the door of the hunting lodge laughing, naked, and in maddening erection even as Derek dismounted from his horse only to be mounting Michel's ass moments later on the bed, or over the arm of a chair, on the dining table, or on the rug in front of the fireplace. Is was a fairytale life, but like all fairytales, it proved to be mere illusion when confronted with the reality of necessity.

Suspicions raised, researched by the dark-side assistants riding into the forests on their white stallions, and confirmed as worse than anticipated, the father cornered Derek and issued certain demands and conditions.

That Derek caved was evidenced by his actions the day he saw the approaching white stallions both in imagination while Michel was riding his cock on feathered bed and in fact through the French doors of the hunting lodge bed chamber overlooking the drive into the meadow hosting the venue of the illicit assignation.

The beat of the legs of the galloping stallions matched the rushing rise and fall of the luscious small French student's channel on Derek's cock, as Derek clutched the young man's sides and Michel bounced up and down on his German lover's cock, burying the palms of his hands into Derek's nipples and moaning the thickness, length, and throbbing of Derek's staff in his orgiastic death throes, knowing—regretting—that this was the end for them.

Thus, when Michel interpreted the horses of Derek's imaginations as *la petite mort*, the figurative death of an explosive orgasms, Derek's interpretation, punctuated by a flinging wide of the hunting lodge's doors was much more down to earth and couched in reality.

* * * *

Derek's eyes misted over as they were prone to do in his last days and the recurring image of the white stallions galloping at him from the convergence line of the narrow forest track was before him again. The image had recurred periodically throughout his long, dull life, at times the only thing that set his heart racing and his emotions jangling on what could have been if he'd made other choices. It had been a comfortable life, and how so he had come to despise that word—*Gemütlichkeit*—comfort. Smug mediocrity. The goal of his father. The goal he'd let his father impose on him.

And what was the outcome? He had been *gemütlich*—so comfortable that it had numbed and smothered him. It still was smothering him. He would died of suffocation from it. One thing was clear—he would soon die. His father couldn't buy his son's destiny from that, just as his father hadn't been able to accumulate enough, been dull enough, to build a barrier against his own death.

Derek had to go back fifty years for any sense of when he'd actually been alive, happy, fulfilled. And when he thought on this time—the brief time with Michel—was when the dreams of the white stallions came to him.

The dreams had changed, though. They were becoming more ominous. The expression of the stallions' faces—their snorted tufts of breath, the foaming at the mouths, the wild, malevolent blazing of their eyes—became more pronounced as they reached him and parted on each side, with each succeeding dream seeming to come closer to him as the brushed by. And over the last year—since he had received a death sentence—the black-clad figures astride the stallions were forming greater substance with each succeeding imagining. The men in black. Swinging shining swords, swishing them ever closer to his head as they roared past him.

With each passing day, he had regretted more the decisions he'd made early in life. That he'd chosen *Gemütlichkeit* over Michel. That's why, as he knew the end was drawing close, he'd drawn away from the life he had so readily allowed himself to be cowed to accept and had moved into the hunting lodge, banning all but the minimum number of day attendants from his presence. Choosing the memories of the closeness of the brief time with Michel over all he had chosen in selling out to his father's world.

He thought he'd scream if just one more person asked him the going price of a ball bearing. Or he would die. Of course he was dying anyway.

"Michel. Never a word from him ever again. If he had really wanted me, he would . . ."

"Foul!"

Derek opens his eyes. A quick roll back to the past. He is on his back on the featherbed in the bedroom of the hunting lodge. Michel, not aged a day, his naked body gloriously the same, is saddled on his cock. He—Derek— is hard as a rock, and throbbing inside the tight, warm passage. He hasn't been hard for a good ten years. The palms of Michel's hands are pressed into Derek's nipples, Michel is rocking his hips forward and back on Derek's cock, forcing the staff to sink deeper into him.

Derek hears a deep moan. Only in echo does he realize the moan is his.

"Michel! Foul? What do you mean?"

"You know what I mean. You knew than what was happening. You know why I never contacted you again. You knew why those two black-clad men, riding up on their white stallions, meant. We'd just discussed it. They meant death. You knew what they came for; what they would do. You saw the death stallions that day. Whose death did you tell yourself they heralded? Not yours. Not your father's. You had already sealed my fate when we last made love."

"No, I never. I—"

"Shush. It's all right. You have paid for it a thousand times over. You realized the dull life you tossed me away for. But you have suffered enough. You deserve one last orgasm. One last *la petite mort.*"

"One last—?"

"Shhh. feel my passage make love to your cock. Explode for me—give me your seed one last time. Do you

178

hear them? Turn your head toward the meadow, the forest, where the lane enters the trees."

Derek moans at the pleasure of the beautiful, ever-young Michel riding his cock, as he turns his eyes to look through the French doors and out into the world. The two white stallions burst forth from the forest opening, and eyes wild, mouths foaming, churning down the drive straight for him. The figures on their back, two men clad in black, swinging broadswords, completely materialized now.

Michel leans over and kisses Derek on the mouth. But, as his body arches up and he rises and falls ever faster on the cock, he pulls a pillow out from underneath Derek's head, places it over Derek's face, and presses down.

Even while fighting for breath and knowing he is being suffocated, Derek can still see, in his imagination, the onrushing white stallions, the swinging of the broadswords. They are upon him, charging through the walls of the hunting lodge as if they aren't even there, swords swishing in the air. Blinding light shines off the descending blades of the swords as Derek ejaculates . . . one . . . last . . . time.

La petite mort.

Men of Thunder

Daniel had walked a good three miles southwest on Highway 411 out of Maryville, Tennessee, southeast of Knoxville, before he decided to try what he'd been told was surefire success in getting him a hitch. He wanted to get as far away from Knoxville as fast as he could. Every time he saw a white Ford 150 truck, he nearly dove into the bushes at the side of the road until he could make out the logo on the side. He wouldn't put it past Steve to come after him even this far out of the city.

It wasn't like he wasn't prepared to do what he had to do to get the hitch or that it wasn't hot enough on the road not to do it without raising the curiosity of regular motorists. Even the late afternoon was pretty warm late in the summer. And the locals probably walked the side of the road that way anyway.

With a sigh, he pulled off his T-shirt and wrapped it around his slim waist and tied off the short sleeves in front.

Sure enough, after he'd done that and turned toward the oncoming road at the sound of a truck, he saw in the near distance, not a Ford 150 nor a semi, but something in between, with a boxy back that hit Daniel as being a refrigerator truck. The vehicle, the first to appear since Daniel turned, bare-chested, and stuck his thumb out, slowed as it approached, almost to a crawl as it passed Daniel. The driver leaned over the passenger seat; took a long, hard look at Daniel; and then pulled over to the shoulder 100 feet or so ahead and put the truck in idle.

Daniel paused for a long moment, having gotten his own look at the truck driver—redheaded and bearded, looking pretty redneck. Not a guy that Daniel would have been surprised to see on a motorcycle with a gang logo on his black-leather jacket. At least thirty, Daniel thought, wearing a sleeveless T and sporting bulging biceps covered in tattoos.

But it wouldn't be light for much longer and Daniel needed to put distance between him and Knoxville. And if the truck driver made demands for the ride, it wasn't any more than Daniel expected or was prepared to accommodate. He'd tacitly accepted this when he'd stripped off his T-shirt. He wasn't running away from doing it; he was running away from the way Steve had brutally been taking it from him. A bit more rough sex to get beyond the reach of Steve as fast and far as possible was something he'd just have to endure.

The passenger door to the truck popped open as Daniel approached, and he had one foot on the runner before he looked into the cab. The man—thin and sinewy—had his thick cock out of the fly of his shorts and was fisting it with his left hand. The man sneered at him.

"You want a ride, boy, you'll have to pay the freight for it."

Daniel sighed, pulled himself up into the cab, plopped on the seat, and pulled the cab door closed behind him.

"Here? Now?" he asked.

"In a bit. Where you headed?"

"Away from Knoxville. Doesn't matter much in what direction as long as it's away from Knoxville."

"Well, then, you're goin' my way. You runnin' away from something in Knoxville?"

"You could say that," Daniel answered. No need to tell him that it was just his boss, Steve, at the landscaping company, who had become possessive and demanding—and very, very rough. It had been OK at first—before Daniel found out that Steve was married and had young kids. Then it wasn't so OK with Daniel anymore.

"Trouble with the law, I reckon."

It was a statement, so Daniel didn't feel the need to answer. Anyway, that would be a better reason than the real one.

"Found the right refuge from that then," the redhead continued. "Me and my friends don't cotton for cops or other rule makers. I can take care of any for you who try to pull you down as long as you're with me." He gestured to behind the seats, and Daniel turned his face, for the first time noticing a rack of three rifles against the back wall of the cab. The driver chuckled, pulling a handgun up from the door side of his seat. "If in we get in close quarters, Betsy here—for the patriot Betsy Ross—will come in handy."

This was getting a bit weird for Daniel, so to change the context, he reached over and touched the guy's cock, which was unusually thick but not unusually long. It took a lurch in length when Daniel touched it. "Nice cock. You want me to suck you off here?" He realized he was repeating something that already had been answered, but he wanted to change the conversation from guns and cops.

"Naw, but turn to me sos I can see how you're built. Hmm, nice. Very nice. Now unbuckle and unzip and let me see what you're working with." When Daniel had fished his cock out, the man laughed, and said, "A real honey you are, ain't you? Got me a real movie star, don't I. My name's Red? What's yours? We're gonna get real well acquainted as we drive up in the Great Smokies."

"John, my name is John," Daniel answered. So, east, into the mountains. That was OK with him. But he'd be happier when he'd parted ways with this one.

Southeast of Maryville, Red turned the truck west on 129, headed up into the Great Smokies. After only a few hours, and with dusk approaching, he entered the broken asphalt pad of a closed gas station and pulled around in the back.

"It's time to pay for the ride," he said, reaching over to wrap a hand around the back of Daniel's neck and pulling Daniel's face down into his lap. At his direction, Daniel had been keeping the cock hard with his hand— but enough in check that the driver didn't spout. Daniel dutifully opened his mouth over the thick cock, which was lengthening even more from his attention. Red reached down for Daniel's cock. Somehow the two managed to get into a sixty-nine position across the truck seat, with Daniel trapped on the bottom, the top of his head pressed into the inside of the driver's door, and each eventually got the other one off. Daniel had voiced his ejaculation in time for Red to turn the cock to splash toward the dashboard, but Daniel got no warning and took a wad at the back of his throat and more on his cheek and chin as he pulled of Red's cock.

Daniel had sucked another guy off before—and even had sixty-nined—but Red had a brutal way of going about it, forcing Daniel to deep throat and hold until the young man was gagging, and sucking hard on Daniel's balls until he cried out for mercy. And he held Daniel tight, not letting him move away from anything. Red just laughed to show how much he enjoyed being cruel.

A group of buildings huddled at the bottom of where the road started to rise at a sharp incline up into the mountains. The only building lit up at this time of the evening, though, was a small, old-fashioned McDonalds.

"Time for dinner. Gotta eat before I get to the camp. Camp food is shit," Red said as he pulled into the fast-food restaurant.

Camp? Daniel wondered. Is this guy going to some sort of camp in the mountains? Red had kept muttering all sorts of government conspiracy stuff and the need for self-sufficiency as they were driving along, and Daniel had just grunted from time to time, sure that some point Red was just going to push him out of the truck, and half wishing he would, but also wanting to get as much mileage between Knoxville and him as he could.

"I'll come in and use the john, and then wait for you in the truck," he said, as Red opened the driver's door.

"You ain't hungry?"

"I'll manage."

"You don't want to spend the money, is that it? Well, for privileges, I'll stand you a meal. You can use the john in there and then, up the road a piece, I'll use the John too. Got it? You said your name was John. For a Big Mac, John takes a big one."

Yes, Daniel got it. But he, in fact, was hungry. And he'd figured Red would fuck him somewhere along the road anyway, even if he didn't agree with it. Red wasn't bulky, but he was wiry, and Daniel assumed the man could break him in half if he took a notion to. So Daniel just agreed to the deal, climbed out of the truck, and headed for the restaurant. Maybe he'd order whatever was the most expensive, he thought. But, of course, by the time he came out of the men's room, Red had already ordered what he was going to be permitted to eat.

The road climbing up into the mountains was windy and it was getting dark when, ignoring the posted signs when a park picnic area was open, Red pulled the truck into the turnoff and parked at the far end of the parking area, which consisted of rows of gravel divided off from each other by rows of overhanging trees.

Daniel prepared to get fucked in the truck, but as he was grasping the waistband of his shorts to pull them down, Red surprised him with a punch on the chin. Shocked and seeing stars, Daniel just sort of collapsed in his seat. Red got out of the truck, came around to the passenger side, jerked the door open, punched Daniel again, and pulled him out of his seat. This wasn't any different than Steve had been giving Daniel. Red had even commented on the bruising on Daniel's face earlier in the drive.

The man was strong. He threw Daniel over his shoulder and walked off into the woods. As he was setting Daniel down beside a big oak and Daniel was clearing his head and steadying himself on his feet, Red punch him again on the chin and followed up with a fist to the solar plexus.

When Daniel could survey his environment again, he found that he was bound to the oak tree, belly and cheek to the bark and his arms encircling the tree, his writs handcuffed to a low-lying limb on the other side. Red was jerking his shorts and briefs down and kneeling behind him, palming his belly to move his pelvis back from the tree trunk, and eating out his ass.

Daniel meekly complied when Red stood, grasped Daniel's hips, and commanded that he move his feet back from the tree and let his ass jut up. Daniel's eyes watered and he gave an internal scream when Red's cock penetrated his channel, but he knew it was useless to cry out for help here in the dark forest, he'd agreed to it, and after the initial thrusts and when a rhythm was established, he wasn't minding the fuck. Of course where they were, that he was handcuffed, and that Red was one crazy dude who had beat him had Daniel scared spitless. Shades of Steve all over again.

After Red was finished, he moved around the tree and released Daniel from the handcuffs. Still stunned, Daniel just sank to the ground by the tree, going into something close to a fetal position in case Red hit him again or kicked him, like Steve would do. But Red didn't do that. He was striding back toward the trunk, when Daniel called out. "Wait. Are you just going to leave me here?"

"Well, now, that's a good question. I'm glad you asked. I could take you with me—to the camp—but you know what you would be getting. It's up to you. If I was you, I'd come along, though. There are all sorts of hungry, creepy things up here in the mountains and I doubt I'll do you any worse than the cops will or than the daddies did to a sweet piece like you in prison. I figure you for a jail breaker on the lam. You took the punches and dick like you were a favorite bitch of black bulls in the pen."

Daniel didn't disabuse Red of that notion. But Daniel didn't have much in the way of options. With a groan, he hauled himself up from the forest floor, pulled his briefs and shorts up, and struggled along behind Red back to the truck. Once inside the truck, Red handcuffed Daniel again to the handle of the passenger door, grinned at him, and said, "Too late to change your mind now, jailbait. Just remember when we get there, to follow my lead and not get any of the guys to notice you. You ain't exactly got an invitation from Brother Joseph."

Red pulled back onto the main road, but he drove for just a few more miles, nearly reaching the summit of the mountain, before slowing, taking a close look in all directions, and then quickly turning onto a narrow track that Daniel hadn't even seen was there until they were on it. There was barely enough width for the truck to manage, and Red drove quite slow. After about twenty minutes or so, Daniel couldn't help exclaim from surprise and fear when the truck's headlights picked out two thuggish-looking guys, bare-chested and in fatigue pants, and with rifles at the ready emerging from both sides of the road. Red brought the truck to a stop, but he must have been recognized, because the two men just saluted and faded into the forest again. Daniel had plenty of time to pick up that they both had cut bodies, probably the result of a military regimen.

Another ten minutes of slowly bouncing along a rocky track, they came to a ditch with a wire fence behind it and a wood-framed gate with wire inserts. Two more bare-chested and armed men in fatigues materialized on the other side of the gate.

Having eyeballed and verified the truck as "friend," they opened the gate and let Red drive through. After a few more minutes they entered an encampment with a bunch of tents and huts strewn around haphazardly under the overhanging tree canopy. There was a log cabin, though, and a couple of sheds and a wooden barn-like structure. Shadowy figures moved through the area and lurked in groups of two and three. To Daniel's eyes, they were all carrying rifles and were dressed in fatigues. All bare-chested with well-worked torsos. Red was probably the scrawniest of the lot, and he was in great shape too.

Lights were on in the house and the barn and in a few of the tents, but most of the area was in an eerie darkness. Red pulled over next to one of the sheds. A light beside the shed door was on, but when Red came around, opened the passenger door, and freed Daniel from the cuffs, he whispered, "No noise from you. Crouch down, and follow me in the shadows."

Red led Daniel to a hut with wood sides and a canvas tent covering and pushed him through the doorway. The hut was maybe nine feet by sixteen feet and was set up as both living room and bedroom with rickety furniture that must have been pilfered from a town dump. Red pushed Daniel down on a single bed with a brass-rung headboard, handcuffed him to the rungs, and gagged him with a red bandana. "Don't you make any noise now. If in you do, it will go bad for you. T'aint should be no outsiders in camp. I have to go unload the supplies from the truck, but then I'll be back to do you proper."

And when Red returned, he did, in fact, do Daniel "proper," roughly and in doggie style. Afterward he led Daniel out to take a leak against a tree, still gagged, but then brought him back to the bed, lay on his back, and made Daniel ride his cock until they'd both come. Daniel was still gagged and handcuffed to the headboard, when Red imprisoned him in his arms, the two men stretched out against each other, and went into a deep snore.

* * * *

Red held Daniel in his tent for five days before Daniel's presence was discovered. He was handcuffed for most of the time and gagged when Red wasn't there. Red was too menacing for Daniel to try to rouse attention, and, in truth, Daniel soon was more afraid of what was going on outside the tent in the encampment than inside.

Four times a day it appeared that those in the camp—all men that Daniel ever saw by peeking through a slit in the canvas beside the camp bed—were called together in assembly, where a man with a commanding voice that changed at will from smooth to harsh harangued them with a bullhorn. It didn't take Daniel long to figure out that this was some sort of antigovernment militia movement. The key word of the man's harangues—the man evidently being named Brother Joseph, as that was how he was answered in a chorus of Amens—was "smite." Quoting the Bible, Brother Joseph spoke of we "will smite the inhabitants of this city, both man and beast" and of the Lord declaring "I will smite them with the pestilence and disinherit them, and I will make of you a nation greater and mightier than they."

Brother Joseph left no doubt that the city and people to be smitten were Washington, D.C. and all forms of authority in the nation and that the nation these fanatics on the mountaintop were to form was their own, forced by arms and domestic terrorism.

It was also a little weird that all of the men Daniel could see through the slit in the canvas were chummy with each other—lots of close contact and arms around each other.

The man with the bullhorn didn't sound crazy—he sounded convincing and smooth as silk, but the words he was using, the concepts he was pushing, and the demands he was making on what this band of men was going to do certainly sounded crazy to Daniel. The man also left little doubt that this group of men were organized for action and had a name. Brother Joseph kept referring to them as the Men of Thunder, who would correct by force of arms and acts of violence the wrongs of the government that was sucking at the teat of the people and disregarding the Constitution left and right.

Still, when Daniel was up in the mountains, he was where Steve couldn't get at him. And, though he was being held prisoner, Red wasn't fucking him more than once a day, albeit roughly, and he was making sure that Daniel was fed and hydrated and that he was able to relieve himself—not in any civilized manner, but certainly not with less privilege than Red himself had, or anyone else in camp. The beatings had stopped when Daniel went completely docile for whatever Red demanded.

In fact, Daniel was finding the sex a little exciting. He was just beginning to look forward to Red returning to the tent after dark with the look of lust in his eyes. The first couple of times Red had punched Daniel into submission before uncuffing him from the headboard, pushing him on his back on the side of the bed, Daniel's head hanging over the opposite side, before using two handcuffs to bind Daniel's wrists to the bed frame on the side of the bed and then raising and spreading Daniel's legs for the deep thrust of Red's cock while he manipulated Daniel's cock like a gearshift. After Daniel had come before Red did, he'd move around to the other side of the bed, slide his cock into Daniel's mouth, and finish by creaming the younger man's face.

After those first few times, though, Red became less hurried and presented his cock for Daniel to suck before climbing up on the bed, covering Daniel's back, and fucking him doggy style.

Daniel made all of the sounds of satisfaction and praise for Red's equipment and prowess that would flatter and please the man.

On the fifth night, while Daniel was on all fours on the bed and Red was crouched over him, mining his channel deep, the door flap of the tent fluttered and one of the other men entered, did a double take, and then, after muttering, "Who the hell is that? He's not from the camp," the man hurriedly turned and left the tent, raising the alarm. Red pulled out of Daniel, quickly zipped his fatigued pants up, picked up his rifle, and slipped out of the tent.

Amidst the yelling going on outside the tent, Daniel heard muffled gunfire. There was quite a bit of gunfire going on up here in the area of the camp, but it had always been during the day, not at night. Some sort of silencers were used on the guns to mute the noise, though. What Daniel heard was more of a pop, pop, pop sound. Then silence. Then the tent flap was pushed aside and three men entered and gawked at Daniel. All of them had rifles at the ready. All of the rifles immediately were turned on Daniel.

It didn't take much imagination for Daniel to figure out that the man standing in the middle was Brother Joseph. He was older than Red and anyone else Daniel had spied as they entered the compound. His body was in just as good a shape, however. The other two men obviously were giving him deference. One of the other men was a scrawny backwoods kind of guy, There were so many of them that Daniel saw wandering around the compound when he and Red arrived at the camp. The other guy was a young, dark hunk, though. The obvious leader was well over six feet; bald, but with a salt-and-pepper beard and bushy eyebrows; solidly built, and with piercing blue eyes.

"What do we have here? What are you doing here, son? Spying?"

Daniel rattled the handcuffs imprisoning his wrists, and said, "Red brought me here. I haven't been anywhere he didn't take me. Ask him."

"I'm afraid that's not possible." For the longest moment as Brother Joseph's rifle remained trained on him, Daniel thought the man was going to shoot him. But he gave Daniel—who was naked—a long, hard look, and then his facial features relaxed. Almost immediately he was transformed into a smiling, fatherly figure.

Turning to one of the men, he said, "Find the key for those cuffs, put some clothes on . . . what's your name . . . ?"

"John," Daniel answered. "I was just hitching a ride and Red picked me up and brought me here."

"Find some trousers for John here, and bring him to the cabin." Turning back to Daniel, he said, "You're gonna have to be blindfolded. Don't want you seein' anything."

The dark-haired hunk, who Brother Joseph addressed as Brother Sam, went scrounging around for trousers to put on Daniel. All the time he was sifting through piles of clothes, though, he was giving the naked Daniel close looks. It may have been so he could determine the size of trousers needed, but Daniel got the impression that it was with more interest in Daniel than that. Brother Sam was someone Daniel thought it wouldn't be hard to develop an interest in too. He went hard before Brother Sam produced trousers, and Daniel saw a slit-eyed smile on the guy's face as he held out the pants. He let the back of his hand brush Daniel's hard cock in the process, and Daniel shuddered—a movement that couldn't have been missed by the dark hunk.

Once the trousers were on, Brother Sam helped Daniel stand up from the bed, his hand palming one of Daniel's pecs and brushing Daniel's erect nipple as he pulled away. Looking down, Daniel could clearly see that Brother Sam was hard too. The signals were going both ways.

For the first time since Red had left the tent, Daniel's heart didn't feel like it was at the back of his throat, thumping hard. If they were going to blindfold him, it must mean they weren't going to kill him right off. They didn't want him to see the operation. Blindfolding was good for him. He had no interest in seeing any part of this operation.

The blindfold was pulled off Daniel when they guided him up the steps to the porch of the cabin and maneuvered him through the door. The cabin was a lot less primitive than the tents had been. It had been a real house at one point and had both a kitchen and a bathroom, Daniel could see as he was led in to bedroom and pushed down in a seated position on the side of a double bed. Someone was keeping the place clean.

While the scrawny redneck Brother Joseph had called Ed stood guard over him from the doorway to the corridor outside the bedroom, the other guy, the hunk, Brother Sam, said he was going to look for a chain. He came back with a long, thin chain with a lock on it. Being gentle and giving Daniel a hint of a sympathetic smile, Brother Sam freed one of Daniel's wrists from the handcuffs, but then he looped the chain in the free handcuff and secured it with the lock. The other end of the chain was secured to a heavy-duty hook on the wall of the bedroom next to the door frame.

"There, that's how Brother Joseph said to do it," Brother Sam said, in a voice in which Daniel could discern some regret. "You won't be going nowhere out of the cabin now, but this will let you move from the bed to the can."

"Whatayou think Brother J will do with——" the one named Ed started to ask, but he was quickly cut off by Brother Sam, who was looking nervously around.

"What do you think he's going to do? You know Brother Joseph. It's what we all do up here. It isn't any business of you and me what he does with this one, though." Ed was already at the door of the cabin, and Brother Sam turned and whispered, "I know what I'd like to do with you."

Daniel blushed and lowered his gaze to the floor, as Brother Sam, after running a hand over Daniel's erect nipples again, turned and left the cabin.

And then they were gone. And it wasn't long before Daniel learned what Brother Joseph would do with him.

Brother Joseph entered the room wearing a long, white robe. He was barefoot, and the robe had a plunging neckline that revealed a muscular, but well-matted chest.

"I can only imagine what unmentionable things that man must have done to you," he murmured in a deep, sympathetic voice, as he sat on the side of the bed.

"I agreed to it for the ride," Daniel said. "Although he only brought me here and kept me a prisoner. I've seen nothing, I promise. He kept me bound to the bed."

"And he took advantage of you?"

"Repeatedly, but I wasn't new to it. I didn't see anything beyond his tent, though." Daniel tried to look both innocent and desirable at the same time. He had little doubt that this man held his life in his hands—and no doubt either what the man was interested in doing to him. That he probably was conflicted in which way to go with Daniel.

"No doubt, but it does raise a problem. We can't have anyone who isn't in the Men of Thunder up here. And we can't just let loose anyone who has been here and

193

knows we are up here. So, it's a question of what to do with you." He was sitting close beside Daniel and had the palm of a hand pressed between Daniel's shoulder blades.

"I'll do whatever you want," Daniel said, trying to give the man a smile. "I heard some of what you were telling your men. It's interesting. I want to hear more. I also would do anything for you that you wanted. Anything . . . like Red . . ."

There wasn't another response Daniel could think of that would keep him alive, at least for now.

"Do you think you could . . . ?"

Brother Joseph let that thought drift. Daniel sank to his knees to the floor of the cabin; turned to facing the other man, who spread his thighs and bunched the robe up to his waist, revealing a thick, engorged cock.

Bidding for life, Daniel took the cock in his mouth and gave Brother Joseph the most satisfying blow job he could manage. After the militia chieftain groaned and released on Daniel's cheek, he pulled the younger man up onto the bed, on his belly. He nudged Daniel up on his knees, with this chest and cheek still flat on the bed, his arms outstretched, and he moved between pulling Daniel's cock through his thighs and sucking him and giving slobbering attention to Daniel's asshole. The man was an expert, and in the short time it took Brother Joseph to recharge, Daniel was moaning and begging for the fuck.

He was well dilated when Brother Joseph covered him and started to slide into him, but the man was thick enough that it took some time and was a belaboring chore. Daniel didn't care. He had known he had to accept the cock and give the militia chief a good ride. But by the time Brother Joseph was saddled and began to pump him, Daniel lost all thought of anything but focusing moaning attention to the cock expertly working his channel.

Before he finished Daniel, Brother Joseph turned him on his side and, without losing purchase of the cock, pumped him slow and deep in a side split, holding

Daniel's leg up to maximize the depth of the cock. Daniel turned his face to the older man and they kissed deeply as they were brought to a mutual explosion.

It became obvious that this was Brother Joseph's bed and that they were going to spend this—and subsequent—nights here until the decision was made on what to do with Daniel. At this point Daniel didn't care that he'd only moved from Red's camp cot to Brother Joseph's double bed. Brother Joseph was the most gentle and proficient top he'd ever experienced.

* * * *

"This here is Brother Dan."

Daniel snapped his head up and turned his face to the door of the bedroom. For a split second, he thought that Brother Joseph was referring to him. He'd given the name "John," so how, he wondered, could the militia chief know his real name was Daniel? But then he saw that Brother Joseph was referring to a guy who was at least forty, had a bit of a paunch, and was ugly as sin. Regardless of the paunch, he had the pecs and guns of a bodybuilder.

He also was grinning and leering at Daniel.

"Brother Dan has done me a service, and he needs to be rewarded," Brother Joseph continued. "I want you to do whatever he tells you to do. I'll be back in a hour or so."

What Brother Dan wanted Daniel to do—after Daniel had sucked the man's cock to as engorged as this underachiever in the sex department was going to get— was to just lie there with his buttocks on the side edge of the bed, with his legs raised, spread and held by the older man, while Brother Dan huffed and puffed and fucked him missionary style.

Every few days after that, Brother Joseph brought other soldiers of the Men of Thunder into the cabin for

Daniel to service. Daniel learned a couple of things from this. Brother Joseph, although he shared the bed, with sex privileges, with Daniel more nights than he didn't, didn't seem to mind other men fucking Daniel, and male-male sex must be some sort of glue and reward system that held this group of men together and solidified Brother Joseph's authority. This confirmed the impression that Daniel was getting from the first day he'd been in the camp. These men were bent in more ways than only politics.

* * * *

"I wish I could believe that those were your real views about the evils of the government and the need to smite the bastards."

"I thought that before I was brought up here," Daniel answered Brother Joseph as they were cooling down from sex on the militia chief's bed, "but I've been listening to your talks to the other men. It's all becoming even more clear to me now."

"Clearer?"

"Yes, I want to join up. I want to be part of the Men of Thunder. You have convinced me."

They kissed, Brother Joseph jubilant at the conversion. "Joining is a process. Can't let you have a rifle yet—and before you get one, there's quite a bit of training."

"I'm ready for that."

"Then I guess it's best that we get this chain off and we find something for you to do in the compound. Maybe the kitchen for starters."

"Whatever you want," Daniel said. It didn't take much to tell Brother Joseph he could have whatever he wanted. He'd taken whatever he wanted from Daniel for the past two weeks, including using him to maintain the loyalty of his men. And what he'd given, in turn, was indoctrination. Daniel didn't know anymore how much of what Brother Joseph had been giving he could resist and how much he was beginning to believe. One thing he did know was that Brother Joseph gave him his dick and Daniel was fully convinced by that.

Brother Joseph gave Daniel greater freedom of the compound, but Daniel was to return to his bed every night—unless Brother Joseph had other plans for the night, which was sometimes to be the case now. During the two weeks, Brother Joseph hadn't come back to the cabin every night—and on a few nights he'd let another man sleep in his bed and use Daniel. One of the hallmarks of what made a soldier of the Men of Thunder, Daniel had learned, was a preference for men, and part of the charisma Brother Joseph used to keep men in thrall to him was to plow the bottoms among them—at least the ones who appealed to Brother Joseph—and to provide bottoms for the rest.

Once assigned to the kitchen, Daniel volunteered to be the runner—to be the one who went to the various sheds and refrigerator rooms to gather supplies for the kitchen. He took on this job so that he could get a lay of the camp and perhaps find a way of escaping the compound.

He didn't find a vulnerability in the camp's defenses. Someone needed to help him over that hurdle. That someone was the young, handsome, well-built, randy man by the name of Brother Sam, who had chained Daniel in the cabin's bedroom and had shown interest in him.

As Daniel moved around the camp he couldn't help but notice that Brother Sam was often nearby, watching him and smiling—smiling that special "interested" smile. Not that he was the only one to do so. It seemed there were more tops—and bold ones—in the camp than there were bottoms. And there was plenty of sex going on, out in the open. This was the primary glue that held the Men of Thunder together. To Daniel's eye, most of the men were here for the sex and were just humoring Brother Joseph's megalomania.

Brother Sam was awfully good looking to Daniel, and increasingly the quiet, dark-headed man was showing his interest in Daniel. Daniel thought it was inevitable that Sam would ask him to go off in the brush with him at some point, and he wasn't surprised when it happened. It scared him, though, but not because he was afraid Brother Joseph would find out. Daniel had already been given to three men by Brother Joseph whose loyalty the militia chief wanted to pin down, and when Daniel asked him if it bothered him that Daniel would be fucked by other men in the camp, Joseph had just answered, "Not as long as condoms are used. Free love between men is one of the tenets of the Men of Thunder movement."

What scared Daniel was what Brother Sam said to him when he finally sidled up to Daniel when the young man was bringing a sack of flour back to the kitchen from one of the storage sheds. Daniel was walking along when Sam came in step with him.

"I've had my eye on you," Brother Sam said.

"I noticed."

"Red brought you into the camp without permission."

"Yes, but I'm with Brother Joseph now. And I haven't seen Red around. Is he—?"

"You don't want to know what happened to Red. And it would be best if you didn't ask. He committed an unpardonable sin in bringing an outsider into the camp."

Daniel had known in the back of his mind what had happened to Red, but it made him shudder to have it confirmed. Brother Sam was still speaking, though.

"I know you're with Brother Joseph now. But you don't really want to be with him, do you?"

"He's fine. He's good to me."

"He's old. You'd rather have a younger man fucking you. You'd rather have me working your ass."

Daniel didn't answer, which was answer enough for Sam.

"And you don't want to be here, do you? Here in this camp, with the Men of Thunder? You didn't volunteer to come here and be part of this. I think you're putting on an act to try to find a way to escape. I've seen you scoping out the edges of the camp. I think you're looking for a way out."

A chill went up Daniel's spine. Had he been that obvious? He thought he was acting out being won over well enough to survive. Why was this man saying this? If he said this to Brother Joseph, Daniel would be dead meat. Did Brother Sam think he had to blackmail Daniel into having sex with him?

"No, that's not true," he said. "But if that even gets hinted around, I'll be in trouble. Why are you saying this? Do you want to lay me? That would be fine with me if it's OK with Brother Joseph. You don't have to go making up—"

"Of course I want to fuck you," Brother Sam said. "Do I really have to get Brother J's OK or have to use blackmail for you to go into the bushes with me? I think you're hot for me."

"Sshhh. I'll go. Just stop talking about me wanting to escape." Daniel turned and started walking into a corner of the camp where there was dense foliage and where he'd seen other couples go.

Sam fucked him up against a low-branched pine tree, with Daniel's legs spread and hanging over low-hanging branches, and Brother Sam crouched between his thighs, their lips locked and their moans in harmony, and Sam slamming hard and deep up inside Daniel.

"I've wanted to do that since I first saw you in camp," Sam said when they had both fired off and were cooling down—and while they both held in place, both enjoying the sensation of Sam going flaccid inside Daniel's channel.

"And I've wanted you to do that since Brother Joseph said I could go with other men here. But you've scared me. If you say anything—"

"You still think we're here, like this, because I'm blackmailing you? The way I fucked you doesn't tell you there's something else to it?"

Daniel didn't answer. It was exactly what he thought, but they'd been so good with each other in the fuck that he didn't want to say that's why he went with Sam.

"I won't give you up. But I need to know if you want out of here. Be honest with me. And I'm here with you because I wanted to fuck you, and for no other reason. But be honest with me. I don't believe any of this stuff Brother Joseph is pushing, do you? You're looking for a way to escape."

"OK, yes. But I don't know if the effort is worth it. I don't have anything to escape to. I'm just not going to take up a rifle and shot people for this cause."

"The sex was incredible for me. For you too, I hope."

"You don't even have to ask about that." And, indeed, he didn't. Daniel had never been fucked this good or been as attracted to another man as he was to Sam.

"If I were to escape too, would coming with me be enough incentive for you to take the risk?"

"Yes. Of course."

"Well, we'll go tonight then."

"I don't understand. How can we? . . . how can you just give this up?"

"I'm not one of them. I'm FBI. The camp is being raided early tomorrow morning. I want to get out before that happens and I want to get you out of here too if you're not part of this. I know that Brother Joseph is going to Brother Tom's tent tonight, so you'll be alone in the cabin. Do you want to come with me or don't you?"

200

"You know I do," as Daniel felt Sam's cock stiffening inside him again, ready for round two.

Retreat to Savannah

Was that really him I'd seen at the graveside, I wondered. It was more than a glimpse and he looked at me in recognition, but then Julio had taken my elbow so possessively, so intent on showing how close he was to Avis and me—or to me, at least. When I'd given him his moment of recognition, I looked back at where I was sure I'd seen David. But he was gone. I pulled the collar of my coat up to my ears and shuddered. Fuckin' long Chicago winters. Frozen stiff by the wind whipping off the lake. How did they manage to chip out a hole to put Avis in?

Not that Avis was in that coffin they were lowering. She'd wanted the pageantry and the attention of a full burial, but she wasn't there. She'd been cremated and her ashes scattered on top of Pedernal Mountain in New Mexico from her beloved Piper Cub plane that she was fond of being photographed next to even if she'd never learned to fly. Thus, her ashes were being symbolically superimposed on those of Georgia O'Keefe. And it wasn't because they had been buddies. Avis would do anything she could, even in death, to upstage O'Keefe.

Not that anyone here, but Julio and I, knew she wasn't in this coffin. She had trusted me to reveal the truth when the sales of her art started to flag—when she needed a boost to connect her to O'Keefe. That was Avis.

202

Always playing the angles, even beyond death. And nearly everything about her fake—except for her art. Her art was genuine, so far eclipsing mine that I'd stuck with her these last five years, living in her shadow, but gratefully so. Doing everything I could to soak up her skill and her inspiration.

Now I'd be flying solo. Or would be if it wasn't for Julio, still standing close beside me, a "comforting" hand on an elbow. As if I were going to throw myself into the open grave in grief.

Avis would like that, I'm sure. But there were enough photographers around this gravesite to hold off the need to play the Pedernal Mountain ash dump for a couple of years.

There was truth in Avis' art, I'd grant her that. But it wasn't anywhere else that I could see in Avis' vicinity. It certainly wasn't in our five-year robbing-the-cradle marriage. That had been one of convenience from the start, me on the rebound from David and Avis thinking she needed to make the *right* statement. The statement had to be about men—and young and stylish men—as she'd had her name linked to a pro women's tennis player, and Avis' big art clients weren't *that* liberal and forgiving. Her real issue was with men, but being hooked up with black truck driver types wasn't seen as in her image interest either. The young up-and-coming artist out of the Savannah College of Arts and Design, SCAD, with the Old Family Charleston background, was just what she needed to rejuvenate her image.

The marriage was a sham from the beginning, of course, but I wanted a totally opposite reaction to the breakup with David, one of my professors at SCAD, and I wanted the further art development Avis would provide me without having taken into account how anyone walking into her shadow withered.

That there was no body in this coffin they were lowering into the ground was another lie, but also what

Avis had died from was a lie. Yes, I guess it could be called consumption, but it was a consumption of men from truck cabs and off the street and from the AIDS one or more of them gave her. Not a glamorous way to go and not one that would write up well in her Wikipedia listing, so the tragic Victorian era malady of consumption was put into play. I certainly didn't object. It wouldn't mean that anyone would look at me as a sexual pariah now, and, at twenty-seven, I was in my sexual prime—and prime in my need for sex. I just never had had sex with Avis. We'd gotten drunk once and had started into it, but we both started to laugh, and it ruined the mood we both worked so hard to pretend was there.

And right at this moment, although I was managing—genuinely—a tear and a look of grief for the passing of my famous wife, what I really could use was being thoroughly laid.

As if sensing that, Julio, Avis' Brazilian business manager and my sometimes lover, squeezed my elbow and leaned his head into mine, "Hold up for just a few more minutes, and we'll be able to leave. I'll take good care of you."

"You always do," I murmured back. And he did, in his overbearing way. Whereas Avis had gone through life assuming it was all about her and correctly taking for granted that her will would be accorded to, Julio was more demanding in his assertion of control. It worked with Avis, because they both essentially wanted the same thing—a well-oiled financial account—and neither could see the manipulation of the other. And it had worked with me to this point because I had a social contract with Avis that left me little breathing room and because I had a weakness for dominating men with big cocks. Julio fit that bill. To Avis, Julio was in the family. He was a safe lover for me.

But then, so had David been—he had left little breathing room for me when we were together. The reality probably was that I needed to have someone control me. Preferably a strong-willed, well-hung man, I now knew after five years of marriage to Avis.

I looked around the gravesite again, but I didn't spy him. It was easier to look for him now than before, because, although the machine hadn't hit bottom with the coffin yet, some of the mourners were already drifting away. There was a reception laid on at the Renaissance Chicago Downtown, centrally located on the shore of the lake, and everyone wanted to be the cause of the stragglers not getting full champagne glasses. Avis was a little optimistic, I thought, about how long she would be remembered in anything but the prices of her paintings now skyrocketing in the market. The people who came today were other artists likely to resent Avis' new price structures rather than the rich Europeans and Asians who bought her art.

"Come here," Julio called from the living room while I was taking off my coat in the foyer after the long drive back to Oak Park. Avis wanted to swirl in the lifestyle of Chicago, so we had a pied-à-terre there facing the lake, but she also wanted to "commune" with the likes of Frank Lloyd Wright for inspiration, so the main house was in Oak Park. Except when I was doing arm candy duty, I stuck to Oak Park, because it did, indeed, have a community of artists that wasn't as full of themselves as Avis' crowd was.

Julio also concentrated his management work in Oak Park, so more times than not, when Avis was entertaining a black bull stranger in our loft studio, Julio was fucking me here in Oak Park.

"On your knees," he demanded when I walked into the living room. He already had his cock out and was holding it, although it looked fully capable of standing out erect on its own. "I know what you need right now," he muttered.

As I knelt in front of him and took his cock in my mouth, strangely enough, I agreed with him. Sex at this moment was comforting. It also put off "what now?" discussions. He fucked me doggy style with my belly plastered to the arm of one of the sofas, my spread knees buried in the cushions of the sofa seat, and my head and arms dangling down to the carpet at the side of the sofa.

Julio was good—very good. And he was divinely equipped. He also was Latin and hirsute, which I had always found arousing. And he was controlling, demanding, rough, and just slightly cruel. I was lost to him when he was fully saddled, had reached down to cup my chin and arch my back up into his hairy chest, and was pumping me deep.

"Oh, shit yes, fuck me hard," I cried out.

He laughed, knowing I was fully surrendered to him—yet again—and straightened up more on the sofa cushion, his thighs between mine. "Fuck yourself," he muttered. "Show me how much you want it." He had pulled nearly out to the surface—which was a long journey back out of my channel. With a sob of need and mindful of the intent to control and humiliate me—to establish who was dominant—I put my buttocks in motion. He held absolutely still as I pumped back on his cock until I could hold myself no more and ejaculated against the inside of the chair arm.

He left me bent over the sofa arm, walked over to the drinks cabinet, and poured himself a stiff scotch. He didn't offer me one. It was as if he was going through the steps to assert total control over all aspects of my life.

So, this was how he intended it now, I thought. A move from paid manager into Avis' place, but with full fucking rights.

"I think I should move in. You'll need someone to take care of you now," he said, as he sipped on his scotch.

I said nothing. I was still panting, having come— knowing he hadn't come yet.

"We can think on arrangements, but I'll pack a bag and bring it over tonight. We'll sleep in your room for a while, but when we can get Avis' things moved out of the master bedroom, that will be more suitable for us."

Again I didn't answer, but I turned my eyes to him. He'd stripped us both down. His body was magnificent. Mature, Zeus like. The dark hair swirling about his body arousing.

"You haven't come yet," I murmured.

"No, I haven't," he agreed.

I turned my body on the sofa to where I was sitting on the cushions. I took the cushion beside me and pushed it under the small of my back as I jutted my buttocks out beyond the front edge of the sofa. Then I grabbed, raised, and spread my legs. "Fuck me, daddy," I whined. "Give me your cum."

Laughing, he put his scotch glass down, came to me, crouched between my spread thighs, entered me strongly, and began to pump again in long, deep strokes that had me crying out for the cruelty of the cock.

I begged him to come inside me, but he laughed, withdrew, and ejaculated on my thighs.

I knew it would take total surrender to him sexually to mark my assent for him moving in and taking control of my life. But I hadn't verbalized my agreement. And I didn't intend to. As soon as he left to pack a suitcase and return, I went to the computer and started looking up long-term rentals. I didn't know where I would look—other than Chicago—before I reached the computer, but, once there, I just naturally keyed in Savannah, Georgia, the image of David floating up into my consciousness.

* * * *

I woke at the sound of a snort. As my eyes flipped open, I assumed that had come from me. But then I realized it hadn't. There was a well-muscled chocolate-

207

brown arm laying across my chest—my naked chest—and there was nothing familiar about the part of the room I could see. It was close enough to dawn for me to pick out shapes if not exact colors. But this definitely was not the loft bedroom in the carriage house I was renting on Savannah's Oglethorpe Square.

I turned my head toward where the snort had come from. God he was good looking. Maybe my age or a little older. Certainly not much older than thirty. I didn't think he was full back, as his facial features were more European—and the skin tone was definitely milk rather than dark chocolate. We were both naked. I could tell that because he had his left leg bent and thrown over my midsection, the knee on my belly and the meat of his calf covering my genitals. His cock, flaccid, was pressed into my hip. I could feel the curly hair of his pubes but other than that his body seemed to be hairless—other than the hair on his head, which was shoulder length and done in dreadlocks. The arm laying over me was tattooed in a colorful design all the way down to his wrist and up to his shoulder and covering his left pectoral muscle.

OK, so I'd been fucked last night by a black man—a black man with a big tattoo. I'd never been fucked by a stranger before, let alone one with a big tattoo. I did been raised to think of such men as scary crazy. Being fucked at all didn't happen all that often that I should be feeling so calm about it as I was. But I just couldn't work up the concern. My head was throbbing whenever I concentrated on my pain centers, so I tried not to concentrate on my throbbing head. Not doing that brought out the soreness in my ass, my muscles there still contracting and expanding. That's how I knew I'd been fucked. I knew how it felt to be fucked in the ass. This was it. And by something big.

He wasn't at all the kind of man I'd usually go with. I hadn't been with black men before. Julio was dark skinned—almost as dark as this man—but he was a

Brazilian. This guy didn't look like the black guys Avis liked to go with either. Other than the tattoo he wasn't thuggish or poor-looking like Avis liked, but, God, he was built.

I felt a moment of panic. I couldn't remember anything about what put me in this man's bed. It certainly wasn't my bed and it wasn't a hotel room. It was some sort of studio apartment. Neat, but Spartan in furnishings. A working man's place. The bed was only a double, and he wasn't a small man, so him being almost on top of me probably was a necessity if we were both were going to be on the bed. There wouldn't be much of a reason for us both to be on this bed if not for sex. And I knew we'd had sex—that he'd been inside me. And on top of me—and with vigor. Our bodies were knotted in sheeting. There still was a pillow under the small of my back. I was a bit sore, which only happened when the man was built big. My legs were slightly raised, my feet flat on the surface of the bed, and my legs were spread—a sure sign I'd been fucked and that he was built big. He was significantly longer than I was and heavier of body, although perfectly proportioned.

I was sore and confused enough that I didn't want more this morning of whatever we did last night— although he was a real hunk and I regretted not having a memory of what we'd done last night and how we'd gotten here. I'd let him do me again, though—when my head was clear. He was that much of a hunk. A rain check. No, I'm not promiscuous. I'd just like to know what I missed.

I'd gone out in the early evening to meet David at a club. That much I remembered. I'd finally gotten up the courage to let David know I was in Savannah on a six-month house lease—just to get my bearings, I told myself. I'd at least pretended I wasn't chasing David down now that I was free. When I called him, he professed delight that I was here, because he had something he wanted to propose to me. My first thought had been that he wanted me to move in with him and maybe I'd been precipitous to rent the carriage house in Savannah's historical district near the river. But then something was in the back of my mind about that thought not having panned out. Something very disappointing. Something that made me angry—both at myself and at David.

Something, maybe that brought me to this black man's bed. This black bull's bed. I wasn't able to help myself. I let a hand move to my hip and take the measure of his cock, a procedure that made me draw in breath. He'd had that inside me—surely even thicker and longer in erection. No wonder I was sore and my ass muscles were still having slight spasms. It was hardening just from my light touch.

He sighed in his sleep and the cock responded to me. I let loose of it like it was a hot potato.

As carefully as I could, I extricated myself from under his arm and leg. He snorted again but was asleep enough that he turned toward the wall, smacked his lips, and began a soft snore. He had his bare buttocks turned to me. They were bulbous and muscular, with deep hollows between the cheeks and hips. I resisted the urge to run my hand over them, and now I really regretted not remembering the sex.

I swung my legs over the side of the bed. A foot came down on swishing film. A spent condom on the floor. No, two spent condoms, both sea slug fat with contained cum. We must have had *some* night—and he must have worked hard to be as dead to the world as he was now.

Our clothes were in the center of the room—or most of them were. I didn't see my briefs, but then I felt them on the bed where the heel of my hand was pressed into the mattress. I lifted the briefs. They had been ripped down the middle in the back. A memory flashed across my brain. Belly to bed with a heavy weight on top of me.

The sound of ripping material and a deep laugh. An arm snaking under my waist, lifting me to my knees. My chest flat against the bed under the pressure of his chest. The initial searing pain of a cock the girth of a baseball bat entering me, through the slit in the briefs.

I dropped the briefs. He could have those as a souvenir if he was into such fetishes. He probably had a drawer full of ripped briefs from the men he had ravished.

Our clothes on the floor were mixed with each other. His trousers and polo shirt were of as good quality and name brand as my trousers and dress shirt. We obviously had undressed quickly, though, anxious to be on the bed—him anxious to be inside me; me anxious to have him inside me. I felt no bruising other than the sore channel. He hadn't forced me—hadn't been violent. Of that I was sure. I had wanted to be here—to be with him.

Something about David. There was some reason why I'd drunk too much, had wanted this black hunk to fuck me too much.

I almost fell down when I stood up from the bed. My legs were cramped. I'd had this feeling before after sex with a guy—a guy who had held my legs spread and raised and pumped me interminably. All of the signs were that I had been totally taken by this black bull—both from the back and from the front. If I wasn't so freaked out at not remembering much of anything from the previous night . . .

But I wasn't really promiscuous. I could count on the fingers of one hand the men I'd slept with in my life, starting with David and ending with . . . whoever this black bull was. This was all unfamiliar and scary ground for me—the part of having different partners—I'd slept with David and Julio on too many occasions to count. Best thing would be if I managed a retreat without him waking up. And then forget this ever happened. Not that I could remember what happened.

I found myself on East Jones Street when I found the stairs and descended to the street. The studio apartment I'd left was over a gray-stone double garage in what had been a carriage house to a larger house, now gone, and replaced by four wooden shotgun houses. I wasn't in one of the better parts of town, but I was still within the edge of the old city. And I'd lived in Savannah before, while attending SCAD, and some of the college buildings were on West Jones across town from here in a tonier section, so, once I saw the intersection of East Jones and Price Street, running north-south, I had some idea where I was.

I was nearly twenty blocks from home and on a side of the city I'd rarely have reason to be in—the rundown side of the historical district.

Savannah had been laid out in straight-line streets within a pattern of thirty park squares. The squares now had been reduced to twenty-two squares, with the line of squares on both the east and west side of the pattern having disappeared over time. I was on the east edge, where squares were missing. My rented carriage house, on Oglethorpe Square, was in the middle of the second line of squares from the river and thus in the center of the historical district and in the high-rent district. It also, unfortunately, was nearly twenty blocks toward the river from where I was standing, so I was going to have to hoof it a good way. I didn't have a car in Savannah; most here didn't keep a car in the downtown area.

I started off, headed north, toward the Savannah River, on Price Street, but within a couple of blocks, I cut west into the center of the historical district because Price Street wasn't looking too safe. I'd only gone those two blocks, though, when I saw a sign over a step-down door in an old brick building. The sign advertised a bar, Louie's, which was familiar to me. And then I started remembering how the previous night had unfolded so that by the time I got to Oglethorpe Square I had most of it worked out.

David had told me to meet him for drinks at 8:00 p.m. at a bar—a gay bar, it turned out—named Louie's. He had given me directions. I took a pedicab there, giddy with anticipation of hooking up with David, my old SCAD professor and lover, again. I had realized within days of retreating to Savannah from Chicago that this was what I wanted—to return to David's bed, which I had abandoned when I married Avis. I wanted the SCAD life again. I wanted to live under David's protection again. I even had visions of teaching art there. I had learned so much from Avis, and my connection with her would help me anywhere I went in the art world.

David was already there when I arrived. So was Kevin, a young, willowy, more pretty than handsome blond student at SCAD. That's how David introduced Kevin to me—as one of the students at the college. All it took was to watch them interact and the way they touched each other and inclined their faces to each other as they spoke to know that Kevin wasn't just David's student. Kevin was also being fucked by David. I could clearly see that, because six years previously, I had been Kevin. And being fucked by David most likely meant living with David too. That's what it had meant for me my last year at SCAD. SCAD was so liberal, eclectic, and off beat that no one raised an eyebrow—at least to my face—when I had moved in with David.

Within fifteen minutes of my arrival at the bar, David had a hand on Kevin's thigh and they had kissed. It was obvious that David was making a statement about David and me. That's when I stopped counting my drinks. It hadn't occurred to me that I'd grown too old for David to be interested in—until now.

It didn't take David long to tell me why he wanted to meet. "There's a lecturer's position for you at SCAD, Ethan, if you are interested. That's why I came to Avis' funeral in Chicago. I had a proposition for you, but I chickened out, deciding that hitting you with an offer

213

when you were burying your wife was the worst of taste. I was going to send you a letter, but here you are in Savannah already. You contacted me."

Burying my wife. David was talking like he didn't know that I was gay and that my marriage had been one of convenience. I left Savannah, sure, but just because I married Avis hadn't meant that David and I couldn't continue sleeping together. He was the one who declared that our arrangement had to stop dead in its tracks. He'd been the one who introduced me to Avis. In hindsight, it almost was as if he had purposely jettisoned me—that he had been handing me off. In that sense, he had deserted me rather than me leaving him. He just resented someone other than him directing my life, even if he'd been the catalyst in that happening.

"A lecturer position?" I asked. "That sounds interesting. I wouldn't mind teaching a course on the Impressionists. Maybe their sense of color and light."

"We rather thought you could teach one on Avis' work," David said. "Having her husband teaching such a course would be a draw for students, we thought."

Teaching Avis' work. Remaining in the shadow of Avis. I'd done all of this preparation in my own field and what I was wanted for was my connection with Avis. It was one thing to use her as cachet to get a position, but it was another thing altogether to continue living in full service to her glory.

That's when I ordered my third drink.

I was somewhat blurry eyed when a handsome, well-built black man came over to our table and greeted David as an old friend. David made the introduction. "Ethan, this is the Louie of this bar's name. He's a sculptor at SCAD too. A very old friend. Louie, this is Ethan Pender. I've told you about him. He was one of my best students—and closest friends—before Avis Blair stole him from me and took him off to Chicago."

"One of your closest friends?" Louie asked in a smooth deep bass voice, turning a winning smile toward me and taking my hand in a firm and prolonged grip. He was one of the most handsome black men I'd ever seen— certainly of those who had dreadlocks down to their shoulders. I didn't think I'd ever be attracted to a black man with dreadlocks, but on him they looked good and natural. The same with the tattooing that showed through the white, gauzy, tight-fitting polo shirt stretching over a heavily muscled chest. The tattooing was in several vibrant colors and covered his left arm, shoulder, and pectoral muscle. I'd always thought of tattooing as being gang member related, but on him it looked sexy and stylish. And a little dangerous and adventuresome. "How close?" he asked.

"Very close," David said, giving Louie a wink.

This was a gay bar. David had his hand on Kevin's crotch who, in turn, had an accepting hand on David's hand. The signaling going on between David and Louie on the relationship I'd once had with David was blatant— as, I'm sure, was the declaration that David no long had a reservation on me.

"Ethan has just come back to Savannah," David continued, "and has, he has told me, taken a six-month lease on a carriage house. I'm trying to convince him to do some lecturing at SCAD. He's a SCAD graduate and an artist in his own right in addition to having studied with Avis Blair."

And married to Avis Blair, my mind screamed, but obviously David didn't want to muddy the waters on possibilities and preferences. I knew David quite well. I knew what he was doing. He was trying to pass me off. He knew I'd come back to reconnect with him and that wasn't in his plans.

Well, fuck David. I tossed off my third drink, as he finished what he had to say. "Nearly everyone Ethan knew here before has moved on. I'm sure he could benefit from making new contacts and friends—having someone to take him on. Ethan is very good . . . a very good friend."

Fuck you in spades, David. I can find my own hookups, thank you very much.

"That would be the distinct pleasure of anyone lucky enough to do that," Louie answered, giving me that stark-white-toothed smile in a handsome chocolate-brown face again. "But look, Ethan—and Kevin here too—need refills. I think a round on the house is in order."

I remembered waving David and Kevin good-bye sometime later—flashing a flip of the bird to David that I was pretty careful not to let him see—and moving to the bar with Louie for another round of drinks. And I remember Louie standing very close to me at the bar. I dredged up the memory of Louie's hand on my butt and then Louie's hand on my crotch as he brought on another drink for me.

I remember him saying he wanted to fuck me. I don't remember saying yes, but I obviously I did.

And then I really couldn't remember much of anything else before waking up in Louie's bed in a studio apartment above a double carriage house garage in an alley behind shotgun houses on East Jones and Price Streets.

* * * *

"Have you thought about the offer on the SCAD lecture position?" David was calling me two days after "the night," giving me time not only to think things out but also to get over both my seethe and my hangover. It was a good thing he had given me the time, because I was thinking more rationally now. Sure I had credentials of my own, but the relationship with Avis was my golden chip to placement, and there was every reason to start into a job that paid and still allowed me time to paint even if it still was in Avis' shadow.

"I'd be happy to lecture on Avis' work," I answered. "But I'd also like to lecture on other topics closer to my own work."

"We can start with a seminar on Avis and Native American abstractism and see where we can fit you in on color and light, maybe next semester, if you're still here. I hear you had quite a night with Louie."

I didn't answer straight off. How in the hell did he know what kind of time I'd had with Louie? I didn't even know what I grand time I'd had with Louie. "I can't say," I answered, truthfully. "I was drunk out of my mind. I have no idea how the night went."

"Louie thought it went quite fine. In fact, he said he was looking forward to hearing from you—which is a word to the wise. From what I know, he's not going to call you. If you're going to get with him again, you need to call him."

"Then I guess that won't go any further," I answered icily. "I don't chase men." Then I wanted to bite my tongue. I'd come back to Savannah to chase David—and there was little doubt that David knew that. He didn't press home the point, though, which wasn't like David. He could be a little tiger in pulling out his little victories. I'm sure he was flattered that I'd tried to come back to him.

But he must really have wanted me to lecture on Avis, because he just signed off, telling me to come around anytime in the next couple of days to make arrangements on the lectures. I went over to SCAD the next day, as I was anxious to get started on something useful. I had roamed my small carriage house for two days trying my best to dredge up the experience of having been fucked by Louie. Every evidence I'd seen indicated I'd had a good time. I just couldn't remember it.

Still, I was trying to resist hooking up with any man that David had thrown at me as some sort of diversion from him and consolation prize.

That proved to be even harder than I could imagine. And imagination was driving me crazy with this man—what had he done with and to me the other night? And was it as satisfying as my imagination was telling me it was?

After I'd talked with David and set up starting with a half-credit course on Native American abstractism, as modeled by Georgia O'Keefe and Avis Blair, in a month's time to allow me to pull the material together, I decided to roam the art department of SCAD to refamiliarize myself with what was there. I told myself that I wasn't looking for Louie Boutan, even though David had told me that he was in sculpting studio and also told me how I could get to the studio.

Surprise, surprise, my walk through the department led me to the sculpting studio. He was working in marble on what could already be seen to be a kissing couple. The two were androgynous enough to be taken as a man and woman, which most beholders would automatically do, but folks like me would see two men. He was being very clever in his execution of the piece.

And he was quite a piece himself. He was using an electric stonecutter's saw that was making a loud-buzzing racket that made me run my tongue over my filings to assure myself none of them needed work done on them— or even now were having work done on them. He was dancing around the hunk of marble from which the heads and hands of the couple had emerged but nothing below yet and was wearing just athletic shorts, sandals, and a safety mask. Both his body and his movements were graceful and sensual, and my body ached for the touch of him. It took him several minutes to realize I was standing there, and I can't say that one of my hands hadn't gone to my crotch in the interval.

When he did see me, he turned off the saw, bringing in an eerie silence; lifted the mask; turned full, divine frontal to me; and smiled.

"You found me again," he said in the smooth bass of his. "I wondered if you would after you left me without a good-bye the other morning. You left me confused. I'd thought you'd had a good time. I certainly did."

"I was drunk as a skunk," I replied. "Honestly, I can't remember much of that night."

"Honestly, I fucked you to heaven. You were crying that you couldn't get enough of me. Wore me out, but you're an ultra good lay."

"I got the part about wearing you out. You were dead to the world when I left."

"I guess the three spent condoms told you why we both were worn out."

"Three? I must have missed one."

"I don't think you missed much of anything. You grabbed me and pulled me inside you the third time."

"I can't speak for how I acted with you. I'm not really promiscuous. I don't just go home with a man like that right after I'd met him."

"You could have fooled me. You were wild for it. I didn't realize you were so far gone on the booze that you wouldn't remember what we did. We practically swung on the chandelier. You wore my dick out."

"Well," I said, looking around the studio. "You certainly don't hold back, do you?"

"I fuck men. David told me you were a great lay. You came to me—to my gay bar. You wanted me to fuck you right there, in the bar. I had trouble getting you home before you jumped my bones. But I found out that David was right; you were a great lay. Is there really any reason to hold back? You did let me fuck you—in fact, I could almost say that you fucked me, you wanted it so bad. And I want to fuck you again."

I cleared my throat and tried to act like he hadn't even said that. Maybe he'd get the message that he was pushing too hard, taking too much for granted. "I've just signed on to teach a class and was looking around the

219

facility. I went to school here, but so much has changed in the last six years."

"Are you changing the subject because you regretted what we did the other night or because you're afraid I'll fuck you on the table over there and you'll love every thrust of it?"

I looked away from him. I couldn't look at his gorgeous body for another moment without starting to tremble. "I don't know. Maybe I'll know some day and tell you which. But not today."

With that, I turned and fled the studio with as much dignity as I could muster. The buzzing of the saw started up again while I was still well in earshot of it.

Rather than walking the dozen blocks, through shaded squares, back to the river and to my carriage house on Oglethorpe Square, I walked south, toward Forsyth Park, a large two-block wide and six-block long park that started up where the historical district with the squares ended to the south.

What Louie had said to me back there made me hornier than hell. But pride had kept me from laying down for him right there in the studio. What if I'd done so and he'd just laughed at me?

I found myself standing in Monterey Square and looking in the window of a bookstore without, for several minutes, focusing on the books in the window. When I did, I saw that the display was taken up almost entirely with copies of John Berendt's Savannah nonfiction novel, *Midnight in the Garden of Good and Evil*, that was set right here in this square. The book was a novelized version of the murder of a gay prostitute by an antiques dealer and leading social figure in Savannah at the time, Jim Williams, in a house on the square originally owned by the family of the songwriter Johnny Mercer. Kevin Spacey had famously played the Jim Williams role in the movie. The house and square had become a tourist attraction, and this bookstore obviously fed that attraction.

Looking beyond the books, into the interior of the store, my eye caught that of a handsome man, probably in his early forties, who was sitting behind a desk and smiling at me. He looked familiar. I walked into the store.

"Hello, are you looking for a copy of the Berendt book?" he asked. "You were staring hard at the books in the window."

After the encounter with Louie, which had aroused me to a hard that I still had and flights of fancy of Louie working my body hard, I was looking for something. I didn't think it was a copy of Berendt's book, though.

Neither did the proprietor of the bookstore. And, almost as if he were reading my mind, he said, "Or were you looking for me so you could say yes to the question I asked you?"

I gave him what must have been a really dumb look. I hadn't asked him a question yet.

"My name is Tyler. We met briefly a few nights ago—at Louie's. You seemed interested at the time; I thought you were going to say yes to my proposition in the men's room. I thought the kiss and mutual feel up had sealed the deal. You've got a great body; you said you liked what I was packing. But when you went back to the bar a black bull took you away. Did you come looking for me? Unfinished business?"

I didn't remember him in the slightest, but there didn't seem to need to be any dancing around if we'd gotten as far as he said we had at Louie's—and I hadn't come looking for him, but I didn't say that. I had a raging need. He already had unzipped and had his cock out. It would do the job nicely.

Tyler lived in an apartment above his bookshop. We fucked on his bed. He was much into sixty-nine positions and a lot of touching. By the time he got around to spiking me, the buildup had been so prolonged that it was thrust, thrust, thrust and he'd filled the bulb of his condom. We lay there stretched out along each other then, with one of his arms embracing me, his other hand slowly jacking me to eventual release, and his face close to mine, giving me what I'm sure he thought were deep, meaningful looks.

"Come for me, baby," he was repeating over and over again as a droning mantra. "Come for me, baby."

It was an effort to come for him—until I shut my eyes and conjured up Louie—but of course I told him it was all good for me and of course I would visit him again. I even bought a copy of the Berendt book. I'd enjoyed Kevin Spacey in the movie. I'd always wondered about Spacey. I would have gone with him in a flash, if he'd asked me to.

But I knew I wouldn't visit Tyler again. All the time we were sucking each other off and he was gliding his hands over my body, I was thinking of a more vigorous, rough, impassioned, total fuck—one that my imagination kept telling me that Louie had already given me—and would again if I could just get over the irritation that it had been arranged by David.

* * * *

It was as dark as a witch's twat at 2:00 a.m. in the shadows of an alley with a view line of the door to Louie's bar on Price Street. I should have been mugged more than once for where I was at this time of night, but mercifully I wasn't. I hadn't drunk anything, but I felt high. I didn't want anything to get between me and full knowledge of what was happening.

I was waiting for Louie to leave the bar and lock the door behind him. And I wanted to be sure he was alone. If he wasn't, if he had another guy with him, I'd just have to do this again—and again and again—until it would be just Louie and me.

When he came out of the bar, he was alone. I followed him the two blocks to his studio apartment in the carriage house over a garage off East Jones. I let him enter his door and counted to sixty before I approached it and knocked.

His eyes opened wide but his mouth went into a big grin when he saw it was me.

"I've decided," I said. "I want you to fuck me, hard, on the table. I want to know everything you do to me this time. And I want you to do everything to me."

We were both hard before we got to the top of the stairs, where we pulled at each other's clothes, paying no attention to the sounds of ripping, as we kissed, tongues swabbing each other's tonsils. I went right down on my knees in front of him when he pushed down on my shoulders after he'd gripped both of our cocks in a strong, beefy hand and had stroked them together. I attempted to swallow him whole, but no amount of swallowing, unhinging my jaw, and gagging was going to help me manage the girth and length of the black cock. For some reason, that made me exhilarated. I knew where else that staff soon would be buried.

Laughing, he pulled me up and tossed me onto his bed. We went immediately into a sixty-nine suck, but it wasn't like what Tyler and I had done in any sense of the word. We wrestled and rolled around, possessing and working cock and balls hard and eating each other's ass out to hear how deep the moans and groans were that we could illicit from each other.

And, at length, Louie jumped off the bed, grabbed my ankles, flipped me around to where I was crosswise on the double bed, my ass on the edge. I lay there, panting and looking at his magnificent body and mammoth erection as he rolled on a condom and wet his dick and my hole with lube. I hardly had enough time to grab a pillow and stuff it under the small of my back to give him a deep-fuck angle, when I was arching my back, rolling my head up to stare at the edge of the ceiling above me, and crying out my need, my surrender, the glorious pleasure-pain, as he brutally grasped my ankles, jerked my legs open and raised, thrust inside me, and began to pump hard and deep.

This was it. This was the way I wanted it. Hard, deep, vigorous, forever.

"Was this it? Was it like this the first time?" I cried out.

"Yes, you were just as wild for it the first time."

"Oh shit, oh Christ, oh FUCK ME!"

Two fuckings later, as the tendrils of dawn light stole into the room; both of us still breathing heavily; neither of us thinking we were finished for the day; my back plastered against the wall by Louie's body, with my knees hooked on his hips; Louie still deep inside me, throbbing, ready to start pumping again, he murmured, "Welcome back to Savannah."

My answer was a very satisfied, "I guess I'll have to look into extending my lease."

Lek's Diary

I have no idea how long the townhouse next door had been empty before someone noticed that the two women living there were gone. I did see the story in the local paper of the two women who drowned on Lake Stanley when their rowboat capsized and thought of it as both sad and a little weird, as no one was supposed to be out in a rowboat on Lake Stanley after dark. Also it happened in early March rather than the summer, and they were reported to be dressed in street clothes. That too was weird—the wrong season to be rowing on the lake and the wrong clothes to be wearing to do it. I didn't connect that report with my neighbors until the workmen showed up next door, though.

I'm not an unfriendly man, although I was going through a bad patch myself at the time. This small townhouse in a reclaimed, once slum area, of the old town hadn't belonged to me when I moved in. It belonged to a professor, Tim. I had been hired as his graduate assistant and had started working in his office at the local university. He was steeped in his research, which spilled over into his private time and which, therefore, spilled over into mine as well. It expanded out from working at the university office to working at his home, my duties gradually broadening to include the domestic and personal. One thing led to another, and, for convenience at first, I was spending nights at his house. And then, again for his convenience, I suppose, I was sleeping in his bed.

When he died suddenly of a flu advancing into pneumonia, I found that he'd left the townhouse to me, as well as everything else he owned. And at his unexpected absence from the university, associate and assistant professors were moved up the chain, and I was brought in at the bottom of the chain as an adjunct professor.

It all happened so naturally and quietly that it seemed to have happened without my full participation. I'd been quite fond of Tim, and I'll admit that his taciturnity rubbed off on me. I too became a bit morose and withdrew into a routine that didn't involve much beyond classes at the university and continued research at home—and doing whatever Tim asked me to do.

The women next door were set in a routine too—for how long before I moved in with Tim, I have no idea. Only one of them ever seemed to leave the townhouse. She was the older of the two and must have been a professional, as she'd leave at 8:15 every morning, almost on the dot, in a tailored, but somewhat severe business suit, and with a briefcase in her hand. There was a bus stop up in the next block, on a busier street than we lived in, that regularly serviced the downtown area. I guess I always assumed she took the bus, but in the news report, they said there was a sedan belonging to one of the women found at the lake right where they would have taken the row boat, so maybe she drove and had the car garaged someplace nearby. She always reappeared by 6:00 p.m., often with a grocery bag as well as the briefcase, and she'd march right up to her door and then look furtively up and down the street before entering the townhouse. I found that odd enough that I marked it in my mind. I wouldn't see her again then until the next morning—

assuming I was looking out on the street the next morning.

My routines and isolation were such, though, that I found I did look for her to follow her routines as well. Observing her almost-on-the-dot departures and arrivals became as much a routine with me as winding Tim's old grandfather clock. That being the case, I did mark when her routine stopped, but I just subtracted those observations from my own daily routine after a few days of change.

Our townhouses were small and bunched together close to the street, with no alley behind, so there really wasn't much of a place to put a car. The woman's townhouse didn't even have a parking pad. There was one for two cars, taking up nearly the whole front yard, for Tim's townhouse, but he never used it for his car. Tim had his car, a fancy Lexus coup he didn't want to leave out in the open, garaged over on the main street. It wasn't a longer walk from the house to where he garaged the car than our subsequent walk from the parking garage to our academic building at the university was. These walks were just about the only regular exercise we got—well, other than what happened in bed, our most active part of the day. Still, we both kept in shape.

We'd used the Lexus almost exclusively to get to and from the university, and I inherited it too. Tim didn't have any family—other than me, and I wasn't really family in any legal sense. I did wait around from some long, lost relative to show up and make a claim, which I would not have contested, but none did. This all happened before same sex marriage had passed in our state, so my claim seemed tenuous.

The older woman, Inger, although I didn't know her name until after she'd died, was maybe in her early fifties and was a big-boned Germanic blonde. She wasn't exactly unfriendly, although no one on this block of townhouses got into anyone else's business much, but she wasn't inviting either. She often seemed to have a weary and pursed-lipped look about her when she came home, and, as I noted before, she had a habit of furtively looking about her before opening her door and entering her house. I found that fascinating and all a bit Alfred Hitchcock in the atmosphere it created.

The other woman was somewhat younger in appearance and was of some Southeast Asian extraction. She was a scared little bunny, sometimes coming a step out of the house either in front or back, but never more than a foot away from an open door in front, through which she'd scamper back into the house at the slightest sound or movement on the block. She did hang their laundry out to dry on a line in their postage-stamp-sized back garden, which I found a bit "last century," but it accorded me an opportunity to observe what she looked like. She was very attractive, but always looked a bit sad— and she too had a tendency to look around with apprehension before settling down to her laundry chore. All mysterious enough to provide me a mental break from my research to pursue flights of fancy about their life.

I didn't learn her name until after they were gone either, and then, first, from the newspaper article without realizing that it was my neighbor. Her name was Lek, and she was from Thailand.

I often wondered how the two women could be so reclusive and what they did in the townhouse, just the two of them. But then I'd think about Tim and me living in here next door to them and how so steeped in his research Tim could be that we could go for days on end not leaving the house when university classes weren't in session. And I thought about some of what we were doing in here alone, and I decided not to think that much about the women next door.

I didn't think about the women next door so much—the interest in observing them having waned quickly once they'd broken their routine and never appeared—that it was maybe a month after I'd read the article in the newspaper without connecting their absence to the article, when I heard a racket start up on the other side of the wall and my own doorbell was ringing.

I opened the door to find a muscular and florid man maybe in his early forties, robust looking in white coveralls with no shirt under them that left his arms bare, showing bulging guns and several tattoos peeking out of the edges of the coveralls. There were construction boots on his feet and his head was topped off with a white painter's cap.

I shrank away from him a bit. Before there had been staid academic Tim, there'd been a brief period in my life when I had gladly lain under such men. I'd had a fetish for muscular construction workers and construction boots. I found when I opened the door that old instinctive arousals didn't die easily.

"Excuse me, sorry to bother you," he said. "But I'm from Falwell Construction. My name's Andy, and I'm the supervisor of the crew renovating the house next door."

"Construction crew? Renovating the house next door? But there are women living next door. And I hadn't heard about any construction."

I trust I didn't sound either belligerent or annoyed. I certainly didn't intend to, but I had just come downstairs—I wasn't a morning person—and only now realized that there had been some strange noises coming from next door since well before I got up. I hadn't had a cup of coffee yet, and so I wasn't really in control of what I was thinking or saying yet.

I briefly panicked with the question of whether I'd even dressed before answering the door—whether I was still just in my sleeping pants and barefoot—but, upon mental inspection, I realized I was dressed more decently than that. Still, the furtive looks the man was giving me when he didn't think I was looking at him made me wonder if I had dressed.

"The house is empty now," he was saying. "Apparently has been for some time. Bank repo. We're clearing it out and cleaning it up for sale. Not much room out here on the street, though, and I've got a truck that has to be here with my crew and we have to bring a dumpster in for a week or so for what we've got to shovel out of the house. Looks like the residents just up and left without taking anything with them."

"Up and left?" I nonsensically said. I was searching my brain for the last time I'd seen one or both of the women from over there and I was coming up with a blank.

"Well, we aren't supposed to know, but these were the women who died in Lake Stanley last month. So I guess they're not coming back and they don't need anything in the house—although it don't look like there's much in the house to be proud of. Place needs a lot of work too. Doesn't look like anyone was in here to service anything in years."

"Oh," I said, just now processing the connection between the women who died in Lake Stanley and the women right next door who I hadn't given a second thought to for more than a month. I was just as glad they hadn't died in the house. I wouldn't have been any quicker, I don't think, to cluing in to the lack of activity over there—and the smell. Some neighbor, I knew, but this really was Tim's house, and, given my relationship with Tim, we hadn't exactly become the neighborhood gadflies.

"Well, the reason why I knocked on your door is that we really, really need space to put the dumpster, and there's very little space around here. I saw that you have a double parking pad without anything on it. I was told to ask you if the construction company could rent your pad for a couple of weeks for the dumpster. We'd keep the dumpster covered when we weren't filling it. The company would pay well for the inconvenience."

"Oh, yes, of course. No need to pay me," I said, giving the man—who was quite presentable in a way that was a whole separate world from what had been mine and Tim's, and therefore of more interest and worth a second look than otherwise. I'd always had a little surge of electricity over men in construction—all that virility and muscle—and Andy met that description well. It was sort of a taboo and two different worlds thing, I guess. I had gone with construction workers in an earlier life, and I'd retained more than a few fantasies of going with a construction worker. And it had been a good six months since I'd gone with anyone—and that was Tim and had become a bit ho hum. Tim was an older man. Of course I did gravitate to older men. Of course, the construction workers who had covered me were older than I was too.

Andy was an older man. Maybe fifteen or sixteen years older than I was. But the construction workers I'd gone with had all been vigorous and meltingly demanding in a way Tim never had been. Tim gave me rather more respect in the coupling than really aroused me. There's no way I ever would have told him that, of course.

The construction foreman named Andy returned my smile and suddenly looked like a million dollars to me. But I knew that wasn't going anywhere—or shouldn't—so we just exchanged pleasantries and I left him to supervising the work next door. That day—and in succeeding days—I didn't get much research or course preparation done, though, as I found myself frequently at one of the front windows, looking at an angle over at the small front yard of the townhouse next door, where there was a double-cab white truck with a Falwell Construction logo painted on the door pulled up on the more-dirt-than-grass verge between the front stoop and the street.

The workmen Andy was directing—all young and well-muscled and jovial men—swirled between the truck and the house, hauling in tools and hauling out split sections of drywall. I wanted to see what sort of furnishings would come out of the house. Maybe there was something I could salvage and use. But they seemed to be doing structural work now. This stood to reason, I decided, since the dumpster hadn't arrived yet.

They also seemed to be having a good time and getting along very well despite being engaged in some heavy-duty work—very well, as a matter of fact. They were all banter and hands and sexual innuendo and "fuck this" and "fuck that" and "ream you a big one" with each other. Andy was directing them, but pleasantly—and in a very friendly manner. Very friendly indeed. More than once I saw him pat one of the young men on the butt or give one a bear hug.

It was, I was sure, all very innocent, but it set my mind aflutter. I hadn't really given much thought to having once had a construction worker fetish—which I sometimes carried out—before I lived with Tim, but those fantasies certainly were stirring now. And I'll admit that they were the source of more masturbatory sessions in the dark of the night than I customarily indulged in after Tim died.

He was a big, heavily muscled, manly musk-scented brute, certainly too powerful for me to fight in any way. We were in an unfinished house, bare wall framing, sawdust on the floor, unfinished floors. I was completely in his control. I had shuddered and gone powerless as he cornered me, putting his hands on me and talking "gonna fuck you hard," "gonna ream you a bigger hole" dirty to me. Just the thought of that and look of him made me putty in his hands.

There was a straight chair, and he had his right leg lifted, his foot, in a heavy construction boot, flat on the seat of the chair, with my right leg trapped up and over his. I was bent over in front of him, both of my arms forced painfully up my back, him needing just one beefy hand to hold them together there in a grip that was painful on my wrists and an angle of stretch that was painful on my arms. I was gasping for breath, panting because he was already thick and long inside me, buried deep but just barely pulsating as yet. His right arm was wrapped around my waist, keeping me bent over there in front of him. My eyes were on the colorful snake tattoo wound around his right calf—and also on his shiny construction boots, polished by my tongue. He'd made me slither across the floor and clean his boots with my tongue—and to beg to be fucked.

I yelped, giving it a hollow sound that assured me that I wasn't really awake, as he began to stroke inside me with his cock. In and out; in and out; in deeper and hold; pull out to the rim of the bulb and plunge, causing me to gasp and jerk and groan. Even unconscious I had the presence of mind to search my memory for whether this had actually happened to me before—or if this was a true fantasy of what I would want if I unleashed my desires and let them run wild. I was ready to come. I screwed my face around to see his and was shocked. As I shot off in an arc over the sawdust-covered floor, the face registered—Andy, the construction foreman working next door.

I woke up in a sweat and with cum dotting the front of my sleeping shorts. I was gripping my still-hard and throbbing cock. I wasn't fully awake, though—just fully satisfied for some reason—maybe for the first time since before I'd met Tim, I had to admit to myself. I went over the scene in my mind, trying to decide whether I was bothered that I'd had a wet dream about the construction foreman working next door. And I should have known it earlier in the dream than I did. Andy sometimes wore shorts rather than bib coveralls, and I'd seen the snake tattoo on his right calf before. I just hadn't realized that the eroticism of it had stuck with me.

The next day I tried to keep myself busy with research. I almost regretted that I didn't have any classes to cover at the university. But my mind kept drifting to what was happening next door. I don't know at what point it hit me that they were working so hard and had been at it for a few hours and therefore could probably use a break and a cup of coffee. It would only be neighborly to offer them a cup of coffee. I went into the kitchen and scrounged around under the counter for the twenty-cup pot Tim had used for class and faculty meetings. After finding the urn I discovered I was out of coffee. There was beer in the refrigerator. Even better, I thought.

* * * *

"What could have made them want to do that, I wonder. They were reclusive, yes, but I can't really believe that taking a rowboat out on a lake at night in early March and both falling out of the boat and drowning was an accident."

"No, it wasn't any accident," Andy agreed. He was sitting at my kitchen table, on his lunch break. They'd been working on the house next door for several days now and I had started making them sandwiches and taking them over at lunch. They were such a convivial crew and so good looking that I felt comfortable and a little bit warm inside to have that bit of connection. I'd already dealt with the wet dream I'd had of Andy. It was just me not having had sex for some time and thinking back to my days before I'd met Tim. I'd given all of that up, though. That was behind me. I'd grown up.

Today, for the first time, Andy came into the house and ate with me while the rest ate over there on the job.

Until now, I hadn't realized how lonely I'd felt without Tim in the house and in this hiatus between semesters at the college. And I certainly couldn't concentrate on research, not with a dumpster sitting right outside my dining room window and me running there each time I heard a clunk to maybe see what was being tossed—and who was tossing it. It didn't escape me that I was more interested in seeing what was what out there than annoyed at the interruption of my work.

Strong, hunky construction workers in those loose, white coveralls, with no shirts under them, giving the impression that was all they were wearing. Heavy-duty construction boots, wide-stance strutting to and from the dumpster like they were heavy hung. Moving with the grace of dancers, contrasting tantalizingly with the hulkiness and roughness of their bodies. All smiles, patting each other on the back and rump intimately. The construction supervisor, Andy, moving among them, more muscular than any of them. Tattoos on his bulging biceps as well as on his calf. Rough, calloused, but sensitive, hands, moving expressively. He so attentive as he sat at my kitchen table.

"There must be some story behind it," I said, "and to think that it was developing just on the other side of this wall from me and I didn't know it was happening—or care."

"You mustn't be hard on yourself," Andy said, giving me a sympathetic look and ever so briefly touching my forearm with his rough, calloused fingers. "That's the way it is with city life. I'm sure you were having your own concerns here."

"Yes, I guess I was." That's when I told him about Tim and how harrowing it was that week that Tim was dying and there wasn't anything anyone could do—or was doing—to prevent that. It, of course, was only a week, though, and whatever was developing next door surely built up over much longer time than that. But Andy was right about urban life. Everyone here husbands their privacy. I couldn't say that either of the women, even the few times I saw them, appeared to be open to approach. Not that I ever gave a thought to approaching either one of them.

"But I guess I shouldn't be so revealing," I said, suddenly not sure of the vibes I had thought I got off this man. What if it was all in my hysterical fantasies—like in the wet dream of the other night? "I hadn't told you before that I'd lived here with a man. I hadn't thought that maybe you didn't . . . and didn't approve of . . ."

"I've seen the photographs of you and an older man. You have them around here on several tables. I figured it out. Don't worry. You two look happy in the photos."

"We were," I said, with a low voice.

"He must have given you everything you needed," Andy said, the edge of natural gruffness in his voice tempered.

"Yes, yes, he did," I answered.

But had he? Had Tim giving me everything I needed? He was an attentive but a pretty tame lover. Were my recent fantasies telling me I wanted more than that?

"He gave me everything I had a right to have from him," I answered, hedging now for some reason I couldn't explain.

Andy smiled, put a hand on my forearm, and said, "You should have everything you need."

It was only after Andy went back to work that I realized that, from my explanation of Tim's death, Andy realized the full extent of the gay relationship we'd had—what positions we took, how I let Tim dominate me as he liked. And yet he hadn't shown the slightest hint of revulsion. Could it be that I'd also revealed that what Tim gave me was a little tame?

"I keep wondering if there is anything in that house that would give a clue to why they did what they did," I said as Andy was getting up to return to work, the stiff rustle of his white coveralls arresting my attention, taking my eyes to the square-cut top with the curly chest hair cascading over it and the deep cut at the sides, showing hard, tanned skin down to his waist, as well as more tattooing.

"I've thought of that too." he answered. "Not much I've found, there isn't."

"Not much? You found something?"

"Well, their tables had photographs on them—of the two of them—very similar to the photos you have here of you and your . . . your other."

"Ah," was all I could think to say.

He pressed on. "There weren't any papers in the desk. There's little furniture, but other than not having taken care of maintenance in the house, it wasn't really cluttered. And nothing really in terms of personal affects that would tell you anything about the women—other than the photos, and they pretty much spelled out what the women were to each other. The lack of maintenance puzzles the estate agent too. There is a tidy sum in the estate; it was like the women didn't care that there was water draining down into the downstairs walls from leaks in the bathroom."

"Strange and mysterious," I said.

"Yes, it is. And perplexing."

"It's almost like they were afraid to let workmen in the house. But, I guess it's not really our place to delve into their lives in death when we didn't do it while they were alive," I said.

"No, I guess not," Andy answered. "It's bad to take too much for granted . . . or to rush anyone into deciding what they want."

He didn't sound too convinced, though. And, more important, he seemed to waver there, as if he wanted to make some parting gesture, some personal connection. But the moment passed and he just thanked me for the lunch—and for the sandwiches for Joe and Mitchell out there, the good-looking guys who were doing the grunt work. And then he left me, to bask in the glow of having had him at my table for lunch. Knowing what that meant to me—how it affected me—but content to let it build apace . . . or not. I went to the refrigerator to see what sort of different lunch I could put together for the workman the next day.

And then I was going to have to make a trip upstairs and indulge in a fantasy.

* * * *

"I found something. And I brought it." That sounded intriguing, but all of my senses were already occupied with Andy's hand that was gripping my forearm at the kitchen table and showed no sign of withdrawing anytime soon. I reveled at the electricity that touch sent through my body. I don't think that I had been as aroused as that by anything Tim had done during our entire relationship.

That Andy's hands were calloused, throwing me out of the academic context I lived in, gave me a guilty thrill. Tim's hands had always been so smooth skinned—an academic's hands. It was like Andy and I were doing something illicit—deliciously taboo—when we were just sitting at the kitchen table and talking.

"Mitchell found it behind a radiator in a bedroom and brought it to me." And then, when I couldn't do more than look at Andy with want in my eyes, willing his hand to move elsewhere, he continued. "One of them was keeping a diary. One of them, Lek her name is, was Thai. Here illegally, it seems. I read the last month of entries before I brought it over. But I want you to read them too."

"Me?"

"Yes. It explains a lot. But it also says some things that I think you need to read. And with me here. Here, I'll open it to where it begins."

"Oh, she's speaking of being in hiding," I said after reading the passages his finger was on—not the fingers of the hand gripping my arm, though. That was still there. "She talks of having been brought from Thailand by a U.S. serviceman who promised to marry her. But didn't. Who was abusive instead. Oh, Inger, the other woman

238

worked as a social services caseworker. I'd never known that. Always wondered what she did—and why she always looked so beaten down when she dragged home."

"Yes. And look there. The Thai woman wasn't here legally if there wasn't a marriage. And she says the guy threatened to kill her if he could find her."

I turned the pages and read random passages. "So, Inger wasn't just hiding Lek. They started up a relationship—an intimate relationship. Lek speaks of how guilty she thought when that started. And then about how the guilty feelings had just eaten up time they could have had together. Well, we're not surprised about that, are we?"

"Or shocked by it, either, I'll wager," Andy said, his voice low and hoarse. His hand had moved from my forearm down to my knee, the grip just as strong, the electricity current that ran through my body even stronger. "Neither am I," he said. "I fully understand their need. The need of anyone who is lonely and is capable of a love like they developed for each other. I particularly understand the Thai woman's regret of waiting so long to acknowledge what she wanted, what she needed."

"But I wonder what made them snap?" I asked. "I didn't hear any fighting through those walls, and God knows I get it from the townhouse on the other side of me. The arrangement seemed to have been working. Do you suppose this bastard tracked Lek down?"

"There are indications he might have been getting close, yes. But look here further along. I think this is what did it."

"Ah. Inger. A diagnoses of terminal cancer. And quickly approaching. I see." And I did, in fact, see. I saw how hopeless their situation had become.

"Do you see it all, though, I wonder," Andy said in a deep voice.

"What is it I should see?"

"Their devotion to each other, yes. But also how fleeting life is, how lonely it can be if you don't seize it, how long it took them to acknowledge what they wanted, needed. How you have to take what pleasures you can get out of life where and when you can get them."

"Yes, I see that."

"Do you really? The pity is that they couldn't see past Inger's condition as a reason to end it all then. They could have continued to the last—and then something could have been done to allow Lek to live on. Just like you have to live on after your own lover's death. Do you see that?"

"Yes," I answered in a low voice.

"They let the situation defeat them without fighting for themselves to the end. You don't really want to give in to it like they did, do you?"

"No." It almost came out as a sob.

"You've invited me into your house because you're lonely, haven't you?"

"Yes, I guess so."

"But not just that. It's because you want something—need something."

"Yes." I had hesitated in answering and when I did, it was with a moan. He had moved his hand again. He was leaning his face in close to mine, his eyes searching mine—seeing what he wanted to see.

"I have my hand on your crotch now. You are hard."

"Yes. Yes."

"You're not moving away from me, or asking me to leave. You want me. You want me on top of you, inside you."

"Yes. Yes. Can't you hear me? I'm saying yes."

"How do you want it—how do you really need it? My guess is that your lover gave it to you soft. Was soft good enough for you?"

"Hard, rough, no prisoners. I want to feel it. I want you to rough me up with your hands. And I want you to keep your boots on. I want to know that it's a rough man fucking me." Each syllable came out of me in a gasp. It was how I wanted it. How I had missed getting it.

He laughed. It was a deep, cruel laugh, and it caused me to shudder in anticipation.

He fucked me upstairs, on my own bed. He showed concern that I wouldn't want to do that—in the bed that Tim and I had shared. And, although the sensitivity he showed within his rough, construction-worker exterior was part of what had drawn me to him, I wanted him to fuck me in the same bed. And I told him that. And I also told him I didn't want him to take any prisoners. I wanted him to fuck me hard, take me roughly, fully. Tim had always been so gentle, felicitous. I appreciated that at the time, but I wanted something different now. Life was too short not to have it all. Lek and Inger had taught me that.

It was clear he was doing this for me. He was solicitous until I let him know that's not the way I wanted it—that I knew this wasn't the way he was doing it with the other workers.

"I don't think you have any idea—" he started to say.

But then I told him about my experience before Tim—that I had been fucked hard, roughly, brutally by construction workers beyond the beaded curtains separating a barroom and the corridor to the bathrooms once when I was in college. That Tim never fucked me that way, and I know knew it hadn't been enough. I only knew now, being with a big man in heavy construction, shit-kicker heavy construction boots and all, that this was how I wanted it.

"How hard do you want it?," he asked in a gravelly voice, as everything off but those construction boots he rolled over on top of me on the bed, his arms wrapped around my neck, his hard dick throbbing up my belly, and came out of a deep kiss.

"Hard. I want it hard," I answered. "Rough. Total. I want to know I've been fucked. It's been too fuckin' long."

He crushed me to the bed, his body heavier and chunkier than Tim's. He was thicker, longer than Tim. He spread my thighs open with his knees and positioned his sheathed cock at my hole. I panted hard as the thick bulb breached the rim and held there, briefly, as, panicked, I fought to open to it, knowing he wouldn't let me—because of how I'd said I wanted it. His expression was lustful now, slightly cruel. I had given permission for whatever he wanted.

I pushed up with my pelvis, wanting the thrust to be straight and as accommodating as possible, and, with a mutter of "You're a little slut for it, aren't you?" and a guttural laugh, he raised himself a bit on his knees to allow me to raise my butt. Neither one of us was acting like the people we were in leading up to this, and I think our earlier interaction was truer—but this was true for what I wanted and needed, and I think Andy was melding to that.

With a thrust, he forced himself inside me before I was completely open to him, letting me know he was going to stretch me to the limit, pound me forever, cause me to scream out in pain mixed with passion, until passion won out, I joined him in the rhythm, and begged him never to stop. And then, when he did in a mutual explosion, begged him to start again, which, with a laugh, he obliged. So utterly different from anything Tim had ever given me, had ever done inside me. And I was so hungry for it.

He filled me, he stretched me, he hit all of the spots. I managed to turn him on his back and saddle myself on his cock, and ride, ride, ride. He had a vigor that far surpassed anything I'd remembered before.

He lifted me off his cock and tossed me to the floor beyond the foot of the bed and sat on the end of the bed, cock in hand, still wearing his construction boots.

"Crawl to me on your belly," he growled, and I slithered to him, kissing the snake tattoo on his calf and moving my tongue down to his boot tops.

He bent me over the foot of the bed, his right leg bent and his booted foot on the bed, while he grabbed my wrists in one hand and pushed my arms painfully up my back. Thrusting up hard inside me, he began to pump again. Mewing my want, I tongued down his snake tattoo back onto the top of his boot and came for him in great gobs of pent-up cum.

We went back up on the bed, Andy on his back, and me riding him until he too had a gushing ejaculation. When we were spent, he rolled me off him and, while his hands explored my bruised and satisfied body, said, "You *were* a little slut for it." I could almost hear the awe and surprise in his voice.

"Yes, sorry," I answered.

"Don't be sorry. You know, Joe . . . and Mitchell too would like—"

"Yes, oh God, yes, please."

All That Argentine Jazz

The dimly lit room showed every sign of transition toward desertion. The closet door was open, the closet empty, other than two sad-looking wire hangers. Two drawers of the bureau were pulled out. Both were empty. Clothes once tucked away in these recesses were strewn on the two chairs in the room and hanging on hangers from the top of the closet drawer. One suitcase was already packed; another one had been moved, open and half packed, to the floor from the bed, where two naked men were stretched out against each other.

The bedclothes were tumbled and entwined the bodies of the two men, indicating both that the two had been going hot and heavy at it and that the battle had not been planned. Such was the case. What also was quite clear was that the older, thinner, taller man had won the battle. They were lying on their sides, the younger man's buttocks nestled into the older man's groin and the older man's arms and legs, caught up in wads of sheeting and coverlet, entwined around the body of the younger man so that the younger man was completely controlled, a prisoner of the older man's desire and sustained penetration. Both men were panting lightly.

The long, thin, slightly up-curved, sheathed cock of patrician and effete visiting Julliard music composition professor, Clayton Ambrose, was still buried to the root in the anal canal of the short, trim, perfectly formed blond, strikingly handsome, second-year Charleston College music major student Neal Burton. Both men felt the cock going flaccid, diminishing in hardness, if not length. Clay knew and Neal strongly suspected that the older man had come almost immediately after penetration.

"You didn't finish with me," Neal whispered, his voice revealing a sense of disappointment. "If it's our last time, I wanted there to be fireworks."

"I was lost in the moment, realizing this is the last time. I would have tried to hold longer, but I felt you were close," Clay responded. "You were close, weren't you?"

"Yes. I hoped we could come together." Close? Neal thought. You'd just started. But Clayton Ambrose had been his mentor and initiator; he wasn't about to argue more deeply than this with him. What he had said had come spontaneously from the disappointment of leaving their relationship like this.

"I want it all," Clay responded. "I do want us to come together. I too want the last time to be special. You know what I want."

"Yes," Neal answered. He'd never done it before Professor Ambrose had come to Charleston as a visiting lecturer and had seduced him, but they had often done it that way since and Neal had become accustomed to it. He turned his face to Clay's and they went into a kiss. For a few moments he thought the professor might harden enough for another finish, as the kissing and Neal's moaning caused by Ambrose's thumb and index finger having found and started to work one of Neal's nipples had caused the professor to breathe heavily and his cock to start to harden—harden enough that the professor could take three more long, shuddering slides.

But then he broke away from the clutch, pushed Neal on his back, and raised and twisted his own body as he reached around to the nightstand for another condom

245

disk. The twisting brought his cock close enough to the surface that the glans dragged across Neal's prostate, causing Neal to jerk and shudder.

"Oh shit, oh fuck," Neal gasped. "Finish me proper, Daddy. Please give it to me."

Basically cruel by nature and pleased with the control he had over the young man, Ambrose dragged the bulb over Neal's prostrate a couple of more times to hear him beg, but then he pulled out. Neal's own cock, thick, and prodigious in its own right in its current hard, throbbing state, stood straight up from the blond, curly V of his trimmed pubes, with Neal flat on his back.

Ambrose laughed and, slipping the condom off his own cock and aiming it for a nearby trashcan, lowered his face to take Neal's cock in his mouth—again listening to the young man's moans and listening for the approach of some edge that would end his play. Before that could happen, though, he released the cock from his mouth and tapped it a couple of times, to hear Neal groan and to feel the cock lose a fraction of its hardness.

They both held nearly a full minute, Ambrose waiting for the wave of Neal's preparatory contractions to cease and listening to Neal begging in a whisper, "Just fuck me, Daddy. Don't tease me like this."

But Neal knew that, since Ambrose had come already, all of this was just play for him.

Without responding, Ambrose placed the disk on the tip of Neal's cock and rolled it down over the sides. Wetting his hand with lube, he slicked up the cock as Neal moaned and then raised up, slung a leg over Neal's thigh in an elegant, fluid motion, fisted Neal's cock until he could get it positioned at his asshole, and slid down on the cock.

Neal was panting and moaning as Ambrose lowered his face to take possession of Neal's lips with his, fisted Neal's wrists, held both of Neal's arms captive above and away from his head, flat on the surface of the bed, and started making love to Neal's cock by raising and lowering his buttocks and sliding forward and back and from side to side on the buried cock.

When Ambrose was ready—and he always seemed to know how close either one of them was to coming—he pulled Neal's right hand down to his cock, which was wrapped in both of their hands when Ambrose shot off up Neal's chest and Neal jerked and spasmed his own ejaculation inside the professor's channel.

Afterward, Neal sat, still naked, on the side of the bed and watched Ambrose move around the bedroom of his Charleston College-owned condo on Coming Street—a name that continually amused Ambrose—and expertly folded shirts and trousers.

Everything was elegant and refined about the professor, from the way he moved his slender, but well-muscled nude frame around the room; to how precisely in place was his flowing, wavy gray hair, despite having just come out of a sex session on the bed; to how wrinkle free his shirts and trousers would be when they got to the end of the journey that marked the close of his residency at Charleston College.

Both men had enjoyed their couplings when he was here; neither had been under the illusion that it was anything more than temporary. For Ambrose it was a necessary servicing wherever he was for any length of time; for Neal it had been the start of a new lifestyle and was worship of an accomplished professor and for the extra time the professor spent with Neal on his music technique. Ambrose had taught Neal a lot about sexual technique too, not least the technicals of edging and of the sexual flip-flop.

That didn't make parting a piece of cake for either one of them.

"When do you drive away?" Neal asked, as Ambrose moved about the room.

"Today. In a couple of hours."

"So, we won't have the night?"

"No." Ambrose's tone had a genuine tone of regret to it. "No. I find I have to leave earlier than anticipated. In fact, you'll see there on my dresser—that envelope—a ticket to the Carlos Ferrari Argentinian jazz concert at the Spoleto Festival tomorrow night. I'd like you to take it— as a parting gift. He's all you are preparing to be in music: a jazz and classical pianist, Spanish guitarist, singer, and composer. I hope you'll go to the concert and think of me and of how important pursuing your desires beyond the music are in honing your creativity."

"Thank you," was all Neal could think of to say on that, but he was having trouble letting go. "You say in a couple of hours. But not right now. And I can see that you're hard again."

"So I am," the professor said. He fucked Neal again on the bed, doggy style, clutching Neal closely from above, stroking him hard and deep, possessing Neal's lips as the young man turned his face to his, and diplomatically not bringing attention to the tears that rolled down the young man's cheeks. Finally, at the finish, giving the young man the finish he'd been begging for.

Clayton Ambrose had done this several times before—picked out a talented, luscious, and willing student, either male or female, to possess for short periods of time. It was usually at least a minor regret he had to leave them, if only because of the investment he put into them surrendering to his needs and whims. He wasn't into looking back. Neal was the most difficult one to leave. He had been so ripe and innocent and willing to do whatever Clayton wanted.

For Neal, though, this was a first—and a momentous first at that. He had no idea if or how he would be able to get into such a relationship again—or even if he wanted to be dominated that way again.

"Do you have any regrets?" Ambrose asked as they were cooling down in each other's arms for the last time.

"Regrets? Regrets for what?"

"That I took your male virginity. That I turned you?"

"No, of course not," Neal answered. "I'm glad it was you. You have taught me so much in all ways."

"It hasn't been just me, has it? I never demanded monogamy."

"No, but not often—not before you and none others that give me what you do."

"Will you promise me one thing?"

"Of course, but what?"

"I want you to take another lover immediately. I don't want you to slip back. You need this for your art, for your craft. Someone who can further hone your artistry."

Neal didn't answer right away. This would be a hard role to fill. He'd actually given the matter a lot of thought already but hadn't made a decision. He didn't even know how to go about finding another lover. Clay had done all of the finding, all of the seduction, most of the fucking and sex education. At no time had Neal felt he had any control over any of it. Neal had had no illusions that Clay had been a predator, taking advantage of his position, and although Neal had struggled against it that first time, letting Ambrose have his way only because the man how power over Neal's future, Neal had been deceiving himself. Ambrose had given him what he had secretly desired and had freed him from indecision and inhibition. Neal had no idea how to go about the hook-up process in more than a casual meeting way.

"Promise," Clay repeated.

"Of course," Neal answered, not sure himself if he'd ever have another deeper-level male lover.

* * * *

"Is this seat taken?"

Neal looked up in surprise and involuntarily smiled, initially mistakenly thinking that Professor Ambrose hadn't left yet after all and had come to the Ferrari Spoleto Festival concert just to be with him. Spoleto was a two-week music, theater, and dance festival, started by the composer Gian Carlo Menotti in the late 1970s, and held in the facilities of Charleston College annually in May. Although Neal was hanging around after the end of the school year to build up his portfolio of musical compositions, he would not have been able to afford to attend any of the Spoleto programs on his own means. The man who was standing by the empty aisle seat next to where Neal was sitting was tall, handsome, elegantly dressed, and of the same late forties age and the same wavy gray hair as Ambrose was.

"No, by all means use the seat," Neal answered, trying to take the edge off his smile. The man smiled warmly back, leaving Neal embarrassed that perhaps he had misunderstood Neal's smile as some sort of come on. Or were Neal's thoughts just too consumed by Clay's request—well, more of a command—to find another lover immediately. Was Neal seeing possibilities where they didn't really exist?

"I do need an aisle seat and the recital hall is filling up quickly. It's surprising there's still this aisle seat available."

"I was sitting in it until a minute ago," Neal answered. "But I could see that I could view the musician's hands on the piano keyboard better from this seat, so I moved over."

"See his hands better—ah, I guess that means that you study music yourself then," the man said as he sank down into the aisle seat. "So, are you a music student?"

"Yes, here at Charleston College. I'm lucky to be able to come to this concert. I am studying the same music styles this Carlos Ferrari composes and plays. Are you a musician too?" The man looked refined and artistic, in the same vein that Clayton Ambrose was. Neal didn't recognize the man as being with the college faculty, but he could be. Neal knew he shouldn't be so presumptuous—or hopeful—but the man could have fallen right into the role of Clayton, and Neal would open to him. Clayton had hinted and Neal had realized that he needed another man like Clayton.

Neal's openness to this—because of the similarities of the men and because of Clay's request still ringing in his ears—did prove to cut through a lot of preliminaries that normally would have been there.

"No, I'm just a banker," the man answered. "But I do appreciate music—especially the music of Argentina. I've done some study of that. And I speak the Argentinean form of Spanish. My name's Peter Wentworth."

He was looking expectantly at Neal, who felt heat coming off the man—not temperature heat; sexual heat. He was so much like Clayton Ambrose. Neal wondered if this similarity in looks and demeanor between this Wentworth man and the professor was misleading Neal into sensing that the man now sitting close beside him was interested in him on a prurient level. It may just be this similarity, he had to acknowledge, but it made Neal tense and trembly and he felt—and hoped the man didn't see—himself going hard. Neal, the wound of losing Ambrose still so open, just went with the flow.

Later Neal was to wonder how many young men other than him had been seduced and made to ejaculate in his shorts by the expert hand of older man while sitting in a crowded hall during a concert. But by the time he thought about, it didn't mean much to him anymore. Ambrose had left him achingly open to the approach. Wentworth couldn't have been blamed for recognizing that, Neal reasoned.

Wentworth was leaning into him and giving him a very warm smile, and their shoulders and forearms were

251

touching—giving Neal a buzz of electricity. But the seats were set close together, so Neal couldn't be sure to read anything into this. The man's hands were sensual, the fingers long and manicured—and hovering as if at the least invitation they would come down on Neal's exposed knee and massage it in a way that could translate—in Neal's fevered imagination—to the feel of it masturbating Neal's cock. Neal was wearing shorts and sandals without socks. He suddenly was feeling undressed—certainly underdressed for the venue, although the festival was pointedly casual and other men in the hall were similarly dressed.

The man's sense of casual was much more refined and stylish than Neal's was, and he was very much aware that he was out of this man's league. But he'd been out of Clayton Ambrose's league too—if you didn't take into account Ambrose's pleasure at debauching younger men.

Neal was aware of the tripping of his imagination on sensual clouds enough to tell him that the fingers on the knee were just his fantasizing. But when he looked down at his knee, he saw that Wentworth, indeed, was lightly massaging it. That, of course, would have been the perfect time to get up and change seats. But he was here first, dammit, and the hall was filling up quickly. And besides . . .

Neal couldn't help himself, he looked over and down at Wentworth's lap. Elegantly cut trousers or no, there was every evidence that the man was hard and built just as long as Professor Ambrose. He looked up to see that the man had been watching him and was smiling as he spoke.

". . . like to meet him afterward?"

"Excuse me, I didn't hear you," Neal said, embarrassed that he was fantasizing about the man's equipment and those fingers on his knee while Wentworth had asked him a question.

"I said that, since you say you are studying the same musical disciplines and techniques as Carlos Ferrari offers, would you perhaps like to meet him after the concert?"

"Well, yes, certainly I would. But I doubt that's possible. There must be others who already have—"

"Oh, he has no other engagements after tonight's concert, and I can introduce you to him. My bank is sponsoring his appearance and I've been hosting him. I am responsible for seeing that he has a pleasant time in the States. I speak his dialect and he speaks very little English. I've been translating for him. Which I suppose means I need to go on stage to usher him out now and introduce him. The lights are going down. Would you be so kind as to make sure this seat is saved for me to come back to?"

Wentworth was rising and moving up onto the stage—and to the back, where a door was opening to let the performer enter. Now Neal knew why the man had said he had to have an aisle seat—and also why he could offer to introduce Neal to Ferrari.

He also knew, with a shudder, that he'd protect the seat next to him with his life.

The introductions made, Wentworth returned to his seat. But before he left the stage, he'd leaned down to Ferrari, who was positioned at a Yamaha concert grand piano, with microphones between him and the audience and a guitar on a stand behind him, and whispered something to Ferrari. The performer looked out into the audience, apparently directly at Neal, and smiled as Wentworth whispered something else to him.

Carlos Ferrari was no taller than Neal was. He was sensitive-looking as many musicians are. Perhaps in his mid thirties, he was dark complexioned, sensual, with black, curly hair—perhaps even permed hair—that reached to his shoulders. He was dressed simply in a white, billowy shirt and brown trousers. Like Neal, he was wearing open-toed sandals. Both his toes and his fingers were long and slender, and, like many Latins, his arms and hands were in perpetual motion as he talked and played.

Wentworth returned to his seat. As he sat down next to Neal in the near total darkness of their row—there was no one in the two seats to the other side of Neal—and in the seconds before the music started, Wentworth leaned over and whispered to Neal, "Carlos is gay, you know. And goes both ways."

Neal said nothing. He told himself that it was just a spontaneous piece of "I am close enough to him to know what he likes" banter, and nothing more. That didn't stop him from trembling or for this to convey to Wentworth where their shoulders and arms were touching.

Ferrari played three songs on the piano. First a busy jazz rendition and then two slower pieces, with rolling arpeggios that made Neal think of the gentle coursing of a river. And, sure enough, when Wentworth went back up on stage to translate a short commentary on the music for Ferrari, he said that these were Ferrari's own compositions and were about life on the river.

"Carlos lives near the Puraná River in Argentina," Wentworth told the audience. "He loves the feel and sound of the river running by his bedroom window. He says the second composition is of an image he once had of his lover having moved down river and of him maintaining an emotional connection with this lover by going to the riverbank and looking down into the water at his own reflection and imagining that the reflection floated down the river to be received by his lover."

After the audience has applauded this, thanks to Wentworth Neal envisioning a male lover in a way that hadn't been revealed to the rest of the audience, Wentworth said the next set of songs would be love songs to this lover.

All the time Wentworth was translating this commentary, both he and Ferrari were looking directly at

Neal and smiling—or so it appeared to Neal. When he returned to his seat and Ferrari was beginning to play his next set, Wentworth leaned over and whispered to Neal, "I told him a music student wanted to meet him and pointed you out. He said he was pleased. He also said this set of love songs was being played with you in mind—that you reminded him of his down-stream lover. The lover is a young man who looks very much like you. I hope that doesn't upset you."

"No, certainly not," Neal whispered back. "I'm flattered."

"And, if I'm not mistaken, you are aroused. Does Carlos arouse you?"

"I am very impressed with him. He makes wonderful music."

"Carlos told me that you were arousing to him. Are you fine with that—in meeting him after the concert. Am I right in having assumed that you take cock?"

Neal paused only a few moments, looking up at the stage, seeing that, although Carlos was playing the piano and singing now too, in a soft tenor, that Carlos was looking out into the audience—in his direction.

"Will you let Carlos fuck you?" the man persisted. "I have to set him up with someone to lay with him after a concert like this. He needs it to unwind."

"Yes, I'm good with that," Neal whispered back. Not exactly a long-term lover that Clay had made him promise to acquire immediately—but a stopgap. And evidence that Neal could manage this himself. Of course, he was actually more aroused by Wentworth.

"As his host, that pleases me," Wentworth said. Well into the second song of the love song segment, Neal felt the tips of Wentworth's fingers on his knee. He moved his hand to cover Wentworth's hand but made clear in the movement that he wasn't trying to push the hand away.

Why was he being so easy, Neal wondered, as he felt the heat of the possessive touch on his knee. It probably was because of what he had promised Ambrose and how nervous he was about how to go about that. It wasn't that Neal was promiscuous. He wasn't—and he hadn't even been voracious for it until Professor Ambrose had come into his life. He'd sucked and been fucked occasionally since coming to Charleston and after Ambrose had shown him the ropes. It was all part of going out into the world, he'd reasoned. And the college was well known for its eclecticism and liberal mindedness. But he hadn't been as casual and open to it before as this. He thought it was from panicking at Clayton leaving so abruptly. Neal wanted to continue such a relationship as that, but he had no idea how to fall into what he'd had with Clayton. He had no experience in casual cruising—not something that fell into a more regular relationship.

This encounter, beyond causing a surge in his libido, was at least a temporary answer to his "where from here?" concern.

Wentworth went back on stage to introduce the guitar segment and when he returned and Ferrari started to play, Wentworth leaned over and whispered, "His music is divine, isn't it?" His hand went to Neal's knee and was rhythmically squeezing and releasing pressure with the beat of the guitar music.

"Yes, gorgeous," Neal responded.

"He says you are giving him inspiration—that he can feel the heat between you across the footlights. He asked if you would lay with him. I told him you will."

"Yes," Neal answered.

"And will you open your legs to me too? I know I've been speaking for Carlos, but you make my blood boil as well."

Rather than verbalizing an answer, Neal spread his legs in the seat and moved his hand to Wentworth's knee. Wentworth's hand was already climbing the inside of

Neal's thigh, traced the line of Neal's hard cock, and grasped it through the material of his shorts, squeezing and releasing to the beat of the guitar.

"Just relax," Wentworth whispered, "and come for me in your shorts. Don't be embarrassed. No one can see us, and I want assurances that you are the young man I need tonight."

Giving a low moan, before that set was finished, Neal creamed his shorts. Wentworth could tell from the young man's jerk and the relaxing of his muscles, that he'd had an ejaculation.

Before rising to introduce the last set, Wentworth leaned over and whispered, "Thank you. I will make it worth your while."

After the concert; after Wentworth and Neal had held back for others to cover Ferrari in adulation, which clearly both embarrassed and delighted the Argentinian musician; after the three of them were alone in the small dressing room assigned to Ferrari and the door to the corridor was closed and locked, Wentworth pushed Neal's back up against the wall next to the door and, placing his hands possessively against the wall on either side of Neal's shoulders, came in for a kiss.

Neal surrendered to him, but his eyes went to Ferrari, sitting at a dressing table, his face to a mirror. Ferrari was all eyes, staring at the other two in the reflection of the glass.

Seeing where Neal was looking, Wentworth smiled and said in a low, growly voice, "Carlos likes to watch at first. He wants to watch me fuck you and then later, in the hotel, he wants you to fuck him. Am I right that you go both ways?"

"Yes," Neal murmured, embarrassed again that he was being so easy—but he also was so needy for it—and giving passing thought to how transparent he must be for the man to assume correctly that Neal would both give and take, something Neal only recently had learned from Clayton Ambrose.

Neal's T-shirt was being pulled over his head. "Carlos wants you to be naked," was the only explanation Wentworth gave. In high heat now, Neal didn't really need any explanations.

Wentworth went back to possessing Neal's lips as he maneuvered Neal's right hand down between them, giving a sound of amusement deep in his chest when Neal shuddered at what his hand encountered when Wentworth guided it to his groin. Neal ran his fingers down the length on Wentworth's cock through the material of his trousers, finding him long, thick, and hard. Wentworth unzipped his fly. Neal's hand entered on his own accord, found the slit in the briefs, and ran his fingers over the flesh of the still stiffening staff.

Ferrari continued to watch, bug-eyed, in the reflection of the mirror.

Neal heard the unbuckling of Wentworth's belt and the belt buckle ring on the concrete floor as the trousers puddled around his ankles. He came out of the kiss, his eyes capturing Neal's gaze, a slight, sneery smile on his lips; looking, no doubt for some sign of reluctance or doubt, but finding none. His hands went to Neal's shoulders and applied gentle pressure. Complying with the obvious request, Neal sank to his knees, his hands sliding Wentworth's briefs down his legs as Neal descended, his mouth immediately opening to take in Wentworth's cock.

After a few moments, Wentworth pulled Neal back up to his feet. As he did so, Neal felt the contours of the disk Wentworth had in his hand, and knew instantly that it was a condom.

"Carlos wants me to fuck you here, against the wall," Wentworth said.

Neal's eyes went to Ferrari, turned from them at the dressing table, but intently watching them through the mirror, his tongue licking his lips, lust overflowing in his eyes, his hand grasping a freed cock. Neal's first thought was, "and what do you want, Mr. Host?" but he already knew what he wanted. "Yes," he whispered.

Neal both felt and heard his own belt buckle being undone, his shorts sliding down his leg, Wentworth's hand on his cock, stroking it.

"God, you're built big for your height," Wentworth growled. "Carlos is going to love you."

Neal felt the slight tug under his knees on both sides, and, understanding, pulled his feet out of his puddled shorts, and climbed Wentworth's hips with his knees. Clayton had done him against a wall before; Neal knew how this worked.

Neal felt the bulb of the cock at his entrance and moaned. "Here it comes," Wentworth muttered in a raspy voice.

"Yes, yes, fuck me," Neal whispered. Then he gasped and gave a little cry as the sheathed cock entered him and started working its way up inside him. He threw his arms around Wentworth's neck, pressed his cheek into the older, taller man's hairy chest, his shirt already having been unbuttoned and flared, and whimpered and groaned as the cock started to mine and pump his passage, increasing in speed and intensity until he, first, came on Wentworth's bare belly, and then Wentworth came deep inside him, with a jerk, inside the condom.

It was only as they climaxed that Neal realized that Ferrari had been singing, his voice rising and its timbre becoming more frenzied as Wentworth's thrusts intensified.

"Now we go for drinks and then to my hotel," Wentworth muttered, while going flaccid inside Neal. Neal was still moaning and trembling in satisfaction.

Later in the night, Carlos Ferrari sat, naked, on a chair in Peter Wentworth's Mills House Hotel bedroom suite, strumming his guitar and watching as Wentworth fucked Neal from behind, bent over the end of the king-sized bed. Wentworth covered Neal's back closely. His fists grasped Neal's wrists, spreading Neal's arms wide on the bedspread on either side. Wentworth's teeth were closed over the nape of Neal's neck like that of a cat holding her kitten steady and still. His cock, as long as Ambrose's, but thicker, pumped Neal's channel deep. He started slow, governed by Ferrari's stroking of his guitar and built to a fast and furious pace as Ferrari added complexity, rhythmic beat, and fast finger picking to his playing. At a loud, discordant chord on the guitar, Wentworth arched his back, jerked, threw his head back, and exclaimed his ejaculation to the ceiling.

He released Neal's wrists then and stepped back from him. Whimpering, Neal drew his knees up into his belly in a fetal position and, still trembling from the ferocity of the fuck, panted and moaned softly.

The guitar music stopped, and Neal felt hands on his knees and shoulders, coaxing him to turn on his back, spread his legs, and let the legs flop over the end of the bed. He complied and looked down to see the top of Ferrari's curly head as he knelt between Neal's knees, ran his sensuous fingers up Neal's thighs to rest at the top of the thighs and thrum Neal's lower belly softly and rhythmically, as Ferrari's mouth swallowed Neal's cock and rhythmically sucked the young music student to a throbbing hard. Thus prepared, Neal watched as Ferrari rose, climbed over his hips, lowered his channel on Neal's cock, and, facing him and looking intently into Neal's eyes with slitted eyes of his own, started to ride him.

Later still they moved into a threesome, with Neal covering and fucking Ferrari from behind, while he, in turn, was covered and fucked again by Wentworth.

They slept in a three-way tangle, which occasionally resulted in a random cock in a random hole, a brief flurry of pumping action, release, and sleep.

When Neal woke in the morning, both men were gone. There was an envelope on his neatly folded clothes on a chair that contained tickets to each of Ferrari's remaining three concerts at Spoleto and an invitation to join Ferrari after the concerts. There also was a check for $500, signed by Peter Wentworth on the Wentworth bank.

* * * *

Neal found that it was exhausting sitting at Carlos Ferrari's bedside in the Paraná hospital and listening for the next shallow breath, holding his own breath until Carlos' next one came—never certain there would be a next one and knowing that at some point there wouldn't be another one. The musician's breathing had become so shallow and the waiting so tedious in the dim sterility of the Argentinean hospital room through the night that Neal fancied he was able to relive a day of their life in each of the spaces between one uncertain breath and the next.

He knew that the time could become perpetual between breaths at any given moment. The doctors had said that it could be any time now. He had wanted to move Carlos down to Buenos Aires, to a more modern hospital and a more experienced set of doctors, but Carlos had forbidden it, saying he'd been born and raised in Paraná and wanted to die here. Such was the respect that the city had for his music that he was receiving the best care they could give him here—at no expense. Carlos had never been one to accumulate money and goods.

Of course he had accumulated Neal, and now, after twelve years, was fading away under the death sentence of pancreatic cancer, leaving Neal with nothing other than memories—or so Neal assumed. Neal didn't begrudge this, but he also knew that he wouldn't receive the regard and support from the people of Paraná that Carlos had. He'd be left, destitute, in this isolated country where he'd not yet, even after twelve years, been able to fully master the Argentine dialect of Spanish—well, the

Paraná dialect, which was distinct from what they spoke in Buenos Aires and of little use to him if he wanted to make money from music in the capital city.

Long after that last breath had been whispered, Neal sat, holding Carlos' hand. Carlos had been everything to him this past twelve years. Neal had given everything up to follow him from Charleston to Argentina—and then to wherever else in the world Carlos' renown as a musician had taken him.

Neal didn't cry at the finish. He was all teared out—and a bit numb. He was just grateful that Carlos, who he had loved well and mutually satisfactorily for over a decade, was mercifully released from the pain he had endured to manage "just one more" composition. Carlos had dedicated the composition to Neal.

Neal felt the pressure of a hand on his shoulder, and some instinct told him that it was Peter Wentworth, even though the three of them rarely—but explosively when it occurred—had met over the years since Spoleto in Charleston.

"You are just a bit late," Neal said in a flat voice. "He's gone."

"I've been here from time to time over the last week," Wentworth said. "I flew down not long after I heard he was ill. Thank God it didn't take long once it was inevitable."

"Yes, thank God for that," Neal murmured. "You have been here for a week but didn't make contact with me? I didn't know you were here." Neal was hurt. Wentworth could have given him some support through this ordeal. Had Peter forgotten everything they'd gone through? Was he abandoning Neal as well?

"I couldn't bring myself to contact you—not until . . . well, you know, out of respect for your relationship with Carlos."

"Yes, I understand," Neal answered. And he did understand when it was put in that light. In all the time the three of them were together, sexually, it had been Wentworth who Neal melted to. Neal could concentrate on pleasing Carlos when it was just to the two of them, but he naturally gravitated to Peter when he was added to the equation. But both of them realized that Neal was there for Carlos, and both of them had restrained themselves in respect for the musician whose talent had brought them together. Wentworth had even declared that they should meet rarely, to avoid the temptation. It was OK that they fucked with Carlos there, but Wentworth really wanted to have Neal all to himself.

"There are no impediments any more. Can you come away now—to my hotel?" Wentworth asked.

"Yes," Neal said, letting go of Carlos' lifeless hand for the last time. There was nothing left here for Neal anyway—at least for this time. There was no reason not to go with Wentworth.

Wentworth fucked him on the foot of the bed in an old, exclusive hotel with large rooms and a shaded balcony. Open French doors led out onto the balcony and the unexpectedly comforting sound of the busy street noises below and let in a breeze to caress the steaming bodies of the fucking men. Neal was on his back, his legs being held raised and spread by Wentworth as, his forehead plastered to Neal's and his eyes capturing Neal's to catch every nuance of Neal's response to the working of the cock inside Neal's channel, Wentworth adjusted his stroking technique to cause Neal's eyes to slit the most and his moans to deepen the farthest.

Wentworth had put a CD of Carlos Ferrari's music on while they fucked, which both men found comforting and arousing. Always in tune with Carlos' music, Wentworth harmonized the working of his cock with the texture of the tune playing on Carlos' CD. This was the first time they'd done this to a recording, though. In times past, Carlos had controlled the fuck with his own singing live.

Afterward, the two lying in each other arms stretched out on the bed, turned slightly toward the French doors and the cooling breeze on their lightly sweating bodies, Wentworth murmured, "Did Carlos ever tell you how we picked you out—picked you up—in the first place?"

"No," Neal answered, surprised. "I didn't realize there was a story to that. I just thought you gauged me as easy—rightly. I still can't believe you were assured enough to just ask me straight out if I took cock. And I can't believe that I answered 'yes' straight out and that you jacked me off right there, in the crowded auditorium during the concert. It wasn't so much that I was easy as that I was vulnerable at that moment."

"Yes, I was told you'd be easy. But I also was told that you weren't really promiscuous, weren't a rent-boy type—that you'd be sweet and with a sense of innocence, albeit willing and pliable."

"You were told? Told by whom?" But just then, the image of a long ago lover—not his face, but the slenderness and grace of his body, the long cock, slightly upturned—entered his mind. "Professor Ambrose? Clayton Ambrose?"

"Yes, Clayton. I knew Ambrose—through Spoleto, of course. I was looking for someone to service Carlos while he was at Spoleto in Charleston. He played with so much more inspiration when he had a young man to fuck him—and the coupling of men to watch. The videos on the Internet were not working. I told Ambrose of my need—I didn't realize at the time that it was my own need as well, but of course it was—and he said he was leaving Charleston and had a relationship with a young music student—you—that he regretted just walking away from. He offered you because he thought it was what you needed, not just because I needed someone to service Carlos during the concerts. I gave him the ticket to the concert to give to you. I hope you're not—"

"No, it's fine," Neal whispered, putting the finger of one hand to Wentworth's lips as the fingers of the other hand went to the older man's rejuvenating cock. "I did have my own need at the time. But I felt like such a slut just to give it that easily."

"Neither of us thought of you as a slut. We both could see your need. You were sweet. Carlos was especially taken with you—although I shouldn't say that. I was taken with you too. But I had host responsibilities. Carlos wouldn't have seen you as a slut to have asked you to return to Argentina with him."

"I can be a slut, though," Neal said, with a little laugh, as he moved his lips down Wentworth's body and swallowed his cock.

Wentworth fucked him this time doggie style on the bed, covering him close from above, as Neal, cheek to bed and arms outstretched in total surrender, gazed out to the blazing light beyond the edge of the shadowed balcony and thought, with appreciation, on his life with Carlos—but also on the restraint he and Wentworth had had to observe, except for the explosive occasional meeting as Carlos watched them fuck. His thoughts also went to his present, uncertain existence.

"You seem sad. Carlos wouldn't want you to be sad at his passing," Wentworth murmured when they once again were stretched out in a close embrace.

"I'm not sad for Carlos. I'm said for me. I gave him everything. I am empty and alone now. I have no idea what to do now. Everything went to Carlos. I don't regret that, but I should have kept something for myself, done some planning, especially in these weeks when we knew the end was coming for Carlos."

"You weren't left with nothing," Wentworth answered. "Carlos has been schooling you in the music since Charleston. He has taught you more, brought out more of your talent, given you more useful experience, than you could ever have learned in that college. You can go on tour yourself now. I can mentor you, just as I discovered Carlos down here, brought him to America, and lifted him up into the international ranks."

"You would do that for me?"

"I've been aching to do that for you. You've been ready for years. Carlos and I discussed that. We were about to offer you some independence and exposure anyway. Yes, I'd do that for you—and you also don't need to be alone. You know how I feel about you. You can come away with me and—"

"Shush," Neal whispered, putting a finger to Wentworth's lips again. "I can be easy for you again. The answer is yes."

Gently pushing Wentworth over onto his back, Neal reached over to the nightstand for another condom and to switch on the CD again, bringing the soft tenor of Carlos' guitar-backed crooning into the room with him. Saddling his channel on Wentworth's sheathed cock, Neal began to ride him slowly as the shadows lengthened out on the balcony—knowing that Carlos' song would increase in volume and intensity as they fucked, knowing that Carlos wrote this song explicitly for this purpose and was watching them from above with approval and arousal.

~

About the Author

Habu is one of the pen names of a former supersonic spy jet pilot, intelligence agent, male model, movie actor, and diplomat. A wild youth in Southeast Asia was spent enjoying whatever sexual opportunities came his way, and much of his gay male writing is about recalling incidents from those days and inventing ones he'd perhaps have liked to experience. He now leads a very quiet and ordinary happily married family life.

An American, he is a published mainstream novelist and short story writer under another name and in another dimension of his life. He has written or cowritten (with Sabb) approaching 1,000 published short stories and over 100 published erotica e-books, primarily of gay fiction but also memoir, straight fiction and ménage fiction. His hand and creative writing can be seen in stories and books by habu, sr71plt, Dirk Hessian, Shabbu, and Stephen Kessel—among unrevealed others that might surprise readers. The fictionalized GM memoir *Flying High, Diving Deep* is loosely based on his life experiences. He can be found at the adults only gay male site www.BarbarianSpy.com, which he shares with Sabb and Dirk Hessian.

Our authors always like to receive feedback, and appreciate it when readers post reviews at distributors and other sites.

FOR LITERARY HEAT

Not all books listed below may currently be on release.
* indicates the book is available in paperback and e-book.

BOOKS BY CHRIS CROSS
Multisexual Adult Romance
Pulaski Square
MF Erotica
Chocolate in Vanilla
BOOKS BY ALEX LOCKHEED
Transgender Romance
Meeting Jenna
Transgender Other
Being Sarah
BOOKS BY DIRK HESSIAN
Xtreme Historical Erotica
The King's Men
Shores of Tripoli
Prophecy of Noto
Pretender's Fate
General Historical Erotic Romance
To the Hessian Hills
Fire Down the Valley*
Constantinople*
The Beautiful Way*
Blue and Gray
Colonel's Treasure
Beginning of Time

Labyrinth
BOOKS BY HABU
Gay Erotica
Memoir Faction
Flying High, Diving Deep*
Xtreme Erotica
Tramp Steaming*
Escape to Girne
Silas' Choice*
Last Call
Choke Hold
Apyko: The Greek Pimp
Visits of the Schlange
Second Coming: Emile La Cour Unleashed
Vortex: Sacrificed by Curiosity*
Dark Angel Sounding *(in e-book & included in
Sounding:Ultimate Control Paperback)*
Sounding: Ultimate Control (*Print Only*)*
Sounding Five *(in e-book & included in
Sounding:Ultimate Control paperback)*
Romance
Turn to Love
Rain Check
Built for Pleasure (Sci Fi)
Danny's Choice*
Pull of the Groove
Sugar n Spice Christmas
Friday Nights with Lenny (Christmas Romance)
Snowy, Snowy Nights (Christmas Romance)
Tank n Bull
Sail to the Sun
War Letters
Ravens Roost
Caribbean Cruise Top to Bottom
Arena Stage
Trading Partners (Valentine's Day)
Four Coins
Lower Than the Heart (Valentine's Day)
Brambleton

Gotta Keep Trying
Finding Amnad
Platres Conclave
Other Novels/Novellas
Temptation's Clutches*
Descent into Chaos
Escape to Girne
Journey Through Abilene
Harmony and Dissonance
Stallion Station
Racing With the Devil (espionage suspense)
Prepared in Cape Verdi
Gilded Cage
House on Park*
Anything for Ambition
Dance of the Ravishers
Hard Knocks U*
My Neighbor's Spa*
Man's Man: Tales of a High Priced Gay Hooker*
Trip Money
The Indian Doctor
Sailorboy
Home to Fire Island
Murder Mysteries
Vanishing Laura
Death on a Ping Pong Table
Clint Folsom Mysteries Compendium Volume 1*
Death to Blonds - Stolen Judgment (Clint Folsom
Mystery)*
Clint Folsom Mysteries Compendium Volume 2*
Gay Erotica Anthologies
Earth Cry*
Shunga
Habu's Christmas Balls
Eight in D*
DevilMENt
Silas' Choices*
Stallion Station (A Novella in Parts)
Eleven to the Dogs*

Fifty Seventy*
Spy Tails 001*
Spy Tails 002*
Doubled*
Doubled Again*
Tails in the Tropics*
Tails in the Med*
Tails in the West*
Rough Riders*
Grab Bag 1*
Grab Bag 2*
Grab Bag 3*
Grab Bag 4*
Grab Bag 5*
Grab Bag 6*
Grab Bag 7*
Grab Bag 8*
Beyond the Beaded Curtain*
Habu's Christmas Balls
The Sporting Life*
Fetish Galore!*
Literary Gay Erotica
Cairo Surrender*
The Handyman*
Homeward Bound
Journey to Mirage*
Bisexual/Menage/Multisexual Erotica
Two Men, One Woman*
Every Which Way
Summer of Denial
Death on a Ping Pong Table
Cruising Gigolo
13 Ways for Halloween
Luther*
The Indian Prince*
BOOKS BY SABB
Driver Reliever
Hiring in Hollywood
The Legend of Holleystone Grange

Surprise Encounters*
She is He
Wrong Man
Loyal to his King
Barbarian Tales - Book One - Traveler's Tales*
Barbarian Tales - Book Two - Journeys Begin*
Barbarian Tales - Book Three - The Inheritance*
Barbarian Tales - Book Four - Road to Persepolis*

BOOKS BY SHABBU

Velvet Interrogation
Finding Jason
Dirty Pool
Operation Black Jade
Cigars!*
Angel in the Barn
Gayly Complicated*
Despoiling David
The Tree of Idleness*
I Met a Man
Rough Road to Happiness

BOOKS BY STEPHEN KESSEL

Gay Romance

The Forever Man
Two Chances

BOOKS BY KIM BLACK

Lesbian Romance

Transfixed on Tammie (F/T lesbian)